OZLAND

BOOK 3

WENDY SPINALE

SCHOLASTIC PRESS
NEW YORK

Library of Congress Cataloging-in-Publication Data available

ISBN 978-0-545-95322-1

10 9 8 7 6 5 4 3 2 1   18 19 20 21 22

Printed in the U.S.A.   23
First edition, May 2018

Book design by Christopher Stengel

My mind, my heart, and my soul are consumed by my three loves: Gavin, Keaton, and Riley. Home is not a house or structure of any sort. It's anywhere you're surrounded by those that love you. You will always be my home.

· GAIL ·

My breath rises in ghostly wisps into the cold evening air as I hold my position. Motionless. Silent. My arrow securely nocked and trained on the shoreline of the icy lake. It's after dusk, and winter has settled in early this year. The woolen cloak and gloves offer some warmth, but the chill bites the tips of my ears and nose. Still, my eyes remain fixed. The nightly cries of the youngest children, the ones that are nothing but flesh over bones, just skeletons really, shriek in my thoughts. They cry for their lost families, for the blistering pain riddled throughout their bodies as the new cure slowly heals them, for insatiable hunger; I can only help with the latter.

I'm the best of the hunters in my village, bringing in the most food out of all of us who take our weapons to the wilderness. But even so, my father, Hunter, our leader, has insisted I travel no farther than the forest's edge.

Beyond the body of water, red lights glow in pairs. They are the eyes of those that are neither human nor beast in these parts. No one has ventured past the lake and returned alive. Terrible creatures lie in wait within the dense forest. Describing them as terrible is generous. They hide in the shadows of the trees, their bodies camouflaged like chameleons—only, they've been known to snap a person in half with one bite from their powerful jaws.

The crackle of dry leaves draws my attention, but I remain still. Heart racing, sweat beading my forehead, I can't allow my fear to shake my resolve. Survival lies in what game I can bring home.

Under the glow of the moon, a shadow emerges from the tree line as the dead foliage rustles beneath the newcomer's feet. The wild sow lifts her snout into the cool evening air, in search of the slightest hint of danger. Although I've been careful, rubbing my clothes and body with oak leaves to cover my scent, my stomach twists, worried that it isn't enough. That my anxious heartbeat will divulge my location.

The sow snorts, as if declaring the area safe, before making her way to the water, only five meters from where I've taken cover.

My fingers twitch, but I don't shoot. Instead, I take in a breath. If I fire now and miss, that will be my only shot before the pig bolts back into the forest. I wait until the animal is lapping at the shoreline. Steadying the bowstring close to my cheek, I take aim.

As I'm about to take the shot, high-pitched squeals break the silence. Four piglets burst through the shrubbery and race to their mother's side on the lake's edge.

My breath catches, hesitancy paralyzing me. I lower my weapon and watch the offspring romp by the lake's edge. They are too young to be alone. With what else lives in these woods, they won't make it through the night. Not without their mother looking after them. Growling, my stomach reminds me that there are those depending on me. Yet, if I don't get back to the village soon, I also might not see the sun rise. It's either them or me.

Again, I take aim, my arrow fixed on the thick neck of the large sow, my hands steady as I pull the string taut.

It takes only a moment to recognize the familiar rumble of a menacing growl before one of the piglets is snatched up by a hideous claw. The poor animal hardly has time to squeal before it disappears into the shadows. My face grows cold as the crack of bones startles the rest of the pigs. Instinct takes over, and I keep my weapon aimed at the adult pig. But I don't have time to shoot. A Bandersnatch explodes from the trees, seizes the sow with its teeth and two of the remaining piglets with its claws. Only one escapes into the wild brush. The horrifying creature abandons the offspring and bulldozes into the trees, leaving behind splintered branches and uprooted shrubs. It takes seconds before the terrifying shrieks of the wild pigs cease, leaving the lakeside as quiet and desolate as it was when I arrived.

Cursing, I throw my bow over my head and quiver my arrow. Knowing the frightened squawks of the pigs have probably warned off any other nearby game, I pack up and take one last look at the shoreline. Everything is still. As I turn away, I hear a quiet whine.

Snatching my bow and an arrow, I target the bushes and find the young pig trembling beneath the lower branches. I drop my aim. Even if I kill it, there's not enough meat on the piglet to make a decent meal for one, much less an entire village. There's no point shooting it, at least not for now. Perhaps I could bring it home and fatten it up. It's better than going home empty-handed or leaving it alone to be eaten by predators. I sit cross-legged on the damp soil and reach inside my rucksack. Taking out some wild berries and nuts, I shake them in my hand.

"You hungry?" I ask.

The piglet cautiously steps forward before it hesitates. I toss a handful of food its way. Squealing, it dodges back into the brush.

"Chicken," I mutter.

The young pig watches as I pull out another fistful and snack on the meager morsels. It edges up to the closest berry with caution. With a guarded gaze set on me, the piglet devours the fruit and nuts. I coax the young pig toward me, holding out another palmful of food. When the warm snout nudges my hand, I pour the snack onto the forest floor. Hungrily, the piglet plunges its face into the pile. It flinches only once when I scratch behind its ear.

"What am I going to do with you?" I ask.

It peers up at me with chestnut eyes before returning to its meal. The piglet finishes off the food and begins chewing at the toe of my silver boot.

"Hey!" I say, pulling my foot away.

A roar rips through the trees. It's the same beastly howl that makes the ground tremor in the dead of night. The piglet sprints for my rucksack and cowers inside, rattling the unclipped metal buckle. My eyes dart upward, hoping the beast is too focused on its dinner to notice me, but I know it's only a matter of time before it picks up my scent.

As the growl dies out, echoing far into the forest, my surroundings become eerily quiet except for the howl of a lonely wolf. I let out a silent sigh, grateful that the Bandersnatch has gone on its way. Standing, I cradle my rucksack in my arms, ready to turn back to the village when the ground shakes again, but this time it is much more violent. Earth-shattering screams erupt from behind me—the Bandersnatch is back, and it's brought company.

I don't have enough time to draw my weapon. Instead, I just run.

The canopy of branches blocks out what little moonlight there is in the sky. I can't see where I'm going as I race between the large trunks of pine trees, dodging low-hanging branches. Twice I nearly fall, tripping over debris scattered throughout the forest floor. The piglet trembles within the leather bag clutched in my arms. The crack of tree limbs chases me like a violent thunderstorm, but I don't dare turn back to see how close the beasts are. Panting, I push my burning muscles as fast as they can go, knowing if I slow down even a little, the piglet won't be the Bandersnatches' only snack.

The Bandersnatches draw closer, and my legs grow tired. Panic riddles my body. I know I can't keep running much longer. Hiding is my only option.

Ahead, a large tree, its trunk almost a meter wide, comes into view. I slip around and press my back against the bark.

Gulping, I hold my breath, afraid that my panting will give away my location.

Three Bandersnatches roar as they sprint past me, and the gust of wind following them ruffles the stray pieces of hair that have fallen from my braids. The younger trees snap like twigs as the beasts burst through the forest. When their long, spiked tails are no longer in my line of sight, I let out the breath I was holding in a cloud of mist. It won't be long before they return. I need somewhere to hunker down until they've given up their search for me.

The pale hue of a rocky hill catches my attention. If it wasn't for the small amount of moonlight casting through a break in the trees, I never would have seen it. Taking one last glance at the destruction the Bandersnatches have left behind, I head toward the stone wall. It doesn't take long for me to find a series of caves. With the chill in the air, more than likely this network of alcoves is a home to a bear or wildcat. But I'd rather deal with a dozen bears than even one Bandersnatch.

Scrambling over the uneven stones, I choose a smaller hollow, hoping that the carnivorous wildlife would opt for someplace a bit roomier.

On one hand and both knees, I clutch my rucksack and crawl through the entrance. The damp soil soaks through my pants as I creep to the back of the cave. Finally, I sit and lean up against the stone wall, thankful for the chill it brings. I inhale deeply, trying to slow my breath. It is the squirm within my satchel that pulls my attention from the anxiety boiling in me.

Reaching inside the bag, the piglet rubs its warm snout against my hand as I search for a candle and matches. Lighting the beeswax candlestick and tucking it into a crevice in the wall, the cavern brightens. Small bones, tufts of fur, and feathers litter the rock-and-dirt floor. Based on the size of the scat, whatever lives in here can't be any bigger than a fox. Relieved, I sigh and watch the shadows dance across the gray rock.

"It's your lucky day, Gail," I mutter aloud.

The piglet peeks out of the bag and tilts its head, as if listening intently.

"Seems today is lucky for both of us," I say, scratching its soft pink ear.

With a single snort, the piglet circles my lap and flops down, lying on its side.

"How can you possibly nap after all that?"

The animal doesn't seem to hear me, but instead breathes deep and slow, lost somewhere in its dreams.

Another roar echoes in the distance. The Bandersnatch may not be outside the cave entrance, but I'm not taking any risks. Not tonight, at least. Besides, I'm suddenly drowsy, my eyelids weighted down by the aftereffects of an adrenaline rush. As the candle flickers, fighting to stay lit, I close my eyes and surrender to the lull of sleep.

· ☐☐☐ ·

Although it's been three months since we arrived here, Evergreen Village has yet to feel anything like home. Then again, after all we've been through over the last year and a half, I'm not sure what home should feel like anymore. From the bustling streets of London, to the underground Lost City, to living in Umberland's Alnwick Castle, and now hiding in Evergreen's treetops . . . home has taken on so many definitions it's become lost in our journey.

Pickpocket and I return to the village after gathering plant samples to stock my medicinal supplies. When we arrive, the armored members of the Evergreen Guard hardly acknowledge us. In fact, I'm certain they aren't pleased that we're here. I can't blame them. More souls to protect. Extra people to account for. There aren't nearly enough bodies left to soldier up for the attacks we've endured from the creatures that were let loose throughout the Labyrinth.

They don't have the time or the desire to watch out for the foreign doctor who insists on picking leaves, roots, and berries he claims will help keep them healthy. They call it magic, even though I can cure most common ailments. The Evergreen Guard care about one thing—keeping as many as possible alive.

No one is left for dead, and anybody or anything that threatens the small community will pay for it with their lives.

That's been the new mantra, the new motto here within the remains of the Labyrinth. Because everybody counts toward our survival not only as a community, but as the human race. They don't voice it to me, but the Evergreen Guards' displeasure toward our weekly scavenges to collect medicinal plants does not go unnoticed in the murmurs as we pass by. Their hypocrisy also doesn't go unnoticed when they come whining to me about a stomachache.

Malevolent shadows lurk in the dark corners of the forest. One distraction could cost a soldier his or her life. Armed with rusted guns fashioned of scrap steel, these are the strongest and fastest of the survivors. Heroes of the Labyrinth, of Umberland and Everland, the Guard are as fierce as they are fearless. More than once they've battled a squadron of bloodthirsty gryphons. Their corpses are ultimately part animal and part machine, cruelly conjured up by the Bloodred Queen, although their wings are an excellent source of metal for creating machine parts. The combination of metal, eagle, and lion, these souls are as tortured as any of us. They are one of many of the Bloodred Queen's ghastly experiments, along with centaurs, chimeras, and satyrs. None of them completely bone and blood, yet none all machine.

I've become numb to the demise of these tormented beings, caught between both living and machine. I've encountered so many. Tried to revive them. But I only know of blood, vessels, muscles, and organs. How they intertwine with metal parts I am left perplexed about. When I lose them, sadness threatens to overwhelm me—not only as a physician, but also simply as a human—so I cut it off. As if that primal emotion is unworthy of recognition. With each toss of soil, every meter into the earth the Diggers breach, and each body they bury, I feel as if I become less of a person myself. I've become as cold as the corpses they've laid to rest.

Those of us from England and the others who've been trapped here in the deadly confines of the Labyrinth have spent the last several months preparing our escape. Right under the Bloodred Queen's nose. Planning a rescue mission to find the missing king of Germany and devising a plan to take down the Bloodred Queen. But it's hardly been simple.

The Labyrinth walls became nothing but ashes when the pwazon pòm tree was set on fire. For days, the maze burned relentlessly, scorching the very fortifications that not only kept the villagers as prisoners but also the fierce creatures that resided within them. Since then, we've battled monsters fabricated from nightmares, nursed as many sick humans as possible back to health, and built an entire army to do the one thing—the only thing—that will ensure the survival of humankind: kill the Bloodred Queen.

Beyond the Guard, the Tinkers—Everland boys who can repair or create, well, practically anything—work feverishly. Hammering, welding, and soldering our fleet of hovercycles. These vehicles are our only hope for the planned mass exodus for safer territory—although I'm not sure if any such place exists.

As we saunter beyond the human brigade of soldiers, the Tinkers greet me with grunts and tired eyes. Even Cogs, the head engineer and normally a pleasant Lost Kid, has been in a dreadful mood lately. Dark circles bruise the skin beneath his hazel eyes, and the glimmer of hope has long extinguished over the months of hardship.

No one sleeps at night. At least not well. Not between the endless ache of hunger or the overwhelming grief for those who have died. Even the slightest noise puts us all on edge. The little bit of rest we do get is vexed with the howls of the forest's predators, warning us that our time here is fleeting. Their song is a reminder that we either escape what is left of the Labyrinth or become their next meal.

Silently, Pickpocket and I climb the ladder made of tightly braided vines to the simple treetop village, the place we call home now. Woven grass curtains flutter in the brisk wind at each hut's doorway, the torchlight within having been extinguished hours ago. The occasional hoot of an owl mingles with the rustle of the dry pine needles. Only the quiet whispers of those who gather near the community bonfire break the still evening air.

"I'm going with Hunter. There are plenty of soldiers to protect the people. You don't need me to stay behind," Lily is insisting. "If Osbourne is indeed alive, as Hunter suggested, he'll most likely be heavily guarded. After all the Bloodred Queen has done, that's one battle I refuse to miss."

A grin grows on my face. She's as kind as she is fierce, although very few get to see the gentle side of her. The girl who was well trained with a sword is not to be trifled with, and most know that. But in the quiet hours of night, when it's just her and me, we can find sweetness in the stars, in the stories of her childhood, and in the mystery of science that runs thick in my blood.

Alyssa, the former Duchess of Alnwick, sits next to Lily, watching her intently. The idea of losing Lily to whatever awaits on the journey to find the king must weigh heavily on her mind. Lily is a valuable soldier. Without her, our war with the Bloodred Queen could be difficult. More than that, though, Alyssa and Lily have become close friends and allies. Both have been passionate about saving those who need to be saved . . . but then again, we all have.

"We need you here," Alyssa says, equally as determined as Lily. Dark aviator goggles rest tightly on the top of her head like a black headband on her long blond hair. "Your contribution to this community has been invaluable. You are our greatest fighter. Joining Hunter on the Emerald Isle will be a loss for us. Even though we have the approximate coordinates to find King Osbourne, nothing is for sure. Who knows what you'll face there."

"Send me. I'm just as capable as anybody. And if my father is alive, I should be the one to find him. Besides, I'm the one who found the key and told you it was meant for that Ginger girl," Jack shouts from behind the bars of his prison. With his cell set on the other side of a narrow footbridge, his words are muffled. But his voice is received with quiet contempt.

Jack. Once a Marauder turned Lost Kid, and then a traitor who ran back to his brother, revealing the location of the Lost City, he has yet again somehow found his way back into our small band. But not without brewing resentment. While Pete couldn't care less about him, I couldn't leave him for dead.

Hook, Jack's only family other than the Bloodred Queen, attempted to murder him with an apple from the tree that Alyssa and, apparently, he and Hook sought. Luckily for Jack, while large doses of the fruit are lethal, it is a sedative in lesser amounts. Having found Jack shortly after he was exposed, it was mere days before he was running his mouth again.

As the stepson of the Bloodred Queen, rightful heir to the German throne, and traitor to all he's interacted with, very few trust him. I can't blame them. After he betrayed the Lost Kids in Everland, none of us dared to turn our backs on him again.

"Don't get your hopes up. You'll be spending a lot of time behind those bars. Trust me, that's a whole lot better than if you were on my side of them," Pete retorts.

"I was and always have been on your side," Jack spits. "I gave up my life as a Marauder for you and the rest of the Lost Kids. I was after that apple to help *you* find the cure. I nearly lost my life, more than once, all for what? To be sure I had that apple so Doc could figure out the cure. I've lost everything because of my loyalty to you, Pete!"

"Loyalty?" Pete stands, pointing his dagger at Jack. "Like when you gave up the location of the Lost City to Hook? Like when you brought him to the sanctuary I created, I built, with the intent to hand over Gwen? *Now* you want me to believe that you 'tricked' your brother by aligning with him so you could get the apple and help us? How stupid do you think I am, Jack?"

Pete's knuckles pale as his grip tightens around his blade.

Lily places a hand on his shoulder. "Let him go. He's not worth your breath," she says.

Pete plops onto the bench and sharply whittles away at the bamboo reeds he's strung together into a flute, not unlike the one his mother once owned before her tragic motorcar accident. The same sort of flute his sister died with in her pocket.

The firelight gives his face a golden glow, accentuating the hollow look in his eyes. He no longer wears leather gloves. There's no medical need for them, but others have opted to keep them on to hide the scars of the disease and my mistake. I still feel ashamed of the damage I caused with the first cure I created. I thought I had found the answer in Gwen and lizard protein, but instead I created something worse: a mutation. With the help of Alyssa and Maddox and a deadly apple, I was able to rectify my mistake. But not before countless others died. Their deaths hang over me.

Pete, though, has embraced his scars. Opting to cover them with ink instead of cloth, he has spent hours with a sterilized needle and dyes, extending the already intricate tattoos on his chest, shoulders, and arms. Only instead of cogs, wheels, and other machine parts, he's etched the names of every important person he's lost. His parents and sister. Names of Lost Kids he's felt especially attached to. Only two scarred fingers remain empty, and I shudder every time I see them, wondering whose name will be next.

Pickpocket nudges me. "I want in on this. What about you?" he asks.

I shrug. "Go gallivanting into the unknown? That idea hardly sounds appealing," I say.

"Hardly sounds appealing? I'd give my right arm to get out of this place," Pickpocket says.

"You and Hook," Pete says with a smirk, noticing our entrance.

"Nice one," Pickpocket says, chuckling. "Anyway, I love a good adventure."

"I'll go, too," Maddox says gruffly. Long gone are the nights in which he hosted the rowdy tea parties in the Poison Garden of Umberland. He's become subdued. As if he's gone from giving up to growing up. He'd have been an excellent Lost Kid.

"Let me guess—you'll offer up a cup of tea and hope that by charming your enemies they won't suspect the sleeping agents you've put in their drink?" Pickpocket asks sarcastically.

Pete peers down at his hands as Gwen interlaces her fingers with his. He holds her hand loosely, a gesture that's become all too familiar. Everland ignited their love for each other. Umberland nearly destroyed it. Here, their relationship has been as uncertain as the environment. In all fairness, Gwen has done her best to patch the damage she did when she pushed him away while at Alnwick Castle, but her cold shoulder has left Pete less whole.

The Lost Boy who once believed we could accomplish anything, who created an entire complex city beneath the ruins of London—his spark has vanished. But who can blame him? Aside from his relationship troubles, he's lost what remained of his family the day Hook dropped his bombs. He tried to piece together a new family, starting with Bella and adding with every Lost Kid he found—Pyro, Pickpocket, Justice, Gabs. Each new kid felt like a small mend to the heartbreak. Yet the original Lost Girl teeters on the brink of here and the afterlife. The damage to Bella's health is far worse than that of any of those who have managed to live. Her recovery has been slow, and she remains the sickest of us all. I'm not sure what more I can do. Since Pete's sister, Gabrielle, died in my arms, we've struggled to repair the close bond we once had. With Bella near death, he's been edgier than usual with me. I understand his blame; I feel it myself.

Life isn't always fair, but when it steals the ones you love so young, so unexpectedly, it's especially cruel.

Pulling a gun from his holster, Maddox forcefully blows out a breath on the metal barrel and buffs it with his burgundy coat sleeve. "Trust me, Pickpocket, if charm doesn't work, I have other means to get what I want."

Gwen shoots Alyssa a tired glance. The prospect of another dangerous journey must be terrifying, even exhausting, to her. She, too, has watched her loved ones succumb to disease and war.

As the group continues to argue strategy and who should rescue Osbourne, the rightful king of Germany, it occurs to me that I have absolutely nothing to offer. My skills are not in warfare but in medicine. Having created an actual working antidote for the virus released in Everland, my job here is done—for now. Without an adequate laboratory to produce the stock needed to distribute worldwide, there isn't much else I can do. Other than the occasional dose of eucalyptus oil to help a nasty cold or stitching up a deep cut, I'm more or less useless. The last year and a half has been one great big nightmare, but the treetop village has served as a temporary asylum from the insanity this world has become. Even more so than Alnwick ever was, but to no fault of Alyssa's. She did the best she could under dire circumstances.

They say home is where the heart is; however, I'm not sure that's true. My heart remains in—even grieves for—London, where I was born, raised, and educated, but now there is nothing left of it. Over the course of my own journey, I've settled with the idea that home is where you find inner peace. These days I'm not sure that concept exists either. With the world diseased and war-torn, peace seems to elude me even in the dark hours of the night.

"I admire your bravery," Hunter says, "but we'll need the skills of your Lost Kids to infiltrate Lohr Castle. It'll take every able body to destroy the Bloodred Queen's reign. Between our knowledge and the abilities your group brings, you have a good chance of taking down the Bloodred Queen for good. As for the king, we've discussed this, and I will be going to find him alone. The scouts have found his approximate location, but we won't know for sure until he's in our custody. If I'm not back by the time you conquer the Bloodred Queen, and I know you will, then you can send help. But there's no use bringing back a king when his throne is still occupied."

The group exchanges an anxious glance, some grumbling among themselves.

"What about Gail?" says Emery, Hunter's wife. "She's excellent with the bow, far superior to anyone else. It makes sense she should go with you to help in the event you encounter trouble."

"No, we have no idea what dangers lie on the Emerald Isle," Hunter says. "Those who have scouted the island claim that it is hostile territory. Our daughter belongs here with the rest of the young folk."

Emery sighs. "She'll insist you take her with you."

Hunter gives a small smile. "As impetuous as that girl is, I have no intention of bringing her with me. I could hardly keep an eye on her within the confines of the Labyrinth. Now that the walls are down, she's constantly running amok despite the rules I've set for her. The Labyrinth is a dangerous enough place for a teenage child, much less the unknown of Emerald Isle," he says.

The Labyrinth isn't safe for anyone, not even someone as fearless as Hunter, I want to say, but I keep my thoughts to myself.

"I offer some of our soldiers to go with you not only for your safety, but for the safety of the king as well," Alyssa says. "You may need help," she adds, shooting a meaningful look at Maddox. He smiles in return, clearly thinking of how Alyssa tried to refuse his help in getting to the maze.

"No!" Hunter says sternly.

Alyssa startles with wide blue eyes. Even though we no longer live within the borders of Umberland, none of us from England would dare challenge her. With the Queen of England deceased, Alyssa is the only one left capable of returning to rule England.

The Queen's death was not wholly unexpected, but we all held out hope that she would pull through. I tried everything I could, but I failed her, too. She was surrounded by all of us from England as she took her last breath. No one could withhold their sorrow, and we mourned for weeks. With her death, like so many others before her, another shred of hope for the return of life as it was before was lost. Only this one hit the hardest for all of us.

Hunter sighs, recognizing the error he's made. "My apologies, Duchess Alyssa, but with all due respect, you have *no* authority here. Not here in my village, nor Germany for that matter. You and your people are guests and thus will be treated as such, with honor and dignity. But any decision that puts lives at risk will be mine."

The chilly night fills with a heavy air of discomfort as the group realize their new role in this strange place. While Pete and Alyssa were leaders back in England, we are not in the Lost City or Alnwick anymore. We really are visitors in a country that is far from home.

"This task is mine because I am one of the few who knows where the king is," Hunter says.

"And how do you know?" Maddox asks with raised brows.

"Along with the Zwergs, I was one of a many who ensured the king's survival," Hunter replies, pulling a chain with a key from his shirt. "Those of us loyal to the king knew that his recovery would be lengthy. We couldn't very well hide him in the castle without the queen finding out. Instead, he was given medicine to reverse the poison apple's effects and placed in a secure coffin that only this key could open. The Bloodred Queen believed he was entombed within the royal crypt. Fortunately, she despised him so much that she wasn't interested in participating in his burial.

"General Ginger, the daughter of the Zwerg leader, took a small army with her to ensure the king safely arrived at the Emerald Isle, hidden away from the Bloodred Queen. In addition to his impenetrable coffin, he was sent with a guard so strong that any who dare challenge it stand no chance."

"Even more reason for us to join you," Pete says.

"Not this time. This is one journey I will take alone," Hunter reiterates, leaving no room for argument.

Hunter can hold his own in a strange land. Of that I have no doubt. Next to his only daughter, Gail, he is among the strongest. And, as brave as my companions are, the toll of the battles in Everland and Umberland are evident in their somber countenances and red eyes. Eyes that have wept over the deaths of the Lost Kids, the citizens of Alnwick Castle, the Queen of England, their families. They have no more strength to fight than I do to pronounce one more innocent person dead. While the battle for Lohr will be costly, at least they won't be alone. It's only because we've had one another that we've come so far. We've become a family of sorts. If we divide, none of our heads will be in the battle at hand. As much as I hate to admit it, I think Hunter is right. Together we stand a chance to defeat the Bloodred Queen. Divided, we'll all die.

"I have not come all the way from Everland, battled through attack on Umberland, only to arrive here and be told where I will or will not go. I say we put this to a vote," Gwen says with defiance, breaking the uncomfortable silence.

Pete squeezes her hand, and his brow furrows. The silent scolding seems to take her aback as she draws her hand to herself. Hurt replaces the anger in her expression.

She, too, has lost more than any one person should bear. First her mother, the one person who secured the escape of so many from Everland. A woman we looked to as a mother after having lost our own. Then shortly after our arrival at the Labyrinth, her sister, Joanna, and brother, Mikey, succumbed to the disease. After all she went through to protect them and rescue Joanna, she took their deaths as her own fault. She could protect her siblings from war, from starvation, and from the Marauders, but ultimately lost them to the disease. However, that falls on my shoulders, and guilt gnaws at me.

Worst yet was the loss of her father, who was presumed dead after the German bombing. Inexplicably, he survived both the bombs and the Labyrinth. Eventually, the disease stole his last breath, too, along with so many others in Evergreen.

The loss of the Darling family affected us all to varying degrees. Gwen is the only one left to bear the family's name. When I first met her and her siblings, they were filled with determination. Despite what they had lost and endured, they radiated with hope we all longed for.

Now Gwen is a shell of the girl she once was.

Hunter turns his attention to Pete. "As for Lohr, your only objective is to destroy the Bloodred Queen," Hunter says, seeming unfazed by Gwen's outburst. "Do it quickly and quietly. Don't draw attention to yourself. Don't do anything that will rouse suspicion. But if the situation calls for it . . ."

Hunter presses his lips together, as if uttering the words might jinx him . . . or them.

The Bloodred Queen dies at all costs . . . even it means losing one of our own.

Pete nods, still carving away at the bamboo flute.

"Doc, you will join Pete," Hunter says.

An anxious hush blankets the group as eyes fall on me.

"Me? Why?" I ask, shifting into the glow of the torchlight.

"Because ultimately, *you* are the one who will save us all," Hunter says. "You will be the one to distribute the cure. Gather what stock you have and go with the assault team. You are to gain entrance to Lohr's laboratory and begin mass production of the antidote. The queen's laboratory was quite sophisticated back in the days when I was there. I imagine with the need to hunt for a cure, she's equipped it with the finest tools she could get her hands on. Tools that will help you produce the cure in mass quantities."

My knees feel weak as Pete's gaze falls on me.

"Doc's not coming with us. Not with me," he says, his voice curt. "Besides, he's a liability. Instead of fighting the queen's army, I'll be more concerned about protecting him."

"Doc is going with you or you'll be pulled from leading the assault team," Hunter says.

Pete shoots me an icy stare. "Fine, but bringing Doc anywhere is a mistake in my opinion."

The brisk words take my breath away and the attention turns to me. They are waiting for a response. Some comeback that puts Pete in his place. But I don't have the energy or the will to engage with him. The dig feels warranted.

Thousands of lives were lost because I was unable to find a proper cure for the Horologia virus. In the quiet of the night, I've cried a dozen tears for every patient I've failed. My well of sorrow dried up, and my job as a physician became mechanical. Lacking compassion. Absent of the emotional investment I've always given my patients.

But if Bella dies, it might destroy me.

"Hunter's right; Doc should go," Gwen says, refuting Pete's open dismissal of my value. His wounded expression tells me this fight isn't over.

Gwen takes in a breath, as if steadying herself for her next words. "My mother's notes state that the virus originated in

Germany and was sent to Britain by an anonymous person with a dire warning that London would be the first target. While the initial research was well supported, after ten years the monarchy was no longer interested and deemed it a false threat. My mother was reassigned to some other project. Look how that panned out."

With London currently nothing but a pile of ashes, there's no rebuttal. It seems like years since our home was bombed by Hook and the Marauders. However, the innocence of all our childhoods was stolen just under a year and a half ago.

"I should stay here. Who will care for the sick if I leave? Who will watch Bella?" I protest. "If I go, I'll be putting everyone at risk. I can't handle knives, swords, or guns like the rest of you. Until Pete's group removes the queen from power, there's nothing I can do. Once she's no longer a threat, I can take the cure, reproduce it in the Lohr lab, and distribute it."

"Time is something we don't have," Hunter says. "The sooner you get started, the quicker we can save what people still remain throughout the world. Second, you may have found the cure, but the threat is far from gone. If the Bloodred Queen contains the original virus, we will always be at risk."

"We should all be immune to it now, shouldn't we?" Maddox asks. "It doesn't matter anymore what she does with it."

"Not if she uses it to create a different form of the virus," Hunter says.

"Why would she do that?" Lily interjects. "What she wants is world power. Killing off everyone makes no sense."

"I don't think she expected the fallout from the original attack. I think she planned to use the destruction of London to show what power she had as a way of intimidating other world leaders to bend to her will. With the virus spreading the way it has, there are only two things that will bring people to her mercy: a cure to the current outbreak and the threat of a resistant strand," Hunter says.

Sweat beads my brow as I consider the possibilities. "He's right. When I added the lizard protein to the original antidote, it stalled the side effects of the virus but created new symptoms. We know the virus is capable of mutating. Depending on who handles the samples, it could be manipulated into something far worse than what we've already seen."

"Worse than death?" Lily asks.

"Yes, much worse!" I say.

"What's worse than dying?" Alyssa says.

Worry lines form on Hunter's forehead. His expression says it all. The horror of the reality he's painted feels like a punch in my gut.

"*Living*," I say, my tone filled with fear.

No one says anything but instead give one another confused glances.

"Living as something the Bloodred Queen has concocted," I say. "You've seen what she's done to the animals around here. The gryphons, the Bandersnatches, and who knows what else lies across the country. What's to stop her from doing the same to humans? You saw how the original cure affected Katt in

Umberland. She was becoming more reptilian by the day. We know Katt sent that cure to the Bloodred Queen. She can use it to buy the loyalty of other nations."

"If the virus hasn't already spread that far," Hunter says, "then the threat of it will buy their compliance."

"And if it hasn't," I say, "if the virus has only spread throughout Europe, a new concoction could be one that ultimately wipes out entire continents. Whoever sent that vial to the biological lab in London knew the devastation it would cause. They were England's ally and understood that in the Bloodred Queen's hands it could devastate nations. We have to find the virus and destroy it for good."

"Of course they were allegiant," Jack shouts. "I've told you already that it was my father who sent the virus! The very same king you intend to rescue."

Pete pulls a dagger from his holster and flings it in one fluid motion. The blade embeds itself into the wood framework just above Jack's head. "The word *allegiant* should never come from your lying mouth," he says.

"You might not like me or even trust me, but you need me if you have any hope of defeating the queen. You'll never get close enough to her to kill her, not with the army she has protecting her," Jack says. "If you won't let me go to rescue my father, take me with you to kill the Bloodred Queen."

Ignoring them both, Hunter continues. "Doc, you need to locate and dispose of all evidence of the Horologia virus permanently. Can you do that?"

"Can't Pete or I take that task?" Pickpocket asks. "We can find the vials and whatever else is left, and smash them or bury them or toss them in the river."

"And contaminate the water, soil, or air?" I ask.

Pickpocket looks down.

Hunter shakes his head. "Your skills are needed on the front line. After what we've encountered in the Labyrinth, I assure you, it won't be just a handful of human soldiers you'll face. This won't be an easy battle."

Emery stands and walks toward me. She takes both of my hands in hers in a motherly fashion. A lump grows in my throat. Again, I'm reminded how long it's been since my own mother looked at me this way. With hope and expectations that are far above what a boy my age should ever have to fulfill. While I attended the finest university in England at age twelve, the neighborhood children played marbles. But that was then. These days the one use for a marble is for creating fire on a sunny day. Only with the clear ones, anyway.

"The Bloodred Queen will find a way to alter the virus, if she hasn't already, only this time she'll raise the stakes. We are counting on you to find and destroy the Horologia virus," she says.

The magnitude of the horrifying possibilities settles over me like ice. The Horologia wiped out nearly every adult in London. Even when I attempted to find an antidote, it came with its own complications. All those years of studying, of sleepless nights with my nose in a textbook, will be a waste.

This is a nightmare we could relive again. This war is far from over.

Unless the source of the virus is under our control, we—no, the world—will always be hostage to the Bloodred Queen.

Either unable or unwilling to process the potential future with the virus still in existence, I nod and turn away, heading toward my sleeping quarters.

Lily catches up and, without saying a word, takes my hand. As her fingers hold mine, I glance at her out of the corner of my eye. She gives me a small smile, and I squeeze her hand in return. I feel the noose around my heart loosen just a little.

We cross the wooden footbridge and turn right, toward the rickety shelters, when my lab coat is jerked, nearly knocking me off my feet. Lily stumbles with me, but I release her hand. Jack grips my lapels, heaving me up against the bars of his prison.

"Let him go," Lily says, drawing her sword.

"Take me with you," he says desperately. "I grew up in that castle. There are secrets no one else knows. Hidden corridors. I know every passage, hall, secret doorway in that castle. If you ever want to take down the Bloodred Queen, you need me."

"Why should I ever trust you?" I ask through clenched teeth.

"Last warning," Lily says, her blade pointed at Jack's heart.

Desperately, Jack grips my coat even tighter. "You'll never take her down without knowledge of Lohr Castle. You—"

The hilt of a dagger smacks Jack's knuckles hard. He yelps and releases his grip from me, cursing.

Pete snatches the dagger still stuck in the wood above the

bars of Jack's cell and sheaths it. He tosses his second dagger into the air, catches it by the handle, and points it at the former Marauder, former Lost Kid, and now prisoner for treason.

"You're absolutely right, Jack. We do need you," Pete snarls. "For bait!"

Jack retreats into a dark corner within his prison, nursing his wounded hand.

"You may have very little respect for me—" he says.

"No. I have absolutely no respect for you," Pete interrupts.

Scowling, Jack continues. "One day, Pete, you *will* know I've been a Lost Kid all along. I promise you that day is coming."

"Only if you live that long," Pete says, running his knife over a steel bar, sending sparks into the darkness.

Jack's voice lowers discreetly. "You need to get close to the Bloodred Queen. I'm her stepson . . ."

"The stepson she wanted dead," I say. "The child she sent into the Labyrinth to be killed, and judging by your story, it sounds like Hook tried to fulfill that wish."

"My chances of getting close to her are far better than any of yours, *especially* because I'm her stepson," Jack argues.

"How daft do you think we are?" Pete asks.

"Seriously! I swear that if you take me with you, I will help you kill the Bloodred Queen," Jack says.

I rub a hand across my face, unable to believe that we're having this conversation. "I'm out of here," I say, tired of the negative air that has grown in our small, frustrated community.

I leave Pete and Jack to their squabble and return to my

hut, hoping to shake the night's conversation and the uncertain future.

"Doc, wait!" Lily says, following close behind. Her sweet scent of night jasmine permeates the air around me.

I throw open the curtain of the rustic hut and storm inside. Running my fingers through my hair, I pace, trying to shake the sense of doubt and helplessness.

Lily places a hand on my arm.

"Hey," she says, her dark eyes fixed on mine. "What was that all about?"

"What?" I say, feeling stupid because I know exactly what she's talking about.

"That back there," she says with a wave of her hand. "The storming off, the fury with Jack."

"I'm not allowed to be angry?" I ask defensively.

Lily shakes her head, places her hand on my cheek, and peers at me with worried eyes. "You're absolutely allowed to be angry, but the ugly looks, the stomping off, the way you spoke to Jack back there—it isn't like you."

Her words are like rain on the raging inferno that has been growing within me since my return to the village. My anger dissipates at her touch. I kiss her hand, grateful for the calm she brings.

"I don't know. I feel useless," I admit. "As it is, I'm not a fighter. Between the two missions, the one to save the king and the other to dethrone the queen, I have absolutely nothing to offer. The only thing I'm good at is medicine, and even in that area I continue to screw up time and time again. Pete's right not to want me to come."

With raised brows, Lily takes my chin in her hand. "Doc, you listen to me. You are a brilliant, sweet man. You care for others so much that you'll do just about anything to save anyone, even that bloke, Jack. You could've left him in that coma, which frankly we'd all have preferred, but instead you did what was right. You gave him a second chance."

I drop my gaze to the floor.

"Look at me," she demands. "All that stuff that Pete said, his continual criticism of you—it's not about you. It never has been. Yes, he projects his anger on you for all the ways he thinks you failed, but the truth is, he's angry with how he's failed those he's loved."

"But at the end of the day, it was my inability to keep them alive that matters," I say, the lump in my throat aching. "And now, with Bella in the state that she's in, I'm questioning my own competence as a doctor."

"Pete respects you, but he just doesn't know how to show it," she says.

"Yeah, right," I retort. "Respect is the last thing he has for me."

Lily smiles. "You don't see it, do you? Think about it—if someone you loved was dying, you'd take them to the person you trusted most."

She's right. If Lily's life were on the line, if she were taken prisoner—there's no one else I'd want to rescue her other than Pete.

I wrap an arm around her waist. Lacing my fingers in her hair, I pull her close.

"Do you know how much you mean to me?" I ask.

Blushing, she shakes her head.

"I would die a hundred times if that's what it would take to convince you that you are a miracle. Not only in my life, but everyone else's out there," I say, nodding toward the entrance. "To live one day without you would be as if the sun burned out. I love you, Lily."

"I love you, too, Doc," she says.

Pressing my lips against hers, I pull her closer and savor the comfort her arms bring.

· KATT ·

Like prey in the open wild, the people of Evergreen meander to their little burrows built high in the trees. Each one retiring for the night into their grass and wooden huts. They suspect nothing, or at least they haven't indicated they do. For the last few days, I've perched in the shadows, hidden in the leaves to gather as much information as possible. Intel for the Bloodred Queen. She seeks one thing: Doc. Even with the poison apple and the stolen research notes, her apothecarists haven't created a proper cure.

The queen doesn't know I've found them. It took a long time to locate Doc and his band of misfits, even with Hook's detailed description of where he last saw Duchess Alyssa in the Labyrinth. The maze was sprawling, with deadly creatures, and once in ruins, it wasn't any easier to find them. Actually, it looks a lot like how the Bloodred Queen left my country. Of course, I may have helped with that in my hunt for the Professor's and Doc's research. I was desperate not to die—I watched the kids in Maddox's garden, night after night, finding relief in death. The bodies piled up at morning light. I refused to be like those fools. And the Bloodred Queen was the best option not only to secure my own survival, but to ultimately overthrow—all in due time. After all, if her apothecarists developed the virus, then surely they could find the cure. Or at least I thought so. With the research journals in my hands, she assured me safe rescue and sanctuary.

What she doesn't know is that I plan to take her crown.

She's still too strong for me to defeat—at least on my own. Doc's cure saved us both, but cursed us at the same time. She's grown even more powerful as the mutated antidote has taken effect. We live, but no longer just as humans, taking on the strength and armor of something beastly. Something only Doc seems to be able to reverse.

In the end, only one of us will receive the real antidote, and it won't be the Bloodred Queen.

For now, I wait for the right time to collect my prisoner. As the former Lost Kids blather on about what is known and what is not, I gain the upper hand. Until then, I continue to bring the queen minimal information to earn her trust.

Fortunately, it appears that I'm not the only one who yearns for the death of the Bloodred Queen. With war plans in the making, I wonder if I should let them take down the queen. I've yet to come up with a plan myself. She is protected by an army made of steel and flesh, so I'll never kill her on my own.

Pete and his crew, however, might be able to accomplish the task. Soon enough she'll have a war on her own soil that she will have to fight. While the Bloodred Queen may have the numbers and strength, Alyssa's group possess skills far superior. Stealth, agility, intellect. It may take only one of them, Pete perhaps, to bring the Bloodred Queen's reign to its knees. If I allow it, the Bloodred Queen will die without a bit of blood on my hands.

And then what? The German people more than likely won't allow an outsider to rule their land. Not unless I become the bride of their king.

King Osbourne may very well be alive, as the people of Evergreen believe, but that piece of information will remain a secret from the queen unless it serves my purpose. Right now, the easiest and most sensible groom would be his son. Jack prattles on about his loyalty to Pete and the Lost Kids, but it is no secret that his allegiance to anyone is wavering.

According to Hunter, the assault on Lohr is only days away, as is the rescue of King Osbourne. If they find him, my chances for the crown become nearly impossible.

So King Osbourne must not be allowed to return to his throne. It's time for me to take his fate into my hands. He must either die or be revealed as a traitor so none will accept his reign. Which fate he meets remains to be seen.

As the final residents of this village bid one another good night, I turn to the Haploraffen next to me. "Back to Lohr," I say. I feel the wires in the circlet crown I'm wearing heat up, casting a golden glow on the creature's primate face. The circlet on my head links me to the creature, part mechanical, part monkey. With a nod, it flaps its metal wings once and turns. I grab the reins and climb onto the steel-and-leather saddle.

I'm about to make the command for the army of winged monkeys to return to the castle when an argument draws my attention.

Jack's face presses up against the cell bars, his coat tight in Pete's grip.

"You've been spouting off at the mouth for months about knowing things that no one else knows," Pete says through clenched teeth. "I'm not inclined to believe you, but my curiosity is piqued. Start talking."

"Oh, I have plenty I could share, but I need something from you in return," Jack says.

"You're not exactly in a position to be making negotiations," Pete says, pulling him even harder into the bars.

Jack shoves Pete and takes a few steps back. Throwing his hands up, he smiles. "Then I guess I've got nothing to share."

He returns into the dark corners of his prison.

Even from where I hide, I can see fury etched in the lines of Pete's face. He slams his hand hard against the bars. They rattle loudly, a sharp clang in comparison to their whispers.

"Fine! But this stays between you and me. Got it?" Pete says.

Jack reappears in the dim torchlight and rests his arms against the horizontal bar on the cell door. "Absolutely."

They continue in bantered conversation, but their hushed voices are beyond what I can hear. I tap my bottom lip with the claw of my index finger. "Interesting. Very interesting," I mumble to myself.

Perhaps I'm being too hasty to leave the Bloodred Queen's fate to the Lost Kids. Whatever Jack is hiding could be advantageous.

I turn to the lead Haploraffen, Kommandt. "Change of plans. Take them captive along with the others from England."

"And the rest of the village?" Kommandt asks.

"Burn it to the ground," I say.

· ☐☐☐ ·

Sleep evades me. As I consider the evening's discussion, fear prickles the hair on my skin. Daily, the Guard encounter the fierce mutated creatures that once called the Labyrinth their home. Now they roam free, taking any unsuspecting victim. Often, their meal is the forest wildlife. Other times, it's one of our own.

With the enormous appetites they have, game has become scarce. We might have survived the Horologia virus and all that's come with it, but it may be for naught. Most of the villagers are on the mend, as slow as it is, but food remains our biggest worry.

The reality is, as much as I hate to accept it, we either risk the dangers of escaping what remains of the Labyrinth, or stay here and starve to death. Or be eaten. None of the options are particularly pleasant. After the bloody battles in both Everland and Umberland, the idea of joining the assault team in Lohr is unsettling, but no more unsettling than staying here.

After staring at the thatched roof of my shelter for what seems like hours, I slip from beneath the ragged blankets and pull them up over Lily. As always, she is restless in her sleep. Most nights she is vexed with nightmares, causing her to cry out. It is the only time I've witnessed her fears and sorrows. During waking hours, she wears a steady, unmoving expression, masking what I know lies beneath the surface. She's guarded with her nightly terrors, refusing to admit that the demons of her past still haunt her. I worry for the toll it must take on her. One can only bottle up their insecurities for so long.

Pulling on my stained lab coat, I retreat back out into the treetop village. Cloaked by the shadows of the night, I creep across the rope bridge, careful not to step on the few weathered boards that I know creak with every footstep.

I'm halfway over the bridge when flashes of light and fire break through the boughs of the thick branches, singeing the dry leaves and pine needles. The hanging walkway sways violently, nearly tossing me over the ropes. I hold on, struggling to get to a platform. When I reach the other side, another explosion rocks the village. Screams ring through the trees in every direction, bringing back memories of the night London was invaded a year and a half ago. The familiar whistle of plummeting bombs, the heat of the fires roaring, and the smell of burning bodies make me double over, vomiting at the recollection of day one when this war began. Surrounded by chaos, my ears are assaulted with the sound of loss, destruction, and madness. The echo of death.

A ball of fire breaks through the branches and hits an unoccupied hut, sending it into a bonfire of flames.

Hunter bursts from the armory building. He takes in the inferno before him, seeming dismayed. He calls out orders, but they are lost beyond the barrage of flames that has set our village ablaze. Heat burns my cheek as a firebomb grazes me, hitting the tightly tied knots of the rope bridge. The fibers burn too quickly, cutting most from escape ladders.

"Lily!" I scream, panic rising within me. I shout for her again, but through the fire and smoke, our hut is invisible.

Hunter grips my arms. "Get the antidote and take cover. Now!" he commands.

Panting, I return my gaze to where I left Lily sleeping safely.

"Did you hear me?" Hunter yells, giving me a hard shake.

"What about you and the others?" I ask.

Hunter shakes his head. "That's for me to worry about. That antidote cannot be destroyed! Without the poison apple, it can't be duplicated."

Quickly, I nod my head. With one last look at my hut, I grit my teeth, only wanting one thing—to save Lily. Instead, I race toward the makeshift laboratory where I've worked the last three months.

The rope bridge to my workshop is severely damaged. Holes riddle the wooden plank, and only one of the scorched fiber anchors remains attached. It doesn't look secure, but there is no way to the other side. Carefully, I grip the handholds and step out onto the rickety bridge. The bridge shakes with each movement I make. The planks groan beneath my boots.

Another whistle of a fire cannon piques my attention. Tilting my gaze up, my skin turns to ice as the blazing ammunition hurtles toward me. With no other choice, I throw myself to the floor. The cannon crashes into the bridge posts behind me, immediately snapping what's left of the anchors. As the walkway falls, I hang on tightly, waiting to plummet to the forest floor.

Instead, I hit against the tree hard, nearly losing my grip. It takes a few seconds for the pain to dissipate. I peer up; the platform is only two meters away. I climb, using the wooden planks as rungs of a ladder. One breaks beneath my weight, but the others hold true.

When I reach the platform, the sight before me robs my lungs of all air. A creature, half primate and half machine, looms over me. And next to it is Katt.

"It's your lucky day," she announces. "While most of the others are useless to me, you are valuable."

"Don't do this," I beg.

Katt tilts her head back and laughs. "Don't do what? Let you run off with the rest of the Lost Kids? I already made that mistake. What I should have done is taken you captive and offered you and the Professor's notes to the Bloodred Queen. That's one mistake I won't repeat."

My stare darts between Katt and my lab as I wonder if I can sprint past her and the beast to get to the antidote.

I dash forward just as she shouts, "Burn it down!"

The creature turns, and with a single shot from the cannons perched on its shoulders, it sets my workshop on fire.

"No!" I cry out too late. Falling to my knees, I watch our only hope of survival as the human race goes up in flames.

Katt sidles up next to me. "Time to go. You've got an antidote to make."

Bolting to my feet, fueled by fury, I tower over her. "Do you know what you've just done? You've destroyed the very antidote you want me to make."

"You lie," she hisses, but I can hear the uncertainty in her voice.

"No. The cure was in my lab. How do you think we managed not to look like you?" I stay near where the bridge once stood, even as the fire eats its way close to us. "I had the antidote that could've cured you."

Katt lets out a bloodcurdling scream. Then, seeming to get ahold of herself, she says, "You made it once. You can make it again."

I stare helplessly at the inferno devouring my lab. My notes, my materials—gone. Months of work.

"Take him to the castle," she demands.

The machine behind flaps its wings, rising in the air above me before digging its claws into my arms.

"Back to Lohr!" Katt shouts. She throws herself onto the riding saddle of another beast. Carrying me through the smoke and flames, the machine leaves behind Evergreen and its residents in a fury of fire.

· GAIL ·

A snuffle startles me awake. Two button-like eyes stare at me as the piglet chews on the last of the food I've brought: a piece of fruit, a handful of berries and nuts, and a few pieces of deer jerky. The pear is brown and bruised, probably from being tossed about in my rucksack when I ran from the Bandersnatches.

"You little thief," I say, tugging my bag to my chest. The piglet oinks in disapproval and continues to gnaw the inedible fruit.

"You're lucky I didn't want it anyway," I say. Sitting up, I stretch to work the kinks out in my body. My neck and back are sore from lying on the hard ground.

Sunshine bathes the cave entrance in a golden glow. Grabbing my bag and bow, I start to crawl through the narrow passage. Halfway through, I look over my shoulder.

"Well, are you coming?" I ask, noticing the piglet hasn't moved.

It sniffs the air before dashing past me and through the opening.

"Wait! Slow down!" I shout.

I give chase, dreading the shame of returning home empty-handed. I peek out of the cavern, but the piglet is gone. The woodlands are eerily still. Even the birds seem to have gone quiet. The hush is disconcerting, making the hair on my arms stand up. A gray haze hovers beneath the boughs of the trees. The smell of burning wood catches my nose. Here in the forest, smoke like this means one thing.

Unable to breathe, I break into a sprint. Sharp branches sting my face and arms as I race past them. Drawing closer to home, the smoke grows thicker. My eyes water and my lungs seize. I pull my tunic over my mouth and nose. Although I can't see the flames, I feel the heat.

When I finally make my way to the village entrance, the Guard are not at their posts. Instead, the trees anchoring my village are ablaze like enormous torches in the early morning sky. I stumble through embers and smoke, searching for any survivors. Bodies litter the forest floor. Most are so charred or disfigured that they are no longer recognizable. Only their garments give a clue of who they are . . . or were. Bile burns my throat.

Among the bodies are the remains of horrifying creatures. Part monkey and part machine, they lie unmoving. Numerous arrows and bullet wounds riddle their carcasses. There is no doubt in my mind that these beasts are creations of the Bloodred Queen.

The smell of burnt flesh hangs heavy in the air. Blood oozes down the trunks like thick molasses from the village platforms above. I can only imagine how many of my community took their last breaths among the tree branches.

Piles of twisted metal from the destroyed hovercycles smolder from the assault they have taken.

"Ma! Pa!" I shout over the crackle of fire. "Where are you?" I cough, choking on the foul air.

The roar of the firestorm devours my voice. Shielding my eyes from the sting of smoke, I make my way through the destruction, dodging the remains of charred corpses and scattered machine parts. A crack rises above the devastation. Turning my gaze up, an icy bite speeds through my bones. I throw myself down to the ground, out of the path of a fiery tree limb as it crashes.

Flames surround me, engulfing anything that will burn. With the smoke growing heavier, I turn back and creep along the forest floor, searching for a way out. My hand falls on a black boot. I know I shouldn't look, but I can't help it.

Lying on a bed of leaves is the blond girl from Everland. Bella. Her blue eyes stare lifelessly at the fiery canopy above. Her copper wings, apparently re-created by one of the Lost Kids, lie beneath her. In the inferno surrounding me, she looks like an angel. A wooden flute sticks out of the pocket of her tunic. I know I don't have much time. My life is at risk if I stay much longer, but I can't just leave her like this. I fold Bella's hands in front of her and close her eyelids.

Although I don't know her well, the stories of her bravery and strength told by her fellow Lost Kids burn in my mind.

"Fly fast and true, Lost Girl," I say, wishing I had gotten to know her better.

Just a few meters away a hovercycle leans against one of the few trees not on fire. My breath catches as the instinct to survive kicks in. Bolting to my feet, I rush toward the vehicle, my arm covering my face to protect it from the flames. As I throw a leg over the deer-hide seat, my gaze falls upon a leather flight jacket crumpled on the ground. My father's name, Hunter, is stitched on one arm with heavy black thread. I rarely see my father without that coat.

Nausea overwhelms me again.

"Pa!" I shout, abandoning the hovercycle.

I find his battered body nearby, twisted and broken beneath singed leaves and twigs. Ash leaves a snowy film on his dark completion. Deep gashes slice his neck and arms. Brick-colored stains coat the fabric of his shirt and pants. A crimson ribbon of blood spills from the corner of his mouth. He pants, his breaths urgent and shallow.

"Pa! I need to get you out of here," I say, panicked, trying to lift him. I am no match for his dead weight, though. After several attempts, I shout for help, but no one answers back. Again, I work to move him. This time, his familiar, strong hand rests on my arm.

"They're gone," he says through ragged breaths. "No one is left."

His words don't make sense. How could everyone possibly be gone? "Shh. Pa, don't worry. You're fine. Where's Ma?" I ask frantically.

He coughs, managing only to say, "Dead."

The gravity of his news hits me like a bolt of lightning.

Intuitively, I knew this the moment I laid eyes on the fiery village, but to hear the words spoken makes it all the more real. My friends, my family . . . my mother. All of them gone. A hollow builds inside of me as I wonder which of these bodies blanketing the forest floor is my mom.

My father coughs some more and blood sputters from his mouth. I wipe his lips with the cuff of my shirt, but it does no good as liquid life continues to ooze from the corners of his lips. I choke back a sob, realizing that even if I could find someone to help, he won't last an hour. Grief consumes me as I struggle to speak my next words, knowing they're a lie.

"Shh. Conserve your energy. We'll get you help. You'll be okay," I say, trying to reassure myself as much as him.

Pa's eyes begin glass over and I shake him, eager to keep him awake. "No! Don't you dare leave me!"

His pupils focus on my eyes. "Take this," he says, unfurling his fingers. Lying in his palm is the brass key from around his neck. I recognize the intricate design instantly. The bow is made up of decorative swirls and arches. It's the work of the royal keymaker. No one else can smelt and create designs like this. It's the key my father took from the prisoner, Jack. He's kept it close, never allowing others near it.

"What?" I ask, confused.

Pa tries to speak, but his words only gurgle from deep within him. He wraps my hand over the key and squeezes. "Go to the Emerald Isle. Find Ginger east of the Wicklow Mountains.

She'll help. Save . . . King . . . Osbourne." His final words fade to a whisper as his grip softens and his hand becomes limp.

"Pa?" My voice quivers, but he doesn't answer. "No, Pa! Don't go!"

Tears burn my eyes. I throw my head back and scream, the song of my sorrow engulfing the roar of the firestorm around me. As the fire closes in on me, I lace the chain over my neck, choking back sobs. My tears leave their mark on the layer of dust and ash on his face.

"I *will* save the king," I say, resting my forehead on his. "For you. For us all." With one last kiss to his temple, I grab his gun, snatch up my rucksack, and stand. There's nothing left of my home, no family here. I throw a leg over the hovercycle, clip the toe of my boots in the foot cage, and turn on the vehicle.

I take one last look at my home. Fire consumes every bit of it.

"Do you hear me? Have no doubt, Bloodred Queen. I am coming for you. You *will* pay for what you've done," I shout. "Your blood will spill when this is over."

I rev the engine of the hovercycle and the propellers beneath the machine whir. Ash whirls in a cyclone of dust and flames as I rise into the early morning sky and head west.

· KATT ·

irelight flickers off the cold stone walls, casting imp-like shadows. Carrying a torch in one hand and lifting the skirt of my white gown with the other, I step over the threshold into the narrow hallway, following the sounds of prisoners' protests.

Cell doors slam hard, echoing throughout the dungeon as the handful of detainees are introduced to their new home.

Driven by rage for having been so close to the cure and losing it, I storm toward the prison. Only a few months ago, these kids were the defiant ones, refusing to honor me with the respect my royal blood was due. Now respect is all they can possibly have for me when their lives depend on it.

I reach the end of the passageway, my eyes meeting each Lost Kid's; they greet me with furious expressions. For now, they are not my worry; they are heavily guarded by the Haploraffen. The mechanical winged beasts are dependable. Certainly more reliable than the queen's sons. First rule of world domination: Don't send anyone to do your dirty work. Which is why this war is mine and mine alone. But to win, I'll need a little help.

At the moment, it's Jack I seek. As I continue down another corridor and into the next bank of prison cells, I think of my future husband, Jack, and his brother, who remain imprisoned in each of their own cells.

Poor, poor Hook . . . I mean, Hanz.

I'm not sure which name is worse.

Sweet Hanz, the Bloodred Queen's only biological son, sits behind thick steel bars, disheveled and gaunt. If gullible had a face, it would be his. Even after doing his mother's bidding, he still is really nothing but her pawn. And yet he openly questions how he could prove his loyalty to her in the dark, damp shadows of his prison cell here in Lohr. I can't really say why the Bloodred Queen has incarcerated him. Perhaps it's because when he was supposed to take over London for the German crown, he left it in ashes. Or maybe it's because after retrieving the poison apple from the Labyrinth, it, too, was left in ruins. Prison might be the only place he can be without leaving destruction in his wake.

Either way, I don't care. One less in the way of my crown.

The irony of the circumstances is nothing less than amusing. Once a princess of England, a daughter into the bloodline that the Bloodred Queen intended to annihilate. Now it's just a matter of time before I take her crown. Here I stand on the very castle grounds of the enemy, unwittingly her closest ally.

The Bloodred Queen sought to take my kingdom; I shall take hers. In due time. Revenge for what she's done to my country, my family, and my future. Granted, my sister was next to claim the crown, but that was just a small barrier. I've dispatched others far more difficult.

As sick as she was the last time I saw her, I can only assume my sister has finally met her demise. It's sad, I suppose. While she was merely a year older than me, we were never all that close. She was too busy learning the necessities of being a real queen in the event our mother was incapable of ruling. Meanwhile, I was left to lessons about etiquette and how to hold a teacup properly so I might be wedded off to a lord. The thought is vile, reigniting the embers of disdain I had for my sister. No longer will I be in the shadow of Little Goody Two-Shoes. She'll be missed . . . on occasion.

Water drips from the ceiling of the musty, dark jail. Wind howls between the thick bars of open windows, sending bitter air into the small room. I stop in front of a cell and place the torch in the metal sconce on the wall. Arranging my skirts around me, I sit on the window ledge with my back up against the frame, facing the brothers in their cells. It must be humiliating to be a prisoner in your own home. I almost feel sorry for them.

"Well, well, look what the cat's dragged in," Hook says smugly. "No pun intended."

"Cute," I reply.

"I have no idea who you are, but trust me, when I get my hands on you, you're going to regret it," Jack says, his teeth chattering. "Do you know how many you killed back there?"

"Believe me, I'm well aware," I say.

"Don't bother with her. She isn't worth your breath," Hook says, carving another tick into the wall of his cell. He's been here long enough that it is full of slash marks counting the days of his imprisonment.

"I have nothing she wants," Jack retorts.

"Of course you do. She's the witch's little minion. There must be something she needs from you. After everything the queen has put us through in both Everland and the Labyrinth, there's never enough torture to find out what that is," Hook growls. "Clearly she enjoys tormenting others as much as my mother does."

"The apple doesn't fall far from the tree, does it?" Jack says.

Hook launches from the floor. He grips the bars, the metal fingers of his right hand scratched and rusted. In the torchlight, his face sneers behind his long unkempt hair. His dark clothes are nothing but rags. Frayed threads line the edge of his eye patch.

"You're no better, little brother," Hook spits.

"Stepbrother," Jack snarls.

"Now, now, boys. Can't we all just get along?" I say as sweetly as I can. Reaching inside my pocket, I pull out an apple and shine it on the pleat of my skirt. Its bright red peel gleams in the torchlight.

Jack wrinkles his nose as if the sight of the fruit disgusts him. Hook looks away, appearing equally nauseated. I slowly walk by their cells, each click of my boots as daunting as the next. But behind their disgust they try to hide their watering mouths—Hook especially since it's been months since he's seen a decent meal.

"What? Were you expecting a gourmet dinner?" I ask,

feigning surprise in their reactions. "You ought to be grateful. If you saw what the chef had planned for you, you'd be begging me for a bite."

Hook props an arm up on the bars and rests his forehead against it. "Let me guess: It's poisonous, right?"

"You have some nerve," Jack says, fury evident in his clenched jaw.

"Suit yourself," I say, shrugging. Closing my eyes, I bite into the fruit dramatically and chew with pleasure. As expected, when I open my eyes both boys are watching me intensely.

"So, what is it you want from us, Katt?" Hook says, his single functioning eye fixated on the piece of fruit in my hand.

"From you, sweetheart, I don't need a single thing," I say.

I step toward Jack's cell, take another intentional bite of the piece of fruit, and watch Jack swallow hard.

"But you—you might be of some use," I say. "Open his cage and restrain him." I gesture to the Haploraffen outside Jack's cell. It does as I ask. Jack tries to resist, but the winged creature is too strong.

Entering the cell, I hold out the apple.

Jack's eyes grow wide as he struggles in the Haploraffen's hold.

"Tsk, tsk," I chide. "You know that fighting will only make it worse for you. Be a good little Lost Kid and sit still. I mean . . . *former* Lost Kid." Jack scowls, rage seething in his gaze.

Smiling slyly, I tilt my head. "Aww, have I hurt your precious feelings?"

Running my clawed finger up his neck, I give his chin a slight push, exposing the scarred skull and crossbones burned just behind his ear: the mark of the Marauders. "Seems to me that a boy who's pledged his allegiance to so many has very little room to be offended."

"Everything I've done has only been to set things right. To do what my father would've done. I joined the Marauders to keep an eye on my lying stepbrother," he says, glaring at Hook. "I became a Lost Kid only to assist the survivors of the Bloodred Queen's destruction on England."

"And what about handing over the Lost Kids to your brother?" I say.

His jaw twitches. "All Hook wanted was Gwen. I stayed true to my father's legacy. Save as many as possible. So I sacrificed one for security of the rest. It never was supposed to end in Everland like it did," he says.

Amused, I laugh at his sense of gallantry. "Sacrifice one for the greater good of the whole. How noble of you."

"Oh, boo-hoo," Hook says, contempt evident in his tone. "You're a buffoon to have believed I'd let any of them go. I needed Gwen. She was the one girl who held the secret to the cure, and those Lost Kids were the bait I needed to bring her to me."

"Yeah, and how did that turn out for you?" Jack asks, gesturing toward Hook's artificial limb, but I see the quick flash of guilt that crosses his face.

"Enough!" I shout. "Jack, you and I are about to become really close friends. In fact, I'd say we are as close as . . . family."

"We are *not* family, nor will we ever be," Jack says, his voice seething. "I demand to see my stepmother."

Leaning into him, I grin and consider his striking eyes. "Be careful, Jack," I whisper close to his ear. "You have no idea who you're dealing with."

His blood is royalty, his skull and crossbones scar is pirate, and his orphaned heart is that of a Lost Kid. Seems only fitting I leave my own mark on him. My claws slice through the soft flesh of his cheek like a sharp knife in bread pudding. Blood stains my fingertips and drips down my hand.

Jack howls for a moment before turning his furious gaze my way.

"So, tell me, Jack, what secrets *do you* know?" I ask.

He peers at me with confusion.

"What was it you said? Oh, yes, I remember. Something about hidden passages and secret doors," I remind him.

Hook grips the bars. His metal prosthetic hand clatters loudly. "Don't tell her anything, Jack! Nothing at all. She's as heartless as the Bloodred Queen," he says.

Jack's gaze darts toward his brother. "Secrets? I don't know what you're talking about," he says, returning his gaze to me.

My spiked fingernails sink deeper into his flesh. Again, he screams until I release the pressure.

"I grew up in that castle. There are secrets no one else knows. Hidden corridors. I know every passage, hall, secret doorway in that castle. If you ever want to take down the Bloodred Queen, you need

me," I say, mimicking his earlier conversation in the forest. "I want to know about these secret passageways."

"Don't do it," Hook warns him.

"Why should I tell you anything?" Jack asks.

Shrewdly, I circle him. "I'm your next queen." I give him a slight shove, but in the clutches of the Haploraffen, he barely wavers. Stepping through the steel-barred doorway, I stop between his and Hook's cells.

A Haploraffen offers me a handkerchief. Pacing, I wipe the blood from my hands, careful to clean beneath each claw. "Here's the deal, Jack: We both want the same thing. Neither of us is particularly fond of the Bloodred Queen. I mean, look what she's done to my country. Turned it into ash with absolutely no remorse. There's nothing left of my home because of her.

"You, on the other hand, are the rightful king of Germany, and she's snatched your crown. That must sting just a little, doesn't it?" I say.

Hook groans. "I don't like where this is going. Jack, don't listen to her."

Laughing, I scrape my claws across Hook's cell bars, sending a shriek throughout the prison. Hook clamps his hands over his ears. Jack growls, unable to cover his own.

"Let's see, Hook: How many times have you either threatened or attempted to kill your younger brother?" I say. Tapping each finger, I feign counting out his transgressions before throwing my hands up in the air.

"Well, it doesn't really matter, does it?" I turn to Jack. "Clearly, he doesn't have your best interests in mind. He never has, has he? Last I heard, he shoved a poison apple into your mouth. He wanted you dead, Jack. Why? Because he knew his mother was on the brink of dying, and he wanted the crown. With you out of the way, he'd be next to take the throne."

"That's not true," Hook says, desperation lacing his voice. "I was trying to save you!"

"Save me?" Jack asks incredulously. "You tried to kill me! You poisoned me and left me for dead. If it wasn't for Duchess Alyssa or Maddox, I'd be a maggot's feast right now."

Hook shakes his head. "It's not what you think. Do you know what my mother's plans were for you? After we returned with the apple, she intended to send you to the gallows. She knew how deadly the Labyrinth was and by sending us both, she doubled her odds for one of us making it back with that apple. But ultimately, her intention for you was to see your head roll."

"And so rather than share the praise and glory of retrieving this elusive fruit, he tried to murder you so the Bloodred Queen would reward him," I point out.

"Reward me?" Hook says. "How is three months in a prison cell a reward?"

Gullible, I think as my eyes fall on Jack.

"Here's what I propose, Jack," I say, strutting toward him. "We both want the Bloodred Queen dead. I want back what was mine, but there is nothing left for me to rule in England. Your stepmother has made sure of that. So that leaves this lovely castle and all who fall under its authority."

"So, what's stopping you from taking it by force?" Hook mutters. "Seems like you've managed at least to get into my mother's good graces to be here to begin with."

"And there's where the problem lies," I say. "While I could hypothetically murder the Bloodred Queen myself and claim the throne as my own, I'm not so sure the people of Germany would take kindly to a young British girl commandeering the monarchy."

"That's the first thing you've said that makes any sense," Jack says hostilely.

"Picture this," I say, ignoring his jab. "The one blood-related kin to King Osbourne, his only son, finally pulls up his big boy trousers and demands the throne. Think about it. After losing their beloved king and years of living under the tyranny of the Bloodred Queen, the rightful heir to the crown demands . . . no, he fights to take his authority back in memory of the good King Osbourne."

"Trust me, Princess, I plan to do that regardless," Jack says.

"That's going to be a bit tough for you while you're rotting away in a cell," I say.

"Who's to say we don't have a secret escape from these cells?" Hook asks.

"Because you would've already fled," I say, rolling my eyes.

Jack eyes me, mistrust evident in his glare. "And how do *you* fit in on all this? As you've already pointed out, no one will allow you to take the crown."

"It's simple, really," I say. "The only way to any crown for me, especially into German royalty, is through marriage."

Hook bursts into laughter. "You want Jack to marry you? That's the most absurd idea I've ever heard."

Turning his gaze to the ground, Jack says nothing. He is thoughtful and unmoved by either my proposal or Hook's amusement in it.

Incredulous, Hook huffs. "You've got to be kidding me. You're not seriously considering her offer?"

Finally, after another few quiet moments, Jack returns his attention to me. "If I do, you'll release the other captives from Evergreen unharmed."

I press a hand against my chest. "It's not up to me whether they can be released. Only the ruling monarch can make that choice. Right now, that's the Bloodred Queen. But that could change."

I know my next words will gut him through and through, so I take my time. My fingers graze the gold circlet around my head. Drawing a breath, I rein in the power of the crown. It buzzes quietly, but its heat circles my brow. "Kommandt," I call out. Within moments, the head of the Haploraffen appears at the corridor's entrance.

"You called, mistress?" Kommandt says with a bow, its voice and movements both mechanical.

"Have you sent your troops to the Emerald Isle to locate Osbourne?" I ask.

Jack's face pales.

"Indeed. They are on the hunt for him as we speak," Kommandt says.

"Very good. You know what to do when you find the good King Osbourne?" I ask.

"Yes. Kill him on first sight," Kommandt says. The leader of the Haploraffen turns.

"No!" Jack struggles in the grip of the Haploraffen soldier.

I hold up a hand and Kommandt stops, waiting for my next instructions.

"How do you know my father's alive?" Jack asks.

"Let's just say I overheard some chatter among the leader of Evergreen, a fallen prince, and a few of his former pals. Something about how King Osbourne still lives somewhere on the Emerald Isle. Oh, and I might have heard plans of some takeover of Lohr, but I suppose I spoiled those. Oops!" I say. "My mistake."

Jack shifts from one foot to the other. "What are your plans for my father and the Lost Kids?" he asks.

"That will depend on your choices," I say, sidling up to him as close as I can. Peering into his dark eyes, I say as sweet as syrup, "Marry me."

"And if I don't agree?" Jack asks.

I turn on the heels of my boots, careful with my reply. "Then everyone you love will burn at the stake, including your father."

"Ha, she's about as conniving as you are," Hook says sarcastically. "You're practically perfect for each other."

"Let me get this right," Jack says, attempting to move, but the Haploraffen grips him tighter. "Will you just get your filthy paws off me?"

The soldier looks to me for my approval.

"Release him," I say.

Freed, Jack wipes the blood spilling from both his cheeks, where I've left wounds that won't heal without some damage to his lovely face. He may be handsome, but after I'm done with him, the people of this land will view me as a mourning bride as they watch me weep over his cold corpse.

"To be clear, you will spare the life of my father and the Lost Kids. In exchange, I will . . ." He swallows hard, his eyes never leaving mine. "I will take you as my bride and queen of Germany."

"Jack, you're making a deal with the devil," Hook says, concern evident in his tone. "You know if Katt could kill an entire village of people, you're eventually going to end up on her list along with anyone else who gets in her way."

"Shut up!" Jack spits, storming toward Hook's prison cell. "You just shut your murderous, lying mouth! I've had enough of your brotherly advice."

Hook is taken aback when Jack reaches for him, but he steps out of his grasp in time. His single eye grows wide. "Jack, you do know this isn't right, regardless of what I or anyone else has done to you. Pledging your loyalty to this girl will only gain you real estate in a graveyard. Nothing else!"

"I don't take advice from you anymore!" Jack shouts. "I make my own decisions. Not you. Not your mother. Not the leader of the Lost Kids. No one!"

Hook is speechless, his mouth gaping open.

"I did what the Bloodred Queen asked by joining you in the fight for London," Jack says, beads of sweat brewing on his brow. "I fought for the Lost Kids. I battled the Labyrinth every single day with one eye on the poison apple and one eye on you because I knew you'd stab me in the back the first second I took my attention off you. And even though I saved you more than once in that infernal maze, you left me for dead!"

Hook shakes his head. "Jack, I'm telling you, it is not what you think. I swear I was trying to save you."

"Save me? How many ways did you plan to see me die? Poison? Suffocation with that blasted apple shoved in my throat? By fire? Or what about when the walls burned down, huh? I'd already fought that Bandersnatch once. Did you plan to leave my body there to be a midday snack?" Jack's knuckles bulge as he balls his fists.

"No. I . . . I hoped the apple would do the same to you as it did to your father," Hook says weakly. "I hoped that you'd go into a deep sleep and eventually someone would find you, which is exactly what happened. My plan worked!"

"You had no idea that Duchess Alyssa would find me," he says.

"If the Zwergs we fought were within the Labyrinth, surely other people were there. It was risky but—" Hook is cut off.

"Risky?" Jack guffaws. "Risky? What if no one ever came? What about that?"

"But they did!" Hook says. "I saw people in the garden as I escaped."

"As you left me for dead!" Jack says, clenching Hook's bars. "And my father, you knew he was still alive? You knew the apple didn't kill him?"

Hook bites his lip. Letting out a sigh, he sits on the ground, pulls his knees up to his chest, and wraps his arms around them.

"The day my mother ordered the execution of your father—" Again, Hook is cut short.

"You mean the murder of my father," Jack growls.

Hook hesitates before he nods. "The murder of your father. We were playing hide-and-seek, you and me. You were the seeker. I found an empty trunk inside the apothecarists' lab." Hook's single eye shimmers. "My mother came in with the apothecarists, ordering that your father be killed, but subtly. She didn't want anyone to suspect that she was behind his death."

"Go on," Jack says, through clenched teeth.

Sighing, Hook continues. "Once my mother left, the woman was distraught over the task my mother placed on her. Instead, she concocted a poisonous tea. One that would mimic death and put its victim in a deep sleep. In highly concentrated forms it can kill; however, a small dose knocks its victims unconscious, slows their breathing until it's unnoticeable, diminishes their heart rate." Hook pauses. "She saved your father, ensuring the king could come back one day."

"You knew all this, and you never told me?" Jack asks, disgusted. "We were best friends. Brothers! How could you keep this from me?"

"If I told you, you'd have insisted on getting your father back," Hook says matter-of-factly.

"Of course I would!" Jack bursts out. "Who wouldn't rescue not only their father but the king of Germany?"

"You couldn't know. If you did, we'd both be dead," Hooks says.

Silence hangs heavy in the air. Jack pushes hard on the cell bars before spinning and pacing the prison hall. Finally, he stops.

"You've betrayed me too many times. You are no brother of mine," Jack says before turning to me. "You have a deal under one condition: You find a way, any way, to bring my father back here alive, and you release the Lost Kids."

This was much easier than I anticipated. Too easy.

I saunter up to Jack and place a hand on his bloodied cheek. "Of course. They'll all be there for our royal wedding. I couldn't marry my future husband without his father and friends in attendance. Upon exchanging vows with me, you will be reunited with them."

"Reunited, yes, but unharmed?" he asks again.

I give Kommandt a quick nod.

"My troops will bring him back unharmed," the machine says, before it turns and retreats through the dungeon hallway.

Jack peers into my eyes. His expression is hollow, reserved. "We have a deal."

"You're making a mistake," Hook pleads.

Ignoring his stepbrother's appeals, Jack holds his hand out as if to shake mine in a customary agreement.

Instead, I take his hand and pull him to me, pressing my mouth against his, knowing that his lips will soon enough be as cold and lifeless as the brewing winter months.

Jack pulls back, appearing disgusted by my affections.

"Until death do us part, my dear Jack," I say.

I turn, pulling out a hankie tucked within my bodice, and wipe away my soon-to-be-dead fiancé's kiss.

· GAIL ·

A shudder rocks me awake. After putting the hovercycle on autopilot with the coordinates for the king's location, I belted the safety straps and cried myself to sleep. Life in the Labyrinth was sheltered, literally. Confined first by living walls and then by horrifying monsters, my home was a prison I could never escape from no matter how much I ached for freedom. Now I long for the things that I may never have again: the stories told by the fire pit, nightly lullabies sung by the young mothers rocking their infants to sleep, the morning smell of wet leaves mingled with freshly brewed tea. My ma and pa.

The sky remains as dark as it did when I left the village. It should be daytime by now. I tap the gears on the dashboard clock. It ticks at a steady beat, indicating that it is functioning properly. I had estimated that the flight would take a day, but I couldn't have slept that long, could I? And surely I'd have arrived by now.

The hovercycle rattles again, but this time steam billows from the engine compartment. The constant hum from the propellers slows, and the cycle begins to drop. Below, a large body of water is as inky as the early morning sky. With as far as I've traveled, it could only be the Manx Sea. Another jerk sends my pulse sprinting through my veins. I attempt to kick-start the engine, but the machine sputters. As the hovercycle loses altitude, I search for somewhere to land.

Torchlight flickers along the edge of a shoreline. In the shadows of the dancing flames, I can barely see the outline of domed huts. Hope and fear mingle in my thoughts as I wonder whether the residents of the coastal town are hostile or friendly. Either way, with the swift descent of my hovercycle, I doubt I will make it to the land before I lose all power.

With no other options available, I'll have to take my chances with the strangers. Aiming for the shore, I prepare to abandon the doomed machine. A chill races through me. Any body of water this far north is cool on a warm day, but with these early winter temperatures, the water is likely cold enough to kill me. Once I hit the water, twenty minutes is all I'll have before hypothermia sets in. Thirty at most.

With a flip of a lever the vehicle switches from autopilot to manual, disengaging the crank arms below the foot cages. The propellers halt, making the craft list. Before it has time to topple me over, I pedal furiously. Although it isn't enough to gain altitude, it does slow my fall.

Within minutes, muscle fatigue sets in. I grit my teeth, forcing my legs to keep moving. The whoosh of the propellers is inconsistent, wavering as I struggle to keep moving. It won't be long before my muscles give out. The shore is hundreds of meters away. I'll never make it.

The whitecaps on the undulating sea draw close. Salty spray

mists my face. I slam my hand down hard on the chrome emergency button, expecting the foot cages to spring open, but only my right foot releases. My left boot remains attached within the toe cage. Panicked, I struggle to pull my foot free.

I take in a breath just before the craft plunges into the water.

The hovercycle bobs once before the sea overtakes it, bringing me down with it. My toes and fingers immediately freeze, and I quickly start to sink. I swing my right leg off the machine, draw my father's gun, and place the barrel on the cage latch. Squeezing the trigger, the locking mechanism shatters when the bullet strikes the metal. Shoving my weapon back into its holster, I kick as hard as my legs will manage.

My lungs burn, desperately needing air. When I break the water's surface, I gasp. I can hardly manage a breath as the brisk wind sweeps across my face. Treading water does not dispel the numbness that wraps my body like a blanket of needles. My teeth chatter and my eyelids grow heavy as I start to swim to shore. The coastline seems miles away. Waves toss me about in the turbulent sea. Each time I go under, I kick and sputter back to the surface.

You're almost there, I tell myself, thinking of whatever encouraging words my parents would give me. *Just keep going. Don't give up.*

My vision blurs. I can't focus on the beckoning light beyond the water's surface.

"Come on, Gail. One arm at a time," I say aloud. My words are slurred.

Fatigue finds its home in my muscles. Unable to kick, I flip onto my back, trying to stay afloat. My throat burns when the icy seawater spills past my numb lips.

I'm dying.

This is it. My life snuffed out like the flame of a candle.

I've let down my father.

The Bloodred Queen will never be stopped.

I've failed the world.

I take one final sweet breath and give in to the roiling waves.

· KATT ·

Agonizing screams once billowed throughout the prison—but not any longer. Other than the snap of a whip, all is quiet. Doc hangs limply from wrist shackles bolted to the stone pillar as the others look on from their separate cells. I check the pocket watch attached to the chain belt I wear. It's a lovely accessory confiscated from one of the Everland girls. What was her name? Ah yes, Lily.

It is almost noon. The queen will be expecting me shortly, so it's time to wrap this up.

I must admit, it is quite impressive how long Doc's lasted. While the cries persisted through the first twenty lashes, the last thirty were met with silence. Even Lily's pleas to end his suffering have become quiet. Instead she watches the Haploraffen soldier flog Doc with tearstained cheeks and a murderous glare.

Behind their own cell bars, the other captives appear defeated. Gwen, Alyssa, Maddox, and Pickpocket keep their gazes to the floor, seeming unable to watch their comrade's torture. Even Jack appears uneasy as he stands by and watches the flogging.

Pete, on the other hand, glares at me, fire in his expression.

These eight are the only survivors of Evergreen.

"You killed her," Pete says through clenched teeth. "You killed Bella. You murdered the entire village."

"Circumstantial casualties," I say with a shrug.

Pete's knuckles turn white as he grips his bars. His dark hair hangs messily in his face. "I swear to you, Katt, I will kill you. For every innocent person you have murdered, and especially Bella, you will die."

I laugh. "Calm down, Lost Boy, you'll be getting your hands plenty bloody in time, only it won't be mine."

Pete's expression draws up into a snarl, but he says nothing. I imagine he's concocting a dozen ways to spill my blood. Fortunately, if my plans go as I hope, he won't be alive by the end of the week and neither will the Bloodred Queen.

The young doctor moans, shifting slightly in his shackles. Deep gashes zigzag across his muscular back, seeping with blood.

Judging by the portraits on the walls throughout the castle, the Bloodred Queen was once quite beautiful. Now she sits on her throne, tapping her long, clawed nails against one another, her skin turning greener by the day. All either of us desire is the antidote to the disease that has consumed us. Yet Doc remains uncooperative, revealing nothing.

"Enough!" Jack says, seizing the whip from the Haploraffen soldier. "He's no good to anyone if you kill him."

I shrug. "I have no plans to kill him. Just to bring him close enough to wishing he were dead so I can torture him again until he gives me what I want."

Jack rolls up his sleeve and exposes his arm. "Just take my blood. I've received the antidote. You can figure out the cure from that. You have everything else you need. The Professor's research, the vial of the virus, and the apple."

"The apothecarists have not found a proper cure, and there are new aches and symptoms every day. I don't have time for them to dissect your blood to find the antibodies they need. Doc, on the other hand, has . . ." I pause, biting my lip before I correct myself. "*Had* developed an antidote that worked," I say, nodding toward Jack's scarred fingers. "He made it once, he'll make it again."

I pace slowly around Doc, the heels of my boots clicking against the rock floor. Each step like the second hand of a clock, ticking down until I rise up as queen. "Either Doc creates the cure, or he'll suffer greatly. One way or another, he'll give me what I want."

Jack grips Doc by his chin and turns his face toward him. The young doctor, covered in sweat and drool, barely opens his eyes.

"Haven't you had enough?" he asks. "Just agree to her terms. She's going to kill you!"

Grinning, I'm certain that Doc will surrender. Especially with the urging of Jack, once a Lost Kid himself.

Panting, Doc stumbles through his words. "I'd rather gouge my own eyes out before I gave either of you the antidote."

At Doc's response, rage courses through me. "I can make that happen."

Snatching the crop from Jack's hand, I land three more lashes.

"Stop it!" Lily shouts, tears streaming down her cheeks. "Please, just stop!"

Hesitating a moment, I stare into Lily's beautiful eyes. It occurs to me that perhaps there's no bodily harm I can inflict that will make Doc bend to my request. However, he is not without his weaknesses.

"You're right. Killing the doctor would do me no good, would it? Perhaps I've been going at this all wrong.

"Bring the girl," I say with a nod to the Haploraffen flogger. Heeding my instruction, it trudges toward Lily, its steel footsteps sounding like a death march. The tip of its finger opens, exposing a skeleton key. It unlocks Lily's cell door and drags her next to Doc. She is thrown violently to the floor. Doc, pale and appearing exhausted, peers at her. Panic sets in as he realizes what's about to happen.

"What are you doing?" Jack says, his eyes wide.

"Leave her alone!" Gwen shouts.

"I'll take her lashings," Doc says, desperation in his tone.

Standing over Lily, I stare into her defiant glare. "I want that antidote, and if you won't produce it, maybe watching one of your own suffer will change your mind."

Raising the whip, I prepare to bring it down violently on Lily. She doesn't turn it away. Only fixes her gaze on me, determined and fearless.

"Wait! I'll tell you," Doc says, his voice weak.

Lily's head turns toward Doc. "No, you won't," she insists. "You know as soon as she has control of that antidote the entire world will be at her command. You can't give it to her. She'll—"

She doesn't have a chance to finish her thought. With the back side of my hand, I slap her across the face with such force that her cheek blooms a bright pink.

"Your voice is not the one I want to hear," I say. Nudging Doc with the toe of my boot, I draw his attention. "Start singing."

"Doc, don't you do it," Maddox growls. "Giving her the antidote will destroy any chance of undoing the Bloodred Queen's destruction."

Jack shakes his head, his gaze darting from me to Doc. Clearly his allegiance lies with the Lost Kids, but I'll be sure to rectify his disloyalty at a later time.

"He's right. The antidote in her hands is as dangerous as the disease itself," Alyssa says.

Doc drops his chin to his chest, choked sobs coming from him.

I kneel and pat his disheveled blond hair. "That's a good boy."

"Hey, Doc," Pickpocket says. Doc looks at him, peering through his overgrown locks. "We've got your back, buddy. You don't have to do this."

Doc bites his lip, seeming unsure what to do. I give him a moment, but only one.

"I don't have all day," I say. Standing, I return to Lily and raise the crop. This time, fear is evident in her expression. "Perhaps a few lashings across that pretty little face of yours will change their minds."

"No!" Doc screams as I bring down the whip hard.

Lily raises an arm and turns her head away. The crop slashes the skin of her forearm. She yells in pain.

"Stop! I'll do it!" Doc says, his words filled with sorrow. "I'll make the antidote. Just leave her alone."

Crouching, I say, "I knew we could come to an understanding. Now there's one last task we need to discuss."

"Katt, I swear, you won't get away with this," Pete says. "You will die; if not by my hand, by another."

Standing, I pace in front of the prison doors before stopping outside Pete's cell. "You want blood to spill, I've got just the offer for you."

"Come a little closer, Katt, and I'll fulfill that offer," he says, fury taut across his features.

"Not mine," I chuckle. "Now, how would that benefit me?"

"It'd put you out of your misery," he retorts. "You were just moaning about how much your body aches. I'd happily help rid you of the pain forever."

"An offer I'll have to refuse, but the blood I can propose to you is the Bloodred Queen's," I say.

"The queen? You've got a whole army of mutant monkeys that can accomplish that for you," Maddox says.

One of the Haploraffen guards growls and bares its teeth in Maddox's direction.

"No offense," Maddox says, holding his hands up. "You're handsome mutant monkeys, as far as mutant monkeys go."

Again, I pace the cells. "That's the thing; while I may control them, they'll never turn on their creator."

"Creator?" Alyssa asks.

Jack drops his gaze to the ground. "My stepmother," he says under his breath.

"The Bloodred Queen made them; she controls them," I say. "Since they would never harm her, perhaps you might make her blood spill."

Pete's eyes narrow. "I'd rather spill your blood. You killed Bella."

"And the Bloodred Queen killed everyone else important to you. She launched the attack on London. She is the one who set loose the virus to begin with. And ever since then, every Lost Kid, every person you've aligned with aside from these here, she's behind their deaths," I say. "And if the rumors are true, she killed your sister."

Pete reaches through the bars, but I'm too far from his grasp. "The mention of my sister on your lips ever again will result in taking a limb, or two, or four, from your cold-blooded body."

I shrug. "I guess I'll just have to let you and your friends rot away in these cells."

Turning, I find Lily and Doc clutching each other, stirring an idea in my head. "Bring Gwen," I tell the Haploraffen guard.

The rage slips from Pete's expression and is replaced with concern. "What are you doing with her?" he asks.

Jack steps in front of me. "Katt, you've made your point. Leave Gwen alone."

"Your opinion was not asked for," I say, shoving him to the side.

The Haploraffen guard retrieves Gwen, ignoring her protests, and places her in shackles. He drags her over to me.

"The extract," I say.

The Haploraffen guard nods and hands me the dose of poison. The golden liquid shimmers within the glass tubing of the small injection needle. Grabbing Gwen's hand, I prick her finger with the tiny needle and press down on the plunger.

Gwen takes in a breath before going limp.

"What have you done to her?" Pete shouts.

"Ensuring that you do what I ask," I say. "That small amount of liquid has put her into a deep sleep much like what Jack experienced, only there's one catch. If you refuse me, I'll give her another dose that will kill her instantly."

Pete rattles his bars in fury. "I swear, Katt, on Gwen's life I will kill you!"

"Promises, promises," I say with a wave of my hand. "I'm giving you a gift, Pete. The chance to kill the Bloodred Queen. Isn't that what you've wanted all along?"

"You just said that these hunks of metal would never turn on the queen," Maddox says, clearly frustrated. "I've had my fair share of poppy tea over time; however, what you're talking about is mad. How do you expect us to kill the Bloodred Queen escorted by her own guard? My math might be wrong, but I don't see us on the right side of this deal."

"They'll never spill her blood, but they won't prevent it either. And while I control the Haploraffen, they'll do just about anything but kill the queen by their own volition," I say. "Therefore, it'll take you to kill her."

"So what are the guards for? Just let us go get the job done," Lily says.

I laugh. "And let you wander the castle grounds on your own? That suggestion is about as absurd as they come."

"Let me escort them," Jack says.

"Even more absurd," I say. "Your history of wavering allegiances speaks for itself, and until I know you're on board with my plan, I'm not letting you out of my sight."

Jack frowns.

"So we kill the queen and get you the antidote. And then what?" Pickpocket asks.

"You can have Gwen back, completely restored to health. When you've held up your end of the bargain, I'll send you back home," I say.

"Home?" Maddox asks, eyeing the rest wearily. "Where's home?"

"That remains to be determined," I say, turning to the Haploraffen guard. "Escort those two to the laboratory. I want guards at the prison exit and one keeping tabs on the rest here in the prison until Doc and Pete return. As for Gwen, I have a sweet little place tucked away where she can slumber until my demands are met."

"Where are you taking her?" Pete growls.

"Trust me, Lost Boy, she'll be well cared for until you've fulfilled your end of the deal," I say, patting his cheek as he struggles in the guard's grip. Turning toward the Haploraffen holding Gwen's limp body, I wave a hand. "Take her to the tower. And, Jack, you'll be joining me."

Wearily, Jack looks at the Lost Kids before following the Haploraffen guard holding Gwen.

"Bring her back!" Pete shouts. "I swear, Katt, you'll be dead by the end of this night."

Sauntering down the hallway to the entrance, I enjoy the sweet harmony as my prisoners protest while the Haploraffen bend to my demands.

· GAIL ·

Water laps at my face. I shiver, my teeth chattering. Barely lucid, I curl into a ball. The murmur of voices surrounds me, but I'm too exhausted. Too cold. The last dregs of night lull me to sleep despite dawn's light. While I dodged one bullet by not drowning, death by hypothermia is an agonizing but welcome friend. I drift in and out of consciousness, catching fragments of images.

Heavy leather boots splash nearby.

Strong arms lift me from my watery grave.

Thick woolen blankets wrap tight around my body.

"Come now, drink up," a gruff older woman's voice says. Hints of cinnamon, cardamom, and ginger tickle my nose. And something else . . . whiskey? A cup is held close to my lips and I sip from it, willing my teeth not to chatter. The warm liquid spreads heat through me instantly, chasing away the icy chill. I cough, feeling the burn in the back of my throat from the alcoholic beverage.

A gentle hand pats my back. "Amzo, I told ye that was too much of your firewater for this one," a boy says, his voice kind and hushed.

"Too much?" the woman's voice says. "'Twas hardly a snifter's worth."

My eyes struggle to focus. Brilliant orange light wavers in

my vision. Sensation burns the tips of my toes and fingers as flickering flames warm them. I sip from the cup offered to me, but this time I'm prepared for the hot liquid. Closing my eyes, I'm grateful for the comfort it brings my near frozen body.

"There ye go. That's much better, isn't it?" the boy asks.

When I open my eyes, a ginger-haired boy smiles wide. "Feeling any better?" he asks.

I nod and take in my surroundings. A dozen soldiers sit within metal machines. With arms and legs, the devices almost resemble a human. Scopes, barrels, and blades cover the machines as if they're one large utility tool. They watch me cautiously, many with curious and even anxious expressions. Within the torchlight, several of them reflect an auburn glow, looking as if their locks are ablaze.

A single machine remains empty and probably belongs to one of the two people sitting next to me: the older woman and the boy, who looks to be my age.

"Where do ye suppose she's come from?" the boy says, poking me with a finger. "I reckon she's a sorceress with her flying about in the clouds like that."

"I'm not a sorceress," I reply indignantly. "I'm just a girl."

He brushes his red hair from his face. "Right, and I'm as thick as two short planks. No one flies around here unless ye be a sorceress or a dragon, which in that case we'd have to kill ye either way."

"That was my hovercycle," I say defensively.

"Yer hover-what?" The burly, gray-haired woman, who must be Amzo, belches, dousing me in the hot stench of old fish and whiskey. My eyes tear up. "I don't give two bollocks what that flying machine was. All I want to know is who are ye and what ye be doing here."

The others chatter among themselves, and their words blur in my head as they speak with thick accents.

Although the warmth of the fire and tea relax me, fear replaces the prickle coursing through my skin. In my grave predicament, I had hoped the strangers would be friendly. Now that dying of hypothermia or drowning is no longer a worry, I second-guess my choice to aim for the beach. While these people appear friendly, I remind myself to remain cautious.

"Where are ye from?" the boy asks again.

"I'd like to know that meself," the whiskey-scented woman says.

"I've . . . been sent to find the . . ." I stumble through my words, the cold and whiskey making me slow.

"Out with it, lassie," Amzo says impatiently. "We don't have all day. What are ye here for?"

"She's frightened enough. Don't ye make it worse for her," the boy says.

"Ye mind yer own business, Jo. Ye have no say here," Amzo chides.

The brusque woman stares at me with dull green eyes beneath a single bushy eyebrow. Sun spots speckle her plump nose and rosy cheeks. Her expression is intimidating. I turn my gaze to the ground.

"I'm here for a friend who was brought over five years ago," I say, my voice trembling.

Amzo guffaws. "Five years ago? Ye was a babe in nappies five years ago. How could ye have a friend from then?"

"Leave her be," Jo says, turning his attention to me. "What's yer name, lass?"

"Abigail, but most just call me Gail," I say.

The villagers whisper my name among themselves.

"What a lovely name," Jo says. He reaches down and grips my elbow. "How about we get ye some suitable garments and give ye a place to lie? Ye must be dreadfully tired, what with that fright ye gave us. Ye're lucky ye didn't end belly-up in those waters. The Manx Sea shows no mercy to those who grapple with it."

As I rise to my feet, exhaustion overcomes me. However, my gut twists, sending alarms to my thoughts. There's no time for sleep. I struggle to stand, scrabbling out from under the blanket. I feel the fabric catch on something, then a tug around my neck, followed by the tinkle of metal hitting stone. Recognizing the sound, I bend down, reaching for the brass key and chain, but I'm too late. Amzo has snatched it up.

"Where did ye get this?" she demands, clutching the key in her withered and wrinkled hand. Her tone startles me. I stumble back.

"Stop it, ye're scaring the lass," Jo says, his words only fueling Amzo's fury.

She rattles the chain in my face. "I said, where did ye get this?"

Words fail to reach my lips. I look to Jo, my only ally in this strange land.

He grimaces before giving me a nod, encouraging me to speak.

I'm unsure if they know of the king I seek. And if so, I have no idea whether they'll help me find him or if they'll consider me a threat. "I . . . I found it," I say, hearing my untruth quiver through my voice.

"Lie!" Amzo says. Gripping my collar, she pulls me close. "Ye're one of hers, aren't ye? Ye hail from Germany! Ye're here to finish what that terrible woman started, yeah?"

Jo stands between us.

"Enough! Get ahold of yerself," he snaps, his face only centimeters from Amzo's. "We don't know where she hails from. She's nearly drowned herself getting here as it is. She deserves the right to speak."

Amzo doesn't flinch, nor does she back down.

"Put her in the locker. No rations until she loosens that lying tongue of hers," Amzo says, brushing past Jo and heading to the empty mechanical suit.

Another soldier reaches a steel claw toward me, ready to take me prisoner. Jo pushes me behind him, shielding me from the metal hand.

"Ye'll do not such thing! This matter is for Ginger to decide," he says.

My breath catches as I recognize the name. Ginger, the same name that my father used when he told me to find the king. My mind is riddled with thoughts. But I don't have a chance to voice the numerous questions I have.

Amzo whirls toward us, rips off a glove, and lifts a blistered hand. "Ye see this? This is the work of the Bloodred Queen. I will not have her cause more destruction than she's already done. This is me land and me people. She'll have no part in the goings-on here. Not by her hand nor through some wolf in sheep's clothing. That girl is the queen's spy, and she'll die before she gets information from any of us. I don't give a bother what Ginger says."

"Amzo, give her a chance," Jo pleads, but the old woman pays no attention as she climbs into the mechnosuit. With a shake of her head, two other women lunge toward me with their mechanical hands. I am wrenched from the sand and lifted into the air.

"What do ye think ye're doing? She's no spy. She's hardly a day older than meself," Jo says.

Jo watches me with striking blue eyes, worry welling in them.

Amzo barrels past the female soldiers, the metal feet of her suit kicking up copious amounts of sand with each footfall. She stops at the entrance to a pathway leading to the remains of an ancient fortress. Turning, she holds up the brass key and presses her lips together.

"Hear me, soldiers of Wicklow. None shall assist this girl or else they'll find themselves in the stockade," she says.

An uncomfortable hush blankets the group.

"Amzo, what are ye saying?" Jo says, distress evident in his tone.

"Do you know what this is, boy? This key is the craftsmanship of the keymaker of Lohr. 'Tis said to be the sole key that will unlock Lohr's most precious treasure. I won't be having some child running off to annihilate our last chance for survival."

As the women drag me along the pathway and toward the fortress entrance, I struggle within their viselike grip. Within moments of arriving at the Emerald Isle, I carelessly lost the last thing my father gave me. He'd never allow such an important item to fall into the hands of strangers.

"Ye must be sloshed," Jo says, glaring at Amzo.

Amzo returns his stare. "Mind yerself, child. This is no business of yers."

"No business of mine, ye say?" Jo steps forward, fists clenched. He rips off his own ragged gloves, exposing a hand so raw with sores that there is hardly any healthy skin left. "I darn well think it is me business. Ye blather on about survival and hope, but all the time ye've lived among us, ye've never spoken of such treasure. If such a thing exists, why have ye not told us before? What blarney do ye speak of?"

Amzo glares at him.

"There's no great treasure of Germany, is there? In fact, I'd wager there's not much left of that vile place anyway. And even if there was, how in heaven's name would ye know?" Jo says.

Amzo purses her lips, fury raging in her eyes.

"Unless ye start talking, I'd suggest giving the lass her key back and letting her be on her way," Jo says, folding his arms. "Or I'll go straight to Ginger meself and tell of yer cruelty to this stranger who has done nothing to warrant it."

Amzo storms toward Jo and leans in close, her armor squealing as she bends.

"I know because the keymaker is General Ginger's da," Amzo spits.

Lily winces as she applies a swatch of fabric from her shirt to her injured arm. Alyssa tends her other wounds as she reaches through the bars in her adjoining cell. A Haploraffen stands guard, waiting for Pete and me, and preventing us from reaching Lily or the others.

I bite my lip while Pete reluctantly dabs at my gashes with a scrap of my shirt. My flesh feels as if it's on fire, but inside I'm numb—like a corpse, cold and dead within my skin. A piece of my soul was ripped from me when Lily was snatched from my side and carelessly tossed back into her cell. And now that I can't touch her, can't help her with her wounds, I feel hollow.

"Hurry it up," demands the guard who executed my lashings.

Lacking a gentle hand, Pete presses hard on my wounds. "Would you care to take over?" he asks.

I swallow the pain.

The Haploraffen growls.

A cure. That's all she wants from me. One that will take her symptoms away and that she could use to hold power over the nations across the world. Once she has it and the Bloodred Queen is dead, she'll no longer have any use for me or the others. More than likely we'll be next on her execution list.

Alyssa does the best she can to tend to Lily's wounds. Thankfully, each cell has a small barred window, probably to taunt its prisoners with the freedom they lack. The weather has turned gray and rainy, allowing Alyssa to wet the torn sleeve from her tunic for cleaning Lily's lashes.

Although I never lost consciousness, I quit counting after the twentieth lashing. The years and expertise in medicine rattle off proper care for my wounds in my head, but I'm in so much pain all I want to do is close my eyes and pass out. My tattered and bloody shirt lies in a heap in a corner, where I shed it as soon as I was brought back to my cell.

Katt has left only one guard watching over us. The other four stand at each entrance of the macramé of hallways serving as our prison.

"How are you holding up?" Pete mumbles. This sign of concern for my well-being surprises me.

Exhausted, I shake my head. "I feel about as well as a tenderized steak, I suppose," I say, groaning as I shift.

"I don't envy you," Pickpocket says, leaning against the far wall of his cell. Curiously, his boot sits in the barred window as the storm sends rain through. "I would've been wailing like baby the entire time."

Maddox, who seems the gloomiest of the bunch, speaks for the first time since we've arrived at Lohr Castle. "There's a remedy for that. A root that eases anxiety," he says wistfully, probably thinking of his garden. He rubs his leg, grimacing. It's been a few months since the Jabberwock skewered his thigh. Although he denies he's in any pain, a noticeable limp has developed in his gait since then.

The conversation dies down. Rain pelts the barred stone

windows, drowning out the hum of the machines. Hopelessness is thick in the air and there's not a thing I can do about it. No medicine, no diagnosis will make any of this better.

"Duck!" Pickpocket says suddenly.

Pete grabs me and pulls me to the ground. Machine parts squeak and sizzle. When I look up, steam rises from the Haploraffen guard as its gears grind to a halt. Behind the creature, Pickpocket stands holding his wet boot.

"I don't know about you blokes, but I'm not about to sit here and starve to death." He slips two metal pins out of the decorative metal adornments on his boot. He easily picks the lock to the cell door.

Lily clicks her tongue. "Impressive! Since when have you stashed lock-picking tools on your boots?"

"Since always; these aren't even my good ones," he says, tugging on the brass button of his vest. The button slips off easily, and clearly it's no regular button. With a flip of the hinge on the back, two metal prongs pop up, looking like tiny chopsticks.

"I've got to get me a pair of those," Maddox says.

"How did you know the water would destroy it?" Alyssa asks.

"Every machine and engine needs a source of energy," Pickpocket says. "In order for that thing to be functioning, it's either run by steam or fuel. With so many in Katt's army, it makes sense to use steam energy, which requires two things: water and . . ."

"Fire," I say. "But why would the queen resort to fire when a simple rainstorm could snuff them out?"

Pickpocket sighs. "That was the hard part." He flicks his wrists, and screwdrivers of all shapes and sizes eject from his fingertips. "Any time it stepped close enough, I gave the screws of its back panel a turn."

Pete and I step behind the Haploraffen. The hinged metal panel is wide open and the burner inside steams beneath a water tank.

"Remind me to take you everywhere I go," Maddox says.

"What now?" Pete asks, slumping against the wall. "Neither Lily nor Doc are in any shape to fight. We have no weapons. We have no idea where Katt has taken Gwen. What are we going to do? Kill the Bloodred Queen and Katt and all their soldiers with our bare hands? This is already a losing battle, and we haven't even started."

Whirling, Pickpocket looms over the former leader of the Lost City. "You know what, Pete, we don't have time for your whining. Ever since the destruction of Everland and then Umberland, you've been nothing but a prat. And now that we lost Bella, you're utterly useless. Where's our fearless leader? That Lost Boy who didn't put up with anyone's excuses?"

"Bite your tongue," Pete growls. "This is nothing like Everland ever was."

Pickpocket shakes his head. "You've given up, haven't you? You're right, Pete. This is *not* Everland. You're no longer in charge. Go ahead, Lost Baby. Sit on your nappy-covered bum. I will not spend my final breath swinging from the gallows all because you're in a foul mood. Get stuffed!"

Pete shoves Pickpocket against the bars. Pickpocket does not take his eyes off Pete, challenging him to take a swing. Pete knocks him against the bars again before jutting a finger in his face. "Watch your mouth!"

"I will not!" Pickpocket shouts, shoving him back. "I have followed you to the ends of the earth. Battled pirates and mutated lizard people. Saved dozens of children. Watched my Scavenger partner and best friend, Pyro, be eaten by a bloody crocodile. If you think for one second that steel bars are going to stop me from killing the Bloodred Queen, you're greatly mistaken. Our plan was to rid this world of the Bloodred Queen, and *that* is what I intend to do. That evil queen will see her grave, even if I have to do it with my bare hands and alone. For all the Lost Kids that have died, for every child who suffered in Umberland, and for every person lost in the Labyrinth. For each life she's taken, you'd better believe I will be sure that vile woman is dead," Pickpocket shouts.

Maddox lets out a low whistle. "He's got a point. And guts."

Pete glances at me. Shock drains the blood from his complexion. It's almost as if he's waiting for me to say something, but I'm hardly surprised by Pickpocket's threat. He's loyal to Pete, almost to a fault, but when it comes making sure justice is served, he can be the judge, jury, and executioner.

"I'm taking her down, Pete, with or without you," Pickpocket says with an eerily calm voice. "I swear to you on my pa's grave that she will bleed. That woman has taken all that I ever loved, all that I cared about, and destroyed it. And she will not get away with it. Not while I'm alive. Either you're with me or not."

All eyes fall on Pete. We all wait uncomfortably for his response.

The leader of the Lost Kids shakes his head. Finally, he looks up at Pickpocket.

"How?" Pete asks, defeat evident in his fallen expression. "The six of us against an entire army of machines?"

"I don't know. But we're here, in her bloody castle; we have to try," Pickpocket says.

"I'm in. I'm not much of a fighter, but I've done my fair share of surgeries. How much different is sword fighting from making incisions?" I joke.

"Count me in, too," Alyssa says, suddenly appearing at the bars of her cell.

Maddox groans and stands. "Well, if she's going, I guess I'm in, too. Someone needs to keep an eye on her. She welcomes trouble," he says with a wave of his hand.

Alyssa rolls her eyes.

"Me too," Lily says. "At this point, we either die in here or we die fighting."

"What do you say, Lost Boy? You with us?" I ask.

Pete nods before a small smile appears on his face. It's the first hint of a smile I've seen from him in a long time.

"Get us out of here, Pickpocket," Pete says.

"You got it, boss!" Pickpocket says, fiddling with Lily's cell door lock first.

· KATT ·

The Bloodred Queen's greenish hand strokes the metal wings on the mechanical raven. It's the very creature that brought the two of us together. A simple hand-scrawled note, a vial of the Horologia antidote, and just like that, we were partners.

"You have information?" she hisses, sounding more like a serpent than a human.

I stoke the blaze within the fireplace, one of many tasks I've taken on since arriving at Lohr Castle. Due to the Bloodred Queen's cold-blooded nature, she prefers the heat. Cold nights tend to make her drift into a hibernated sleep. While cooking and cleaning is hardly what I belong doing, it's sufficed since I've arrived here at Lohr. It makes me look useful and, for now, that's what I need the Bloodred Queen to see me as.

The antidote had affected her much differently than those of us in England. While most of the adults who survived the queen's initial onslaught died rather quickly after taking the antidote, the younger ones gradually morphed into having reptilian qualities. But nothing like the woman who sits before me. It's almost painful to look at her.

Sitting on her ominous throne and peering at herself in the ornate mirror set just behind her seat, the Bloodred Queen reflects what I will be unless Doc creates the cure. While the antidote saved her life, it did not spare her beauty. Once known as the loveliest woman in all of Europe, it is difficult to look at her without pity. She spends hours each day staring at herself in the mirror, obsessed with her transformation. Furious that it's happening, but unable to stop it or look away.

"Although most of this is hearsay, it is believed that King Osbourne was never entombed in the royal crypt as once thought," I say.

"Those tales have been rumored for years," the Bloodred Queen says. "This is nothing new."

Placing one more log on the fire, I continue feeding her bits of information, waiting for her to bite. "They say he is being kept on the east side of the Emerald Isle."

"Lies! The king is dead. I watched him take his last breath with my own eyes." She stares at me, daring me to say more.

"Of course, Your Highness," I say, bowing my head.

She regards me for a moment longer, and I keep my eyes on the floor. Then, finally, she speaks again.

"Tell me what you know of this ridiculous story of the Emerald Isle," the Bloodred Queen.

Climbing the scarlet-carpeted stairs, I approach her throne. She expects me to kneel or at least curtsy. It's what I always do when addressing her. But today I do neither. Instead, I run my hand over her chair. Its elegant ruby-encrusted metal twinkles under the lamplight. Soon, I promise myself. This throne will be mine.

Dismayed, the Bloodred Queen watches me as I rest on the

arm of the chair. I delight in the horror on her face. No one else would dare approach her throne, much less sit on it. But in this moment, she has no choice. I suppose she could always behead me like she has so many others, but then my knowledge will go with me to my grave. And with the possibility that King Osbourne still lives and may one day return for the crown, she won't harm a single hair on my sweet little head. Not yet, anyway.

"According to my sources, the coffin is indestructible and can only be opened with a key," I say.

"What key?" she asks.

I wave a hand in the air. "Oh, that's the least of your worries. What is disconcerting is that I'm not the only one who knows this, and if this information falls into the wrong hands," I say, running a finger over the seat back, "this elegant seat may no longer be yours."

"And how do you know this?" she says, a calculating look on her face.

"Because for my queen, I would find out anything," I reply coyly. "And seeing as this is vital information, I figured you'd want to know right away."

If she knew how long I've really known about it, I have no doubt my punishment would be swift and painful. Worse yet, if she'd discovered that I'd destroyed the actual cure, she'd have me killed.

Seeming satisfied with my answer, she sits back in her chair. "Tell me about this key," she demands again.

I look up, meeting her eyes, wanting to capture her expression when I tell her that those who served her also betrayed her.

"The key was made by the Zwergs," I say.

The Bloodred Queen bolts to her feet and I step back. "That can't be. They were taken care of years ago."

"Yes, but not before they entombed the king," I say. "A coffin made on your orders."

Appearing to realize the timeline fits, anger flashes across her face.

"Again, this is merely theory," I say, not wanting to reveal too much to her. "According to those I have spoken with, the Zwergs were a skilled group of people. Not only were they collectively coal miners in the southern regions of Germany, they were also trained in other trades. Many of them offered their expertise to the crown before they were imprisoned in the Labyrinth." I pause. "When *you* sent them there."

Her frown twitches.

Standing, I pace between her chair and the large mirror. "The Zwergs suspected you were behind the king's death and together, with their combined trades, an impenetrable but life-sustaining glass coffin was built, sealing the king inside until he had the strength to return and defeat you. The Zwergs were fiercely loyal to the king, and they saved his life. But before they could retrieve him, you'd imprisoned them within the Labyrinth, making it impossible for the keymaker to take the key to the Emerald Isle."

"Bok?" she snarls. "Of course he'd be the one behind these tales."

"Indeed. Only the single key made by Bok could open it. Bok sent his daughter, Ginger, to look after the king with the promise that he'd follow soon. The plan was to release the king after he recovered from the attack on his life, return him to his throne, and kill the one who attempted to assassinate him."

The Bloodred Queen turns her gaze away, refusing to meet my stare, confirming what I've assumed all along. Rumors were whispered in the days following the announcement of the king's death. Although someone eventually hanged for his assassination, it wasn't his murderer who swung from the gallows. His killer watched an innocent man die from the comfort of her royal balcony.

"When you ordered that he be entombed, the Zwergs paid a heavy price to have his body discreetly taken from the castle and escorted to the Emerald Isle by ship. And there he still resides," I say.

The Bloodred Queen rises, giving me a slight shove to the side, and stands before her mirror. Her gold eyes glow with rage. With a swipe of her hand, she runs her claws across her reflection, leaving four deep cuts in the glass.

"How foolish I was to trust the Zwergs would turn on their king," she says, the tone of her voice low and thick with fury. "I should've killed him myself."

She spins on her heels, whirling toward me. "He must

be killed, but this time I'll be sure he's dead," the Bloodred Queen says.

"Your Majesty, I've already taken the liberty to dispatch your army to find and retrieve Osbourne," I say, slipping the gold circlet from the silk ribbon tied around my waist.

"Where did you get that?" the Bloodred Queen hisses.

Ducking my head, I hand her the crown. "I found it in your sleeping quarters as I was making up your room. When I heard that Osbourne was alive, I assumed you'd want him to be found right away, but now I return it to its rightful owner, Your Majesty." I bow and turn away, descending the steps, waiting for the queen's next move.

"Halt!" she says. I turn back to her. She stands boldly in front of her throne, fury etched in her features. The Haploraffen guards in the room draw in close to me, waiting for her next command. "Your open lack of respect for my authority begs to be disciplined harshly. Lesser offenses have resulted in beheadings."

A flare of panic ignites in my belly, but I steel myself. Again, I bow. "I beg for your forgiveness, Your Majesty. I only did what I thought was right. I don't know how many others know of the king's existence. Had I not done what I did, the king may have very well been rescued before your army found him. That is, if he hasn't already been discovered."

The Bloodred Queen's next words are clipped. "Despite my displeasure with you removing things from my room, I'm pleased that you took the incentive to act upon the information you've received—for now."

She tosses the circlet back to me. "You will use the Haploraffen Halo only to conduct the king's retrieval and to have him brought to me immediately. And you will return the halo once Osbourne is in custody." Her stare fixed on me, she makes her way down the stairs, almost like she's slithering. She holds a scaly finger to my face. "Let me remind you, Katt, that my army is first and foremost loyal to me. Don't think of trying to double-cross me."

"As you wish, Your Majesty," I say humbly. I bow once more and place the circlet on my head.

"I expect a report by the end of the day," the Bloodred Queen says.

Giving her a slight nod, I hold back the grin creeping to my face and prepare to exit the room. Perhaps I'll save my last surprise for later. It's only a matter of time before she'll be as dead as the skin she sheds regularly. As if on cue, the clock tower dings, counting off another hour of her life.

"Katt!" the Bloodred Queen calls. "Just one more thing."

When I turn back to her, she is within centimeters of my face. Startled, I take a step away.

"That's a lot of information from a girl who hails from England," she says, quickly snatching me around the throat. "May I ask how you know all this? Are you certain the king is indeed alive? Who revealed this information to you?"

I cough as her scaly fingers press against my windpipe. "The traitor was one of your own," I choke out.

"One of my own?" the queen says suspiciously.

I try to nod, but end up coughing more. "Your Majesty . . ." The world is a little fuzzy at the edges. "Yes . . . a traitor . . . with proof." I motion frantically for her to put me down. She loosens her grip enough that I can gasp in air, but her nails still rest dangerously on my throat.

I raise a hand, gesturing for the winged machines, and croak out, "Bring him." After a moment, both guards return, dragging Jack between them. Jack shouts through the gag tied around his mouth. With his wrists bound, he looks quite adorable in his helpless state. He is shoved hard to the floor in front of the Bloodred Queen. He groans but doesn't look up at his stepmother. She drops her grip from my neck, and I'm grateful to take in a full breath of air. Crouching, I grab Jack by the arm.

"Don't you forget our deal. Play along or we're both dead," I whisper in his ear as I yank him to his feet.

"Jack!" the Bloodred Queen hisses. "First your father and now you? You're supposed to be dead!"

"But he's not," I dare to say. I can feel her wrath pulsating from her as I add, "The same apple you fed to the king, your son, Hook, fed to Jack. Proof that the king could also be alive."

"Impossible!" she screams as her pupils nearly disappear in her eyes.

"Not impossible. He's far from dead and singing like a songbird. That's usually the way I like my prisoners, don't you?"

"That means . . ." The Bloodred Queen stiffens.

"That means you're not a widow after all. Your husband still lives," I say. I have to bite my tongue to keep from adding, "You must be so relieved." But I don't need her to direct her anger at me.

"Why would he whisper such vital information to *you*?" the Bloodred Queen asks.

I wave a hand in the air. "Why not? He's got nothing to lose except his life. And what better person to provide information than the one person who has managed to infiltrate the Marauders, the Lost City, and the Labyrinth's townsfolk. This boy has been doing a lot of listening to campfire talks about the good King Osbourne. The fact of the matter is that just like Jack, the king still lives and intends to retake his throne."

"He can't be trusted," the Bloodred Queen says, glaring at her stepson. "He speaks lies."

"Hmm, perhaps," I say, shrugging. "It's possible given his history of deception we shouldn't listen to him." Jack squirms by my side.

"But if I may," I venture. "He is the son of the king. It'd make sense that he'd know of his whereabouts if anyone did. Even if there were whispers of where the king might be, he'd surely be the one who would benefit the least from the king's return. Think about it: If King Osbourne is indeed alive and he returns, he and his followers will destroy you. Have no doubt about that. But where does that leave poor Prince Jack?" I brush his long dark hair out of his eyes. "Still just a prince—and a traitorous one at that. But if the king were dead, then Jack's only threat is you, Your Highness." I have no idea if Jack ever wanted the throne, but it doesn't matter now anyway. He's going to ascend it, if only so I can kill him upon it and take what was stolen from me.

"Never!" the Bloodred Queen says, rearing back in horror. She spins, her gaze fixed on the ground as she considers the situation. After a few moments, she turns back to me.

"Kill him!" she declares, pointing her clawed finger at Jack.

The Haploraffen lunge for him.

"Stop!" I shout.

The guards turn in my direction, waiting for their next command.

"With all due respect, Your Majesty," I say quickly, "I'm not so certain that is the right decision. Jack is valuable. He not only has information on the king's whereabouts, but he lived in Everland and the Labyrinth, with the young doctor who has created the proper cure. He may know things, and if not, perhaps we can use him to our advantage."

"How so?" the Bloodred Queen asks, staring at me suspiciously.

A crooked grin grows on my face. "I think perhaps we should go for a stroll through the castle. I have a few others you might like to meet."

· GAIL ·

Steel bars cover a cavern dug within the hillside. Amzo opens the door and unceremoniously shoves me in. I fall onto the hard ground. Bolting to my feet, I race for the opening, but the cage slams shut with a loud clang. Gripping the bars, I lean my face against the cold metal. "Let me out!" I shout.

Amzo grins, revealing a mostly toothless smile. "Not until you tell me how you got this key and what your intentions are with it."

Frowning, I stand defiant. There's no way I intend to tell this woman where it came from, much less what its purpose is.

"Suit yourself. You're not the first, nor will you be the last. There are those who have heard the stories and come barreling in demanding to know its whereabouts. But they're all just as young and naive as you are." Amzo chuckles. "They all end up dead."

"But if you know what that key is for, why imprison me? My being here with the key means the treasure must be retrieved," I say.

"That's not up to the likes of a child," she says, sneering. "Ginger will decide what to do with you."

With those parting words, she turns in her mechnosuit and leaves.

Shouting for her to come back and release me is pointless. It will only fuel her power over me, so I search for someone who might be willing to help me.

Boys and men scurry about, tending to the daily domestic duties of the coastal village. The women, however, stand guard in their mechnosuits, armed and ready for anything. It occurs to me that every soldier on the beach was female other than Jo. I'm not sure what sets him apart. Clearly, he was supposed to be with the rest of the men.

While the village appears peaceful, there is an air of vigilance, as if an attack on the community is imminent. If someone like me could heighten their anxiety, I can only imagine what they've endured.

No one pays any attention to me. I shrink down to the ground and lean against the bars. With my head tilted back and my eyes closed, exhaustion overwhelms me.

I'm not sure how long I've slept when the sound of music stirs me awake. Jo sits just beyond the bars, resting on a rock and playing a sad song on a fiddle. The long, weepy notes dance mournfully through the air.

Nearby, a bowl consisting of carrots, potatoes, and some sort of meat in a thick gravy is emanating a scent that makes my stomach growl. I've eaten nothing in nearly three days, and I devour the stew. When I'm done, I place the bowl outside the prison bars.

"Hey, Jo!" I call out. When he doesn't respond, I call for him once more. He ignores me until the end of his tune. Then he slowly rises from the rock and saunters over.

"What do ye want?" he asks, blinking at me.

"I need to speak to Ginger," I say. "It's urgent."

He sets his fiddle and bow down and folds his arms. "Ginger, ye say?" he asks.

I nod. "Yes, is she here? When can I talk to her?"

Jo rolls his eyes. "Yer chance with Ginger is gone. What with ye flaunting yer key off, ye're lucky to be alive."

"Look, that key is why I need to speak to her immediately," I beg.

"Well, now that Amzo caught ye, I doubt ye'll ever see General Ginger," he says.

"But you know where she is? You can take me to her, can't you?" I ask.

Before he can reply, a blare of sirens cuts him off. Shouts rumble throughout the village. Dizziness overwhelms me as I wonder if the alarms are for me.

"People of Wicklow, take up your weapons and prepare for battle!" a woman shouts. She is also armored in a mechnosuit, only instead of the dark steel armor the soldiers wear, hers stands out in a tone so bronze, the sunlight reflecting from it blinds me. She clearly is the leader of this army. This must be General Ginger.

Her long auburn hair sits high on her head, a single white lock hanging to the side of her heart-shaped face. Explosions detonate around the village, sending dust and pebbles raining over us. I dodge out of the way of a large rock that breaks loose from the ceiling and hide in the corner as blasts detonate one after another.

Outside my prison, the community shouts unanimously in a language I don't understand.

"*Faugh a Ballagh!*"

Confused, I glance at Jo, hoping for an explanation.

"It's the battle call," he says. "We're under attack!"

Boots pound the soft earth, each footfall in unison with another. As if this isn't their first invasion, and with how organized they appear, they obviously don't expect it to be their last.

Another blast rocks the town, this time just outside my prison door. I'm hurled to the floor as loose dirt beats down on me. When the earth stops shaking, I cough, surrounded by a cloud of dust. I move slowly, checking to be sure nothing is broken.

My prison door hangs precariously, its bars twisted and bent. Quickly, I scramble out of the cell.

"Jo?" I say, choking out his name. Wiping the dust from my eyes with the back of my hands, I blink, trying to clear my vision. More explosions kick up dirt and shrubbery around me. Nausea twists my stomach as I search the destruction for any sign of Jo.

Within minutes, I find him crumpled beneath a tree, like a tossed-aside toy. I rush to help him to his feet.

"We need to get to the beach quickly," he says, coughing. "They'll need our help. Follow me."

I don't know what help I'll be without my bow and arrows, but I go anyway. Jo leads as we travel through thick brush. Villagers run in different directions, and I'm not sure which way leads to the soft sand I landed on this morning. I'm surrounded by greenery; nothing looks like it did when I first arrived.

"This way," Jo shouts over the ruckus. He chases after three soldiers armored in their mechnosuits.

Sunlight shines down, reflecting off the armor of the fallen soldiers. The closer we get to the beach, the more bodies we pass. Scattered among the dead are numerous wounded. From deep lacerations to missing limbs and disembowelment, their injuries, if not fatal, are disfiguring. Those who survive this assault will never be the same.

The ground quakes with the detonation of another cannon-ball. We race through a rugged pathway until the brush opens up, revealing a white-sand beach and fierce waves. Soldiers, standing nearly twice their size in their armored mechnosuits, fire high-powered, futuristic-looking guns that encase their arms. Smoke rises from the barrels as bullets fly.

Just beyond them, the sky is littered with flying machines that possess wings, and the body of a monkey. Spheres of fire shoot from cannons affixed to their shoulders.

As one Wickloreon soldier takes aim, a flaming orb rockets toward her, striking her in the chest. The armored suit is no match against a ball of fire. With a loud crash, she is thrown past us. When I turn back, she lies lifeless. Hot liquid metal from the melting suit pools inside the hole in her torso. I turn away, burying my head in Jo's shoulder.

"Hold them back!" Ginger shouts. Her hair blows as gusts of wind rage across the shoreline. Patinaed coils adorn her waist, wrists, and neck like jewelry, gleaming as she grips the levers in the mechnosuit.

"How can we help them? We don't even have weapons," I say.

"There's an armory cache nearby," Jo says.

I shake my head. "This is far bigger than anything I've dealt with."

"Ye want that key back?" he asks, pointing to Ginger. "She's got yer precious key. The only way ye're getting it is by proving ye're worthy to hold it or by prying it out of her dead hands."

Considering my options, I watch Ginger command her troops while she holds her own against the attack. My father insisted I find this woman, telling me she'd help me find the king. If she dies, my journey here will be for naught.

"Show me where the cache is," I decide, not all that sure that I'm qualified to wield anything inside of it.

Jo leads me away from the firefight and down a short stony path. He picks up a palm-size stone from the ground and turns it over. Instead of a smooth granite surface, three metal spikes protrude from the rock. Jo easily slips the protrusions into the barely visible pits of the large boulder. With a twist, the stone appears to be a door handle. A slab of the rock opens toward us, revealing a pathway descending into the earth.

Jo grabs my hand. "Stay close," he says.

We take only a dozen steps before we find ourselves in a dark cavern. Jo reaches inside his pocket, lights a match, and tips it toward a lantern he must have known was there. When the light chases away the shadows, I find myself surrounded by arms of all sorts: swords, katanas, guns, maces, throwing knives, and other weapons I don't know the names for.

"Pick yer weapon of choice," he says.

Shaking my head, I'm not sure what to say. "I'm only skilled with a bow. Those creatures are made of metal. Those arrows will never pierce their armor."

Jo selects a bow and quiver and shoves them at me. "Attack them like ye'd attack any game. Go for the soft spots. They're not entirely made of metal."

Jo picks a modified antique-looking gun for himself. He snaps a cartridge filled with bullets into the side of the weapon. Reaching into a trunk filled with ammunition, he pockets several more cartridges.

Seeing my hesitancy, he gives my shoulder a good shake. "Do ye want that key or not?"

Reluctant, I join him as he dashes out of the underground cavern.

When we reach the beach, he steps next to Ginger and takes aim.

"About time you got here. Where have you been?" Ginger asks, her question clearly aimed at Jo even as she keeps shooting.

If she's angry, she shows no sign of it. Tossing a glance over her shoulder, she peers at me and frowns.

"Who's your friend?" she asks. Her dialect is familiar, not at all the Emerald Isle accent the others have.

"Gail's here seeking yer help," Jo says as he fires his weapon. Two bullets speed from his gun before bursting, sending a spray of hot metal toward the oncoming army.

Sending my own arrows through the air, not hitting anything, I plead my case with her. "You have to come with us."

General Ginger's eyes narrow. "I don't know who you are, girl, but the last person to demand something of me and not regret it was my father."

"I'm here *because* of your father," I say, pointing at the brass key, which now hangs around her neck.

"Let's be clear about one thing: This is *my* key," she growls, switching a lever. Two cannons rise from the forearms of her suit. She squeezes the triggers with both hands, sending bullets flying. Several of the flying machines are hit. While some plummet into the ocean, others barely waver.

Pressing my lips together, my gaze stays fixed on the chain looped around her neck. "That key was given to me to bring to *you*."

Ginger's cheeks burn scarlet. She retracts the barrels of her weapon and turns to me. "Where did you get this?" she asks, holding the ornate metal up.

"My father. It was found in the Bloodred Queen's Labyrinth.

He instructed me to find you and to save King Osbourne," I say bitterly. After all I've lost—my parents, my home, my friends—I can barely contain my anger at her lack of understanding, even appreciation that I've pretty much handed her a gift. Not only does she hold the key to saving the world, but *the* key constructed by her own father's hands.

Meanwhile, my father . . . is gone. A lump wells up tight in my throat.

She considers me for a moment. "My father would never have given this key up. Not willingly."

"Listen here," I say, marching up to her. "My parents, my village, and everyone I know is dead. That key is the *only* relic I have left. Now, you either help me or I'll take it and find the king myself."

Ginger's jaw tightens. "I'm sorry for your loss. However, I merely meant that my father would not relinquish this key to anyone unless he couldn't bring it here himself."

When I realize what she's saying, I feel ashamed. As it turns out, we have that loss in common. My severed heart confirms this fact. However, comfort isn't anything I can offer her. Only that the key was given to Jack with instructions to return it to Ginger.

Another fiery missile strikes nearby, sending dirt and grass into the air.

She purses her lips and tightens her grip on the key; then she turns. "Amzo, you're in charge of the militia. Get those birds or monkeys or whatever those machines are out of the air."

"Yes, General," Amzo says before shouting out orders to her soldiers.

Without saying a word, Ginge passes Jo and me again, only this time heading back into the village.

"Wait! Where are you going?" I ask, chasing after her. With her suit's long strides, it's hard to keep up with her. Jo follows behind.

"It's time to wake the king," she says as the ground shudders from another bomb. "You two had better find shelter. This one looks like it is going to be a long battle."

"You're not going without me," I insist.

She turns. "You are a child. A little girl who should be back at home learning how to aim better, instead of being out here shooting your ridiculous arrows at flying metal chimps."

"What makes you think you'll fare any better?" I challenge her.

Ginger shakes her head. "I've faced far worse than those winged rats. And if you think they're bad, you'll be sorely disappointed. They're kittens compared to what's guarding King Osbourne. You're not cut out for this, kid. Go back to the others and take shelter."

Sprinting ahead, I stand in her path. "I'm going with you."

Ginger gives me a crooked grin. "You're cute, but you're becoming a nuisance. This is not a task for a child."

"I'm not afraid. I've outrun creatures you could never dream up. I've left a half dozen arrows in beasts that can only be concocted from a nightmare. You don't know me or what I'm capable of. You either bring me along or you'll never know the information I have on that key or King Osbourne," I say, hoping she buys into my lie.

"You have no information," Ginger replies.

I only smile, never breaking her stare.

Ginger bites her lip, clearly annoyed with me. She steps aside and waves a hand toward the west. "Well, then, go ahead."

I watch the scene behind her: smoldering machines and dead Wickloreon soldiers piled on top of one another as others step up, taking the place of the fallen. If worse battles lie ahead, I can't fight them alone.

"Go on. If you're so brave and fierce, go find the king yourself. I'll even give you the key back." She loops the chain over her head and holds it out to me.

I don't move. The key dangles in front of me, but I don't have the courage to take it. If I do, I'm not sure that she wouldn't let me just wander out into the unknown on my own. Forward is not an option. Not alone.

Smiling, Ginger tilts her head. "That's what I thought. So, I guess this puts us at a standstill. You with whatever information you hold. Me with the key and the ability to save you when you find yourself in trouble. And trust me, you will." She turns her head and shouts, "Jo, you're to stay here and assist Amzo with anything else she commands."

Jo shifts uneasily, standing several meters away. "But . . ." Jo doesn't finish his sentence. Whatever he was going to say is snatched by the torrential wind stirred up by the beat of the machines' wings overhead.

"And as for you," she says, pointing my way, "I guess we're taking this journey together." Ginger loops the chain back over her neck and tucks the key beneath her shirt. Her fury is evident as her lips press together.

I adjust my bow and secure my quiver. "I guess so," I say.

· GAIL ·

Between the onslaught of explosions and the dust hanging thick in the air, I can hardly see where I'm going. The unarmed villagers scream, running away from the bloodbath happening at the shoreline and around their hometown. Ginger bulldozes her way through. Even struck with fear, the villagers give her the right of way. I follow Ginger, nearly losing her in the throng of people.

In the early rays of sunshine, rolling hills come into view. I shield my eyes from the blinding light of flames burning grass and trees on every side. It takes only a few steps before I am struck with disbelief, unable to move. A sea of villagers and machines lies lifeless across scorched fields, flagstone walls, and barbed-wire cattle fences. Others run for safety but quickly join the legion of dead. The winged machines bombard those fleeing the coastal village with fiery cannons. A convoy of Wickloreon guards stand their ground, taking aim at the invaders to protect those who still live.

A ball of fire strikes next to me, its percussion throwing me several meters away. I slam to the ground as rocks, dirt, and grass shower me. The explosion reverberates in my ears, making the world go temporarily silent. I shut my eyes from the dizzying images in my vision. When I open them again, the world spins and a piercing ring assaults my ears. Rolling onto my hands and knees, I crawl toward a stone wall, hoping to shield myself from further strikes.

Once I find myself in the security of the rock barricade, I peer over. Choked by the sight of dozens of bodies that blanket the green field, I feel as if I've fallen into a nightmare. A deadly game far from home. This journey was meant to be a rescue mission and yet casualties follow me. Tears well in my eyes, but I don't have time to shed them.

The ground shakes as something crashes in front of me. Shielding my eyes, I blink, trying to take in the dark figure before me. Sharp fangs gleam in the early morning light as it bares its teeth. The beast stands, towering over me with its wings spread wide. Its jaws open and inside its mouth a ball of fire ignites.

My breath catching, I crawl backward, looking for anything to hide behind. My foot slips and I lose my balance. Before I can stop myself, I slide down the edge of a grassy embankment and fall over a rocky ledge. Below, a vast lake expands in nearly every direction. Clinging to the craggy ledge, I dangle helplessly. With my feet, I attempt to stand on any foothold of the rock structure, but the slick shale crumbles beneath me. I try again, but only succeed at sending more rocks crashing below me. The mechanical monkey peers over the ledge once, lets out a yowl, and takes flight. I half expect it to light me up in flames, but it doesn't come. Instead, it joins the others as they continue to shower the hillside with bombs.

I growl in pain as the muscles in my hands and arms grow tired. My pulse roars through every vein in my body as I glance down. Jagged rocks jut out of the watery grave that awaits me. Above me, the slaughter continues. My hand slips when an explosion hits nearby, but I recover.

Squeezing my eyes shut, images of my home back in the Labyrinth pass through my mind. A childhood lived within the boughs of the Black Forest's trees. Friends and family. I struggle to keep my grip, but I can't hold on any longer. My heartbeat throbs in my ears as my fingers slip. With quick, panicked breaths, I wait for my body to be crushed along the rocks.

But it never happens.

Instead, something latches on to my arms, legs, and waist, bringing my fall to an abrupt halt. My breath is taken away momentarily. I gasp and lift my chin only to be met by copper coils that cover the cliff face like vines. Stunning rust-colored blossoms decorate the latticework. The petals quiver in the brisk wind. Protruding from the wall, several of the coiled vines lace up my body, keeping me from falling to the ground.

I let out a breath, thankful that my body isn't in a thousand pieces. The machines fly over the cliff but don't seem to notice me.

The nearest blossom draws close, and I swear it's scrutinizing me from head to foot. When it reaches my face, a light, pleasant floral smell tickles my nose. I lift a finger to touch the petals. As I do, the coils around me tighten, cutting off my circulation.

"I wouldn't do that if I were you," a female voice says.

At first, I don't see her among the green coils; she stands on a narrow walkway, leaning up against the cliff wall with her arms crossed. It's Ginger. She's ditched her mechnosuit but is still as ominous as ever.

Another vine crawls up my legs and torso. Panic sets in as the vine twists around my neck. I reach for it, but my efforts are met with restriction to my airway.

"You see, girl, that there is the blossom of the Clinging Vines. Trust me, it might be pretty, but looks can be deceiving," she says.

I try to wrench my hands free from the copper coils wrapping around my wrists, desperate to pull the vine from my neck.

"Stop," Ginger calls to me. "Struggling only makes it worse. The more you move, the more the vines sense that you're still alive, and alive is not what it wants you to be. It'll choke you to death before it tears your head and limbs off your body and makes you an afternoon snack."

As if on cue, another vine wraps around each arm and leg. Slowly, it pulls my limbs from their sockets. My shoulder and hip joints protest in excruciating pain. I try to swallow, hoping for the smallest gulp of air, but my throat is too constricted. As spots bloom in my vision, another blossom's anthers dig into my thigh like long, thick needles. My scream is muffled, as the one around my neck tightens even more.

Ginger leaps from the narrow ledge and pulls from a holster on her back a revolver with a hand-size circular saw on the end of the barrel. Gripping the handle, she brings the sharp blade down on the plant. It takes her less than a second to cut the vines from me. Right before I drop, she wraps both legs around me and grunts, taking on my weight.

We are showered with thick black oil spewing from the severed vines as they recoil into the rocky wall. They squeal like rusty hinges, but I know that no amount of grease will quiet their wails.

We land on the ledge with a jolt. Gasping, I cling to the wall, grateful for the crisp air in my lungs. As I inhale deeply, I notice the flying machines give out a piercing cry, each one returning the call. En masse, they head west.

Ginger shoves me against the wall and unhooks a vine from her belt. "Let's go," she says.

My knees feel weak, but I refuse to let the general see me as frail. She races ahead. I follow her, barely able to keep up with her pace. The slate walkway is not only damp and slippery, but it's no more than half a meter wide. Some parts are eroded, leaving large gaps to hurdle over.

When we reach a dirt path, I look back. The severed vines hang limply from the cliff. Oil stains the rock in a black sheen.

"Why are you so bent on saving the king?" Ginger asks, thankfully drawing my attention away from what was almost my demise.

"My dad" is all I can say.

She waits, but I don't add anything else. "Look, it's not like we have adolescent girls on crazy hover machines carrying the key to save King Osbourne drop in on us daily," she says. "I don't know what your story is, but you're better off going home. Just tell me what you know and be on your way."

"I'm not leaving," I insist.

At the top of the path, her mechnosuit sits abandoned, over-looking the cliff. To the northeast, just beyond the continuing battle, is a dilapidated stone keep appearing abandoned. I take in its beauty. "What is that place?" I ask.

Ginger flips a switch on her mechnosuit and it buzzes to life. "The Black Keep. It's our watchtower. We keep a lookout for intruders, especially those wanting to get to the king," she says, giving me a disapproving look. "There are three others. One in each direction from here, so don't get any funny ideas about tak-ing off to reach him from another route."

I chuckle bitterly.

"What's so funny?" Ginger asks.

"You've been living, sleeping, protecting your own from within the Black Keep," I say.

"And you find this amusing?" Ginger asks, her brows raised.

I shake my head. "No. It's just that I've done the same thing back in my home. Back in the Black Forest."

"While I fail to see the humor in this, the coincidence is strange," Ginger says.

"See, perhaps we are more alike than you think," I say.

Ginger grins. "Don't push your luck, kid."

When Ginger seems satisfied with the setting on her armored suit, she turns to me. "Now that we're all buddy-buddy and I've saved your life, I think I've at least earned information from you. What do you know of the Bloodred Queen?"

"The queen?" I question, taken aback. "Why would I know anything about her?"

"That freak show," Ginger says, pointing at the flock of machines, "can only be the creation of one person alone: the Bloodred Queen. Last I heard, she's still ruling Germany. You are from Germany. And since I've never seen those creatures before, I find it ironic they arrive shortly after you show up. Therefore, I can only conclude that you have something to do with it."

"No," I say, stepping back. "I don't know anything about them."

Ginger's brows rise as she steps forward with every step back I take. "Is that so?" She pulls a gun from inside the cockpit of her suit. Her fingers slide into the grip of the weapon, giving her the appearance of having brass knuckles. I was grateful for Ginger when she used her strange weapons to save me, but now with one pointed at me, my blood runs cold. She lifts her weapon to my throat.

"Maybe you didn't hear me. What do you know?" she asks, teeth clenching.

"Nothing," I say, wondering if I could notch an arrow and make a lethal shot before she shoots me.

Ginger's face flushes. The arm of her suit slams me to the ground, and she stands over me. Placing the heavy foot of her suit on my chest, I can barely catch my breath.

"Look. While you appear brave, this is *not* a task meant for you. Not only that, I'm not all that sure you can be trusted," she says.

I meet her eyes, determined to get my point across. "I made a promise to my father that I would save the king, and I'm not about to break that promise because you think you can intimidate me with your fancy weapons and armor. I will save the king, with or without you," I manage to cough out, each word choking me.

Grimacing, Ginger releases me.

Gasping, I roll over to take in a breath.

"Seems we have more in common than I thought," Ginger says, unsympathetic to my shallow pants. "My father sent me here, making me swear to protect the king while he was in his weakened condition, knowing it would take time to recover from his attempted assassination. He said he would follow behind soon with the key to release the king once he and the other Zwergs planned an assault on Lohr to take out the Bloodred Queen." She looks to the sea. "That was the last I saw of him."

My father's ash-covered face comes to my mind. His plea for me to take on this burden, even though I've never been more than a short distance outside our village. His last breath.

My throat constricts as I consider Ginger's brave face. It is a reflection of my own.

She tucks the gun beneath the control panel and pulls a lever, arming her vehicle. Lifting her boot, she trudges just a few meters before she looks over her shoulder.

"What are you waiting for?" she asks. "We have a king to rescue."

It takes Pickpocket only a few minutes to open the locks to the other prison cells. He races up the stairs to scope out our escape and returns equally fast.

"The exit is guarded by at least four Haploraffen. I doubt I'll be able to take off the panels as quickly as I did with this hunk of metal," he says, banging on the steel chest of the disabled soldier.

"Jack would be extremely useful right now," Pete says, leaning up against the wall with his arms crossed. "If there really are hidden passageways, I'd about kill to find the one that leads to Gwen."

Pickpocket heads toward the opposite hallway. "Maybe there's a way out in this direction."

"Right. Like Katt would leave one exit guarded and not the other," Maddox says.

"The snide remarks are getting old," Pickpocket hollers from far in the dark passage.

Lily struggles to her feet with Alyssa's help. I rush to her and gently wrap my arms around her. She's hurt, but her strong arms wrap around my neck.

"How bad is it?" I ask through the lump in my throat. Seeing her in this condition hurts me more than the wounds crisscrossing my back. My beating was severe and long, but even one strike of the whip to her is far worse to me than the fifty I received. I brush my hand across her cheek, where one of the lashings struck. She smiles and shakes her head, but I know she's covering up her pain. I'm not surprised. Lily is never one to show weakness. Being the only one with training and experience in medicine, I can call her bluff. She knows it.

Her dark stare falls on mine and the crease between her brows gives away the pain she's in, but I won't reveal her secret. Instead, I'm lost in her gaze, and the conversations around me fade away. I hold her close to soothe the nightmares that rage through my thoughts, but it helps only minimally.

Like the rest of us, Lily has lost all she knew of siblings, parents . . . of family . . . the day Hook and the Marauders invaded our home. The only difference is, her family was murdered in cold blood by the Marauders right before her eyes. I can only begin to imagine the anguish she must feel on any given day.

"Gwen is our priority," Pete says, drawing my attention back to the conversation. "Once we find her, we'll get Doc to the lab, kill the Bloodred Queen, and then go home . . . wherever that is."

"Gwen is *not* the priority right now," Alyssa says sternly. "Killing the Bloodred Queen is."

Pete's expression grows cold.

"She's right," Maddox says. "We have to think about the big picture—save one or save the world."

An icy silence fills the air, and no one dares to speak. Pete drops his eyes to the floor, accepting the fate that lies ahead. I turn my attention back to Lily.

"I have to find the antidote, even if that means going alone," I tell her.

Pete's stare grows hard. "With the Bloodred Queen and Katt in charge, it won't matter if we have the antidote or not. Your job is to do what I say. Stay back while the rest of us take down the queen, and then you can get the antidote."

"I'm not waiting on you," I say. "Go get the queen. Kill Katt. That's what *you're* good at. Me, I will stay out of your way by going to find her lab," I snap.

Pete shakes his head. "I'll give it to you—you're good with mixing stuff and keeping us all alive, but you don't stand a chance venturing out on your own in this castle."

"You know what? I'll be just fine," I shout. "I can handle myself without you or anyone else. And you're right, Pete! I might not be like you, saving lost kids, rescuing those in need, but I keep everyone from dying. So don't you dare discount my abilities!"

I wait for him to fight back, but he says nothing. I let out a breath.

"We lost everything when the village was burned to the ground. I made a cure in Everland, I made a new one in Umberland, I remade it in Evergreen . . . I'm tired of making and remaking cures that help only a handful of people. It's time for me to end the destruction of the Horologia virus for good. Your enemy is the Bloodred Queen. Mine is the virus," I say, feeling both frustration and a surge of guilt.

There's a long pause, and finally Pete nods. "Fine, I'll escort you to the lab, but the rest of you will find Gwen."

I stare at Pete. I know he wears his heart on his sleeve, and I can see how hard it is for him to not take off after Gwen this instant.

"Then we take out the Bloodred Queen," he's quick to add.

"Look, Katt said the Bloodred Queen was much too strong for her to kill," Alyssa says. "Why would she openly admit that and then just set us free to do the job for her?"

"Well, we're not exactly free. She had no intention of just letting us loose without those hunks of metal on our tail," Maddox says.

"Yeah, but something's not right with her story," Alyssa says.

Before anyone can respond, Pickpocket calls out from down the hall. "Look who I've found. Seems like someone who could be useful to us, don't you think?" Caught by his shirt collar, Hook struggles in Pickpocket's grip. Pickpocket shoves Hook in Pete's direction. Face-to-face again, the archenemies stare each other down. "Seems like our old friend is now the queen's prisoner. I think I've swayed him to be on Team Pete for a change."

Pete lunges for Hook, but Maddox and I grab him by the arms and hold him back.

"Hook," Pete sneers. "I thought I smelled cod."

"Nice seeing you again, too," Hook says, brushing the wrinkles from his shirt.

Furious, Pete pulls from our grip and clenches his fists. He spits on the ground. "You're a murderer, Hook. And murderers, in my book, don't deserve to live," he growls.

"As if you haven't killed a few people yourself along the way," Hook retorts.

Pete lunges for Hook again, and this time he slips past our reach and shoves Hook up against the stone wall. "I'd watch my mouth if I were you. You're not exactly in good company."

Hook shoves Pete back. "Everland was a mistake," Hooks admits. "I'm not as callous as you think. My mother led me to believe that England was the enemy. That England needed to be contained. I had no idea what her true intent was. I was her son, doing what she asked. Nothing more, nothing less."

Pete throws a swift punch to his face before Maddox and I can pull him off. "Pete, enough!" I shout.

He wrenches free from our clutches and juts a finger in Hook's direction. "You killed everyone I loved. Maybe not directly, but your choice to attack London took everyone who was important to me away, starting with my sister."

My throat grows tight at the mention of Gabrielle. She was my first love. My heart and soul. The day she took her last breath, it was in my arms. When I turn my attention back to Hook, hurt becomes fury. "Pete's right. You *are* a murderer."

All eyes fall on me. I swallow hard. "You've also killed those I cared for."

Pete's brow furrows. Our friendship has been contentious, at best, since the death of Gabrielle. However, no one standing here knew her but us, and they never will. They'll never know her beautiful smile that brightened a room wherever she went. Nor will they know her generosity, her kindness. Although paralyzed from the waist down, she never used that as an excuse to keep her from living a full life. An orphan, just like her brother, Pete, what very little she earned by busking Gabrielle still gave to those in more need than her.

I'd intended to marry her, but now she's gone.

When Pete brought her injured and broken body to me after the bombing, there was nothing I could do to save Gabrielle. Her death left a hollow in my heart. One I never thought could be filled again.

Lily laces her fingers with mine and the pain eases, but only slightly. I wonder for the briefest moment if there's room in my heart for both Gabrielle and Lily.

Pete glares at our intertwined fingers before turning back to Hook. "You're also responsible for the deaths of the Lost Kids. All the Lost Kids, every single one, are gone because of you. You set the virus loose, killing their families and eventually them. And—" His voice cracks. "And Bella. You killed Bella."

Hook drops his gaze to the ground. "All I wanted was to please my mother. To make her proud just once. For one moment to see an inkling of love from her." Hook throws his hands up and peers around the dungeon. "But despite everything I've done for her, in her eyes, I'm no different than you.

I'm expendable. She doesn't see me as her son. I'm just another soldier in her cause or prisoner of her wrath. I have no one I can call family any longer either. I am no different than you. I'm . . ."

"A Lost Boy," I say. "Parentless, homeless, and in need of a family."

The comment obviously stings, as Hook peers down at his tattered and filthy clothes. One moment he's the cause of the Lost Kids' deaths, the next he is one himself.

"Let's get one thing clear: You are not a Lost Kid, nor will you ever be," Pete says, anger in his tone.

"Understood," Hook says.

A hush fills the air. I wonder if everyone else feels the nervous tension that simmers in my gut.

"Look, there is nothing left for me here at Lohr," Hook says, breaking the silence. "I never wanted royalty. The title, the wealth, it means nothing to me. It never has. All I wanted was a mother. It's silly and childish, but it's the truth. And now I know it's something I'll never have."

"Why should we trust you?" Alyssa says. "You've left my country in rubble."

"Because," Hook says quietly, "I have nothing to gain by helping you, and everything to lose if I don't."

While the arm that he lost by Gwen's sword in Everland has been replaced with a mechanical one, the other remains gloved. He tugs on each finger of the glove until it slips off. Wincing, he holds his hand out.

Immediately, the smell of rotten flesh makes me want to gag. While I've been around my share of dead bodies, this is far worse. Like so many I've treated, his hands show signs of the original Horologia virus, only his skin is blackened and sloughing off. At first glance, it looks like a third-degree burn. However, I know that he was exposed to the virus like the rest of us. Only, we received treatment, and he returned to Germany. I'm unsure if the return home slowed the disease or the exposure to the mutated virus has caused his symptoms. Either way, his wounds appear incredibly painful, and there's no question in my mind that if his other extremities are equally as bad, he will die.

I can't help but ask, "Did you take the antidote?"

"No." Hook shakes his head. "My mother threw me down here upon my return. Told me I didn't deserve the cure. That I could let the virus kill me, slow and painful. Judging by what she and Katt look like, she might have done me a favor."

Pete glances at me, silently wanting my assessment of his situation. I suck my bottom lip in and nod. While he may not care less about my opinions, as a doctor able to diagnose Hook's prognosis, I'm useful. "Hook will die without the cure," I say, leaving the choice up to Pete whether to save him.

"Fine! We'll take you with us, but if I smell anything fishy from you, I'll end your misery. Are we clear?" Pete says.

"What? You're going to trust this guy?" Maddox says. "After everything he's done?"

Alyssa sidles up to him. "Let's at least give him a chance. Maybe he knows the secret passageways that Jack was talking about back in Evergreen. With the Haploraffen guarding the entrance, we could use all the help we can get."

Maddox says nothing.

"Right now, all I care about is finding that lab and creating the cure," I say. I glare at Hook. "Where is it?"

Hook snorts. "You'll probably have better luck than the apothecarists. They've been working on it for months."

"What do you mean?" I ask.

"The Professor's notes and all your work on the Horologia virus were brought here by Katt. When I returned with the poison apple, it was confiscated. Everything was taken to a lab where they've been working on a cure," Hook says.

"How far have they gotten with developing it?" I ask, alarm building within me.

"I don't know. I was imprisoned shortly after returning. The Bloodred Queen wanted nothing to get in the way of creating the cure. Especially her son, who's failed her repeatedly," he says bitterly. "What I do know is where the laboratory is and that I can get you there undetected."

"What about the queen?" Pete asks.

"You'll never kill the queen, not in her condition," Hook says. "With the antidote she's taken, her scales are like armor. Combined with the fact that she ultimately controls the Haploraffen army, a hundred of you could never bring her to her knees."

"Well, then, perhaps we ought to just return to our cells and die," Maddox says sarcastically. "I certainly hope you've got better news for us."

"The apothecarists dislike the Bloodred Queen about as much as any of us," Hook says. "I have no doubt that they'll assist you with anything you need. Maybe they can come up with a way to weaken her."

"Weaken her? From what you've said, it doesn't sound like a steam train could take her down. It seems pretty far-fetched. I'm still opting for the cells," Maddox says, rubbing the scruff on his chin.

"Hook's not that off base," I say. "The symptoms of the original antidote were caused by the inclusion of the reptilian proteins. Everything from the scales to the changes in the eyes and claws—it was all because we use the lizards' blood. The only thing that really makes her strong is the armor covering her skin."

"How do we get rid of it?" Pete asks.

"Leave that to me," I say. "I just need to get to the lab."

"What about the Haploraffen?" Alyssa asks. "We won't get far with them patrolling the castle."

"Maybe I can tinker with this one to see if we can gain control of them," Pickpocket says.

Nervous, Hook looks at each of us. "The only way to control the Haploraffen is to kill the queen and confiscate the crown that Katt wears. But that's it; I won't tell you anything more, not without something in return," Hook says.

"Something in return?" Maddox asks. "The murderer of hundreds of thousands, maybe a million or more, wants a favor? This is simply mad. You're not going to listen to this nonsense, are you?"

"Name your price," Pete says suspiciously.

"I'll take you wherever you need to go, but when it comes to killing the Bloodred Queen, she's mine," Hook says.

Confused glances are exchanged among us, unsure if what we've heard is real.

"You want to kill your own mother?" Lily asks.

Her doubt doesn't surprise me. The girl who lost her own mother and was taken in by Gwen's can hardly comprehend such a desire. The Professor was a mother to us all at one point. I'd give anything to have her back. Her knowledge was invaluable. Her kindness, abundant. Her nurturing nature . . . a painful reminder of my own mother, but a welcome blessing considering our predicament.

"I not only want to end her life . . ." Hook reaches for his eye patch. Lifting it, he exposes the empty socket. "I want to get even before I take it."

Pete holds out his hand. Hook grips it with his metal prosthetic.

"An eye for eye," Pete says, with what sounds like approval.

I wave my hand at the unmoving Haploraffen and ask, "Pickpocket, is there any way you can reconfigure those cannons so they can distribute the antidote?"

"I'm no Cogs, but I know a thing or two about some things," he says.

Pete sighs and drops his gaze. Our chief Tinker and an original Lost Boy was one of the many causalities of the attack on the Labyrinth village.

"We need weapons," Pete says.

"Not a problem. I'll take you to the weaponry," Hook replies.

Pete nods. "Once we arm ourselves, Doc and I will head to the lab to see what we can find to get rid of the queen's scales," he says. "We'll return as soon as we can. And then—we attack."

"Sounds flawless," Alyssa says sarcastically.

Maddox wraps an arm around her waist. "I can just see the ticker-tape parade that will be thrown for us for our gallantry and superb tactical planning. Of course, we'll be dead, but what does that matter?"

Lily frowns, worry creasing her brow. Cautiously, I wrap my arms around her, knowing we share the same stripes of defiance across our skin. "Don't worry. I'll come back for you. I promise."

Her dark eyes shimmer. "How can you promise something like that?" she says.

She's right. I can't control what will happen to me or her after we leave this prison. We may both be dead by the time the sun sets. But I just can't believe—won't believe—that this is the end of our story.

With one hand on the back of her neck and the other tangled in her hair, I pull her into me. Her lips are as soft as satin, and for this moment, nothing else matters. When I pull away, I know in my heart that today is not our last together; whether it be on this side of mortality or the other, we will be together.

"I'll never leave you, Lily. Not in life or death," I say.

They're not the words she wants to hear. I see it in the flash of disappointment in her eyes, but it's all I have to offer her right now.

"Wait, guys, what about Jack?" Alyssa says. "He's clearly aligned with Katt."

Pete stiffens. "Don't worry about Jack. He won't be a problem."

He knows something. I can see it in his expression. Of all those standing here with us, I've known him the longest. I'm not sure what secrets he's hiding, but there's definitely something there.

Maddox cackles. "Jack? You out of everyone should know that he's allied to no one but himself. He's his biggest priority."

"Trust me," Pete says, his green eyes as sure as I've ever seen them.

· GAIL ·

There is no road. Not even a dirt trail. Instead, we trek through tall grass and wildflowers. Although the fields are wide and trees are scarce, there is an ominous feeling as we silently head toward the setting sun. While the welcoming golds, pinks, and lavenders paint the sky ahead of us, western winds blow dark clouds our way.

My stomach feels uneasy. I have no idea what lies before us. Worse yet, my thoughts return to Wicklow, and all those we left behind. I don't understand how Ginger could leave her home, especially while it's under attack from such vile beasts. They're not my community, and still I worry about whether Jo and the others have survived the invasion. But Ginger trudges forward, seemingly unmoved by the possible destruction of her home. What I wouldn't give to be back in my own village, to have those I love close to me. While tears sting my eyes, I know to let them find their place on my cheeks is futile. My family has been murdered. My friends killed by the Bloodred Queen. Crying won't bring them back.

Perhaps Ginger has resigned herself to the destruction of her community, has accepted her duty as a warrior for the rebirth of Germany, and knows that though her home and those she's called family and friends continue to fight a losing battle—none of it means anything. Maybe, just like me, she longs to be embraced by the arms of a father she will never see again and so this is all she can commit to his memory. Both our fathers wanted to see the Bloodred Queen's rule end and King Osbourne returned to his throne, and no matter if we live or die, that is our goal.

I guess we are more similar than different.

My heart splinters as the loss of everything washes over me.

There's no place like home—or family or community or the simple pleasure of laying your head down at night knowing that in the morning, you and those you love will still be alive.

Ginger reaches inside a satchel and pulls out a hooded gas mask with a respirator and numerous valves. A small, shallow tin is attached at the forehead, and a glass lid reveals a green effervescent fluid inside that shines brightly. It's not a torch or a gas lantern, but it is impressive nonetheless. I run a finger over the glass.

"Cold light," she says, handing it to me. "It's from the sea. When the water is disturbed it glows. Sort of like a firefly, but in liquid form."

The cool green radiance provides sufficient light to see my way through the darkness. However, it's the mask that concerns me the most.

"Why do I need this?" I ask.

"You'll thank me later. Now just put the thing on."

Reluctantly, I slip the hood over my head. The lack of air-flow and the overwhelming scent of leather makes it difficult to breathe.

Ginger flips a lever on her mechnosuit. Slabs of glass rise from the suit and link above her, enclosing her within the armor. She looks like something from the future.

We trudge through overgrown grass and rolling hills. Nocturnal animals begin their nightly call and small animals scurry when we step near them. My gut lurches with each moment, half expecting the machined monkeys to rise from the brush and wipe us out. The other half is uneasy with the few words Ginger's spoken since we've left Wicklow.

After an hour or so, a thick mist rolls in, obscuring our visibility. The headlamp does little to help, but instead casts a green glow in the dense fog. I can't see my own feet, much less a meter in front of me. The tall grass trails behind us, disappearing altogether as we find ourselves in a thick bed of flowers.

"Make sure the straps on your mask are tight," Ginger commands, her words muffled behind the thick glass. "The pollen will knock you straight into dreamland. And don't fall behind."

"Pollen?" I ask. Beneath my silver boots, bright petals peek through the ghostly haze. Tugging the leather strips tight, I follow her cautious lead.

Again, we trudge forward in silence. Only our boots and the distant hoot of an owl interrupt the quiet.

My mind wanders, contemplating the incidents over the last few days and the toll they've taken on me. One by one they play out in my head: the Bandersnatches, the village on fire, witnessing the death of my father with my mother nowhere in sight, my abrupt meeting with both the Manx Sea and the

Wickloreons, escaping my prison, the carnivorous vines, and my not-so-certain allegiance with General Ginger. It's all been overwhelming, and with as little sleep as I've had, the weight of each tragedy, each fear-inducing event, suddenly feels like it's too much to take on.

I'm about to suggest a rest when Ginger stumbles and collapses. Her fall is far from silent as her mechnosuit hits the ground hard. I race to her side.

"Are you okay?" I ask, knocking on the shield of her suit.

Beyond the thick glass, Ginger is motionless. I bang once more, but she doesn't stir. Feeling around the windows of her mechnosuit, I search for a way to get to her. I'm not sure what Ginger meant by *dreamland* when she spoke of the pollen, but I can only guess that's what's affecting her.

My fingers slip over a rough crevice in her glass shield. Investigating it, I find a single spot in which the glass is chipped, enough to leave a breach in her closed space. I reach for a nearby rock and work on the slivered shards until it leaves a hole large enough for me to reach her.

I loosen the leather straps of my gas mask, ready to throw it over her head the first chance I get. Yes, I risk falling into the same dream state as Ginger, but I'll never get her out of here on my own. If I'm able to wake her, she can get us both out of this place before I succumb to the pollen.

Taking several breaths, I release my mask. As I pull it over her face, something buzzes by my head. After years of living near a mosquito-infested river during our hot summers, by instinct I lift a hand to swat at the insect. The back of my hand slaps against the hot metal of its wings, forcing me to draw my hand in. Gasping, I peer down. Under the green light, the raised burn marks leave loops and swirls scorched into my skin. The dull hum around me grows, sounding like a convoy of hovercycles.

My eyes grow heavy as I reach for Ginger and shake her. She stirs, but I can hardly keep my eyes focused on her. The sleepy pollen draws me in. Ginger squints as she tries to shake the lethargy away. She sits up, seeming confused. Relieved that she's conscious, I rest my head on the soft red petals of the blanket of poppies.

I blink, struggling to keep from giving in to sleep's alluring call.

"Stay with me, Gail. We have to leave, and quickly," she says. With her mechnosuit arm, she reaches inside a panel and retrieves another mask.

Between the exhaustion of my travels and the pollen, I fight to keep my eyes open.

"You'll be fine," she says, placing the second mask on my face. "Just breathe."

After several minutes, the lull of sleep passes. Only sheer fatigue remains, but I'm able to get to my feet.

"You all right, kid?" she asks.

"Let's just get out of here," I say, sounding mechanical through the respirator.

We cautiously tread forward with Ginger leading the way. After a while, the hum of unseen creatures fills the silence of the evening air.

"Stay away from anything that comes close," she shouts over the growing roar of gears grinding on one another. We swat away anything that buzzes near us, but the swarm grows thicker, making it hard to decipher what is flitting around us.

Soon, I lose track of Ginger. The swarm has become so dense, I can't see my own hand in front of my face. I call out to her, and she responds just ahead of me. I rush forward, and she comes into view. On the shoulder of her mechnosuit, an exquisite gold butterfly flutters its ornate wings. The decorative design matches the burn marks on my hand.

"On your shoulder," I say, in awe of the insect's beauty. "It's stunning."

Another settles on the broken shield of her suit. Even beyond the glass I see her face pale. "That thing is hardly stunning. It's deadly," she says. Frantically, she flicks a lever on her console. Barbed spears erupt from the left arm of her suit and spin blindingly fast, sending sparks into the air as they strike the metal butterflies. Made up of some foreign metal, the flying creatures barely budge when struck.

With a push of a button on her console, fire erupts from the clawed hand of her armor. In mere seconds, both insects are set ablaze, the metal wings melting like butter.

My breath catches when she turns her gaze toward me and breaks into a sprint, her torch aimed at my head.

"Run!" she hollers.

"Ginger?" I say, terror rendering me motionless.

Still somewhat foggy from the poppies' pollen, her advance toward me is halting and jerky.

"I said run!" she says, shaking me with one hand and batting the robotic butterflies with the other.

Blindly, I run through the swarm and the dizzying blur of scarlet poppy petals.

Ginger races nearby. She darts in and out of my vision. Heat stings my face as I dodge the flames of her mechnosuit while she holds the insects back. My foot catches on a rock, and I find myself flat on the ground. Several butterflies flit about, their wings on fire and melting.

"Watch yourself," Gingers says as red-hot metal drips just centimeters from me.

Ginger offers the hand of her mechnosuit to me, helping me to my feet.

"Let's go. It isn't much farther," she says, breaking into a trot again.

I follow, but we don't get very far before several more of the nasty insects fly near her, their spiral tongues straightening into sharp blades. Before either of us can react, they tap on her mechnosuit, creating weblike fissures throughout the thick metal.

Others surround me, their gossamer wings deceptive of their capabilities. One lands on my left arm, and before I can dodge it, its tongue stabs through my clothes, biting into my skin. Fiery pain explodes in my bones and muscles. Every nerve within my body shrieks in agonizing protest. The scream that bursts from me is deafening. My knees go weak and I drop to the ground. With the little strength I have, I pull an arrow from my quiver and nock it. My vision blurs, smearing the green reflection of my cold-light lantern from the metallic wings of the butterflies. Fighting the pain, my hand shakes, making my aim impossible. The arrow ricochets off the nearly indestructible body of the butterfly.

"Ginger!" I howl. Nocking another arrow, I take aim at the insect buzzing above me. Suddenly, the image before me splits into dozens of replicates and I don't know which to kill first.

Just as the swarm of butterflies blind me in a cloud of gold, I am scooped up from the ground. Within seconds, I feel as if I'm flying, the world whirling by me in a kaleidoscope of colors.

"Hang on, Gail. We're almost out of here," Ginger says.

The poppies blur beneath me into a sea of red, their petals no longer discernible. I half wonder if I'm awake or in an awful dream. I close my eyes and breathe through the dulling pain, shutting the world out. At least for now.

· KATT ·

Morning sunlight casts a haunting glow on the grim village below as I pity them from the balcony of my bedroom. Peddlers sell their meager wares in the town center. Coal, grains, and other goods hardly fill their small, rickety wagons. With coins no longer holding value other than for the metal they're made of, bartering has become the new way of life for this small village.

They, too, suffer from the effects of the virus. The only difference between here and Umberland is that some adults still live. With the detonation of the biological weapons lab in London, over seven hundred kilometers from Lohr and separated by the North Sea, the impact of the virus has been gradual on the townsfolk. Still, the adults show evidence of infection, including lesions and respiratory difficulties, but they don't know why. All they know is that they suffer and there is not a thing their queen can do about it.

Had I just held out a few more days, been a little slower with my trigger finger, I would have known that the cure was mere meters from my hideout in Evergreen. Not only would I be well on my way to health, but I'd have enough to have wagered the favor of everyone. With time, I would've had the respect of the entire world. And now I'm back to making bargains and threats to get what I want.

The thought of how close I was boils my blood.

If I hope to live long enough to reign, I'll need that cure from Doc. Sovereignty only arises when there are those who depend on a ruler. What is a queen who has no one to rule over? And until I have something to offer them, they'll never accept me as their monarch.

A young woman with an infant in her arms points to the sky. "The Haploraffen have returned!" she yells.

Appearing on the western horizon, the leader of the Bloodred Queen's army returns, escorted by a court of his own. There aren't nearly enough of them to terrorize the community, but their fear is not unwarranted.

It's only been a few days, and I'm surprised to see them so soon. The only reason they'd return early is that there is news to be told. I straighten the Haploraffen Halo on my head as they descend on the village.

The villagers quickly gather their belongings. A grin creeps to my lips as they race like ants, scurrying to find shelter. While the peasants have never witnessed the extent of these machines' capabilities, they've experienced enough to know better than to challenge them. One cross look from an indignant commoner promises pieces of their burnt corpse scattered throughout Lohr.

The four escorts perch on the tower peaks above my balcony as the leader, Kommandt, hovers at the window. Its metal wings send a light breeze through the room.

"Status report," I say.

Kommandt bows its head. Its gears grind as the machine speaks. "We have not found the king."

A flicker of anger erupts within me, but I stay calm. "And why not?" I ask.

"We've encountered some resistance, which we assumed was protecting the king, but he was not among them. Only a few have escaped, but we are on their trail," it says robotically.

My jaw aches as I clench my teeth. "You *will* find Osbourne and bring him to me. I don't care how many are killed to make that happen."

"I understand, but you ask much of my troops," Kommandt says. "I've lost many. Your open disregard for their lives are noted. Mind yourself or you shall find yourself on the other side of our battle."

"Is that a threat?" I say, seething.

Kommandt bares its razor-sharp teeth. "My legion is loyal first to the Bloodred Queen," he says. "She's made no orders to kill the innocent. Enough blood has been shed on your behalf."

"You will do as I say or you'll find yourself melted into a rubbish bin," I order.

Kommandt growls. "I answer to the Bloodred Queen. You may wear the halo, but you will not win. With it, we can do no harm to you, but your time is coming. You will not rule my army for long."

"We'll see about that," I say, hiding the fury building within me.

"Yes, you will," Kommandt says, before calling to its court in a song of monkey-like grunts. With the speed of a steam train, the Haploraffen race into the horizon.

· GAIL ·

My vision blurs and tears stream down my face. The pain in my arm is excruciating. Although my body no longer has the intense burning feel, the stinging sensation remains at the injection point.

Wood splinters as a thick branch strikes Ginger's metal armor, but she races forward at a dizzying pace. I'm grateful to be out of the field of poppies, but I can't help but wonder what other dangers lie ahead of us on the Emerald Isle.

A rumble in the distance roars across the valley. I feel the heat before I see the flames. The sky ignites in an orange glow as a plume of fire rises in the distance.

"What is that?" I ask, slipping the mask from my face.

"*That* is Ozland," Ginger says. With me still cradled in her arms, she breaks into a sprint faster than any hovercycle I've seen. I try not to get sick as with each step, she covers nearly five meters, and within minutes we are several kilometers from where we began.

I'm rendered speechless as we reach our destination. A single tower stands before us, made of green marble and stone. It looms ominously, casting eerie shadows beneath the flames rising above it. Metal statues of soldiers scatter the grounds, positioned as if in battle. As I pass by one, a young woman wielding a sword, I almost feel as if she's watching me.

The entrance of the tower is a sheer face made up of coal-colored machine parts. Gears, wheels, springs, and chains spin in opposing directions, sending a rumble through the earth beneath my feet. The clank and squeal of metal upon metal does not deter from its foreboding facade.

My heart slams in my chest as a sound like thunder rattles the ground again, but this time fire bursts from the top of the wall. I shield my eyes from the bright flames that illuminate hundreds of charred and broken skeletons embedded within the machine. Brackets snap over long bones that appear to have once been arms and legs. They serve as levers for the moving parts of the machine before us. Wires string through rib cages, keeping them from tangling with one another. Empty eye sockets from skulls serve as grooves to hold moving gears.

Horror replaces fear as I make out the few skulls within the components of the wall. How many people have endured the field of poppies and deadly insects only for their lives to end encapsulated within this machine? Clearly, we are not the only ones who have attempted to enter Ozland.

The flames die down, leaving smoke billowing from the top of the fortress. Only the whir of the wall's metal elements can be heard, and an uneasy feeling grows in my gut. But that lasts only a moment. Lights spark behind two windows made of etched, colored glass, casting an emerald-green glow over Ginger and me.

As fortified as the tower is, I have no doubt that King Osbourne is inside.

"Keep quiet and, for the love of my father, I certainly hope you're better with that bow than you are battling butterflies," she says.

Pulling an arrow from my quiver and nocking it, I take aim. "If that thing is as horrible as those butterflies were, you better believe I'm taking this one down before it gets me."

"Trust me, this is far deadlier."

"Deadlier?" I say as a sickening feeling stirs in my gut.

Ginger grins. "Hold on to your britches. This is going to be a tough battle."

Swallowing hard, I stand shoulder to shoulder with Ginger.

"Why have you come to Ozland?" a deep, gruff voice grumbles from somewhere deep within the machine.

"We've come for King Osbourne," Ginger announces.

"It has been quite some time since anyone has come to see the king. Who seeks his company?" the machine asks, its words muddled beneath the clank of its parts.

"Ginger, daughter of Bok, King Osbourne's closest companion and royal keymaker," she says. "I'm here to bring King Osbourne back to Lohr."

"I am the Guardian of the Gate, created to protect the king," the machine says. "No one sees King Osbourne."

"My father and the other Zwergs, your creators, built you to protect the king until his release was imperative," Ginger says, unmoved by his dismissal. "That time is now."

"A claim made by others who have come before you. Where

is your proof?" The deep, haunting voice surges through me, pulsating under my skin.

Ginger pulls the decorative key out from beneath her shirt and holds it up into the firelight. The initials cast a shadow onto the doors: *OZ.*

A moment passes before the machine responds.

Fire blazes into the sky and the ground shakes. "I shall consider your request. Return here tomorrow to hear my answer."

Lifting my bow, I aim for an opening in the center of the moving part. "We don't have that much time. We're leaving with King Osbourne today."

"So much for keeping your mouth shut," Ginger says.

I don't care that I've broken her rules; the idea of waiting another day is too much to bear. We're so close.

"How dare you make demands of me," the voice growls. "Leave now or face the consequences."

Again, I have the sensation we are being watched as I turn my attention to the statues throughout the garden. While they remain still, I could swear they have moved. No longer in the same location, their poses have changed.

"We are not leaving here without King Osbourne," Ginger says, tucking the key back into her shirt. She flips switches on her console. Her mechnosuit whirs to life, gun barrels slapping into place on her arms. Two cannons rise from the shoulders of her armor. She almost looks like a steel-clad tank, and for an instant I'm jealous of her weaponry.

"You're not leaving," the voice says. "At least—not alive."

The gears squeal to a sudden halt. Within seconds they reverse direction. Parts of the wall shift, moving out from the surface. Another section lifts, giving it the appearance of a metal forearm. A leg extends from the fortress and settles on the ground.

Other components at the top of the wall shudder. I go cold as the machine swings from the face of the castle. The head of a warrior stares at us through what I thought were extravagant windows. Now the green glow narrows, one spotlight on each of us. The enormous soldier steps from the wall. When it is no longer a part of the tower, it slams the base of its spear to the ground. The force of it throws both Ginger and me to the earth.

"No one challenges me and lives to tell about it," the machine says. It slams its spear into the ground repeatedly, a rhythmic quake with each strike. "My purpose is to protect the king. Many have come for King Osbourne and none have passed. You two are no match for me."

The earth quakes again, sending stones from the castle's edifice barreling to the ground. Metal gears grind behind us. From where I stand, it is clear that the courtyard soldiers are as machine as the Guardian of the Gate.

Ginger unclips a strange-looking gun from the arm of her suit. Constructed of a glass tube, a coil heating element, and long metal double barrel, the weapon looks deadly and sleek in her hand.

When she slaps at a switch on the roof of her suit, a compartment opens in the back. Inside is an arsenal of weapons. With another push of a button, a grisly-looking bow juts out from the compartment, along with a quiver of barbed arrows. The weapon is not like anything I've seen before. Made with polished steel, it reflects the firelight in a fiery blaze. Decorative gears on either end of the bow keep the string taut. Curved spikes protrude from the front of the bow for what I assume is hand-to-hand combat when ranged is not an option.

Ginger snatches the weapon with her mechanical claw and hands it to me. "That little toy bow and arrows you've got isn't going to take that thing down," she says, motioning to my old bow. "This one is made of steel, and those are diamond-tip arrows."

"Thank you," I say, admiring the weapon.

The soldier lifts its spear and drives it into the earth next to us. Standing at least four meters tall, the tip of the spear slices through the dirt with ease. Beyond the dirt and stone that rain down on us, the statues spin and face us, armed and angry.

"Stay close," Ginger says, breaking into a sprint toward the tower. Her mechnosuit whines as she races to the entrance, but it doesn't compare to the metal footfalls of the statues that follow close behind. We dart past the enormous legs of the soldier, barely dodging the machine's weapon as it swings by us. "And try not to get hit," Ginger yells as a throwing star whizzes by us. Although the massive gates to the tower are only fifty meters from us, it feels like safety is kilometers away.

When we reach the entrance, I have a fleeting sense of relief. There are no handles, and when I push the door, it doesn't budge. A gilded metal stamp in the shape of a heart is embedded into the metal door where the handle should be.

"You think it'll be that easy?" Ginger says, spinning around to send bullets and missiles at the mechanical soldier and the dozens of statues. "Those doors aren't opening until that big guy is dead. The handle to that door is the heart of that machine."

The soldier's spear glows red as he tilts it in our direction.

"Watch out!" Ginger shouts. The hands of her suit reach for two levers affixed to metal panels that make up the armor of her legs. She snaps them up, using them as shields as she dodges in front of me.

Liquid fire shoots from the end of the Guardian's spear. Ginger battles the jet stream with the two shields, barely able to hold her ground.

I try the doors again, but they don't budge. "There must be another way in," I say, scanning the entrance.

Ginger snorts and continues to fire. "You're welcome to search for yourself, but until that scrap of metal is disarmed and we get the handle, those doors aren't opening. So quit talking and start shooting!"

Spitting jets of hot metal and nearly knocking us over with each drive of its spear into the ground, the Guardian approaches us. Surrounding him, the metal statues aim their weapons at us. I haven't a clue how to destroy the machine without being turned into courtyard decor.

Wrapping my hands around the grip, I nock an arrow, aim, and fire. The arrow flies from my bow like a missile, striking the machine in the neck. Roaring, the Guardian rears back.

"Nice shot," Ginger says, impressed. "But it's going to take more than one arrow on this big guy. Keep shooting."

Between Ginger's hits and mine, dozens of small holes and arrows riddle the contraption, but it doesn't seem to slow it down. The inner workings of the machine rattle and spin, churning like an engine, and are barely exposed by minor gaps we've managed to create.

Surveying our situation, I have an idea.

"Distract it," I say, slipping the bow over my head and shoulder. I climb the pins that held the Guardian's gears to the wall. My braids whip in the wind, swiping against my face. Halfway up the wall, a shout freezes my ascent.

Ginger grabs two blasters from within the console and quickly climbs out of her mechnosuit as the molten metal hardens the legs of her armor. The Guardian aims and shoots again, this time entirely consuming her suit.

With her exposed and in the open, I know I have to work fast. I scale the castle wall quickly, my hand slipping only once. When I reach the top, I stand on a marble ledge, far above the ground. The height is dizzying, but I shake off the sense of vertigo, fixing my stare on the Guardian of the Gate. Shouting, I wave my arms, trying to get its attention. The soldier takes aim and spits a column of liquid metal at Ginger. The smaller statues draw close to her.

"Ginger!" I shout, but it's too late. She ducks into a crevice within the marble wall. As the metal strikes, it quickly cools, sealing her in the crack.

Drawing the main soldier's attention, I take a breath, suddenly nervous. I glance a few times at Ginger's tomb and weigh whether I should save her first or defeat the monster.

But then the Guardian roars a terrifying battle cry, creating gusts so strong I nearly lose my balance on the narrow shelf. With fierce force, the soldier drives its spear onto the earth, rocking the tower. I cling to the stone walls.

When the dust settles, I ready myself. I'll only get one chance, provided I'm not turned into metal myself. As the machine draws closer, the gears at the joints of its jaw drop, unhinging what was already a terrifying mouth. It occurs to me that I never considered how the skeletons became a part of the machine, or why, for that matter. Judging by the way the Guardian glowers at me, I'm certain I'm about to find out. By the end of this I'll either be another forgotten skeleton in the pile or I'll have defeated them all.

The machine aims for me, ready to strike. Just before it does, I jump.

Seconds slow and my surroundings blur as I lunge toward the Guardian. My right hand catches hold of something as my body slides off the metal. Grunting, I struggle to pull myself up. When my eyes fall upon my handhold, I nearly lose my grip to see my fingers wrapped over a bony spine anchored with steel bolts. Quickly, I pull myself onto the chest plate of the creature.

The machine shudders, attempting to shake me free, but I hold tight.

Where the left plate attaches with bolts and screws, a gap reveals a melon-size engine. Chains snake from within the hunk of metal and trail off to other sections, giving the illusion of blood vessels. The links disappear into piles of metal and human bones. Clipped to the top of the machine is a piece of metal with loops and swirls designed in the shape of a heart. An ornate handle attaches to it. It is more decorative than anything else on the machine. I can only conclude that it must be what opens the door. I slip my hand into the crack, but it's just out of reach as my fingertips graze the metal handle.

I slide my bow off my shoulder. Grateful for the curved spikes on either end of it, I carefully lower the bow into the torso of the dragon. When the spike catches hold of the heart-shaped key, I pull it up and tuck it into my quiver.

The Guardian of the Gate roars and shudders, but I hold the bow once more over the opening in the metal plates. With as much force as I can muster, I plunge the spiked end of the bow into the torso of the beast.

The ferocious roar that bursts from the Guardian rattles within me. Each part, one by one, disengages, catching on the metal shaft of my bow. Bits of hardware clank against the hull of the Guardian's body as it howls.

A violent tremor erupts from the metal man and my bow shakes lose. It plummets to the ground. Although the Guardian holds tight to its weapon, fire blooms in its chest as it lists to the right. We barrel to the ground, our demise only moments away.

Gauging the distance to the ground, I wait until I'm closer before I release my grip. I fall hard. Pain crawls through my left shoulder, but I've never been so grateful for the discomfort and its assurance that I'm alive. The Guardian of the Gate strikes the earth in an explosion so tremendous that the world quakes beneath the sky. As I watch the remains of the Guardian smolder, my attention is drawn toward noise coming from the tower wall. At the top of the fissured stone, chunks of the seal crumble to the ground. I race to the crevice, dodging the fallen metal statues that now remain motionless, no longer controlled by the Guardian. Picking my bow up along the way, I chisel through the cracked metal with its steel curved tip. Finally, Ginger and I manage to create an opening wide enough for her to fit through.

Grunting, Ginger pulls herself through the small opening and hops to the ground. I let out a breath I didn't realize I was holding. I watched her imprisoned in the wall with dread, sure I'd never see her again. I should've known better. As determined and resourceful as she is, it'd take more than being enclosed within a crevice of the tower wall to seal her fate.

She dusts herself off. Loose red locks hang in her face, having fallen from her ponytail. She lets out a long sigh. "Now what? That handle was our only way in. It could take days to sift through the wreckage to find it," she says, taking in the fiery scene.

Reaching inside my quiver, I pull out the heart-shaped knob.

Ginger grins. "Nice job, kid. Ready to rescue the king?"

Hesitating, I turn back toward the wreckage as something gnaws at me.

Ash and embers lift into the wind as a storm brews to the east. What remains of the Guardian burns hot, an orange glow undulating within the chest of the machine.

A human skull lies nearby, safely far away from the blaze. I kneel and carefully lift it up. Peering into its empty eye sockets, I wonder who this person once was. Was she here for the German treasure people spoke of? Did she know the treasure was King Osbourne? Did he have a family of his own?

Placing the skull back onto the ground, I turn it so it faces the bonfire that lifts into the morning sky. With the clovers that bloom throughout the tower's courtyard and a piece of wire shed from the Guardian, I create a living crown and place it on top of the skull.

"You're finally free," I say.

My body aches as I turn back toward Ginger.

"Let's save the king," I say.

Leaving Pickpocket to tinker with the downed Haploraffen, the rest of us crawl through a small opening behind a false stone wall located in the farthest prison cell. Led by Hook, we travel damp, dimly lit passageways.

Spiderwebs brush my face, occasionally leaving behind an unwanted passenger on our journey. Water drips in the distance, making the clandestine stone passageways feel more like a cave than part of the castle. Ascending a stairwell, Hook holds a torch in front of him, cautious with every turn he makes. Pete follows with Alyssa, Lily, Maddox, and me close behind.

"The weaponry is this way," Hook says, leading us to a door. He presses against it with his ear. Seeming satisfied, his metal hand reaches for it, his fingers wrapping around the brass door handle. He hesitates, his single eye focused on the mechanical body part. I trust Hook as much as I trust Jack, but for that moment I can't help but wonder what is going through his head. What it must be like to lose your eye, your arm . . . and your soul to a woman you call mother. Sometimes the villains in life are not so obvious. Sometimes they're the ones we think love us the most. Or the ones we love unconditionally.

He turns the brass knob and steps inside a dim, cold chamber.

Weapons of all kinds fill the room. Racks of swords, sabers, and maces hang from the walls, and an arsenal of guns and bullets fill shelves. Some of the weapons are so medieval-looking I briefly wonder how many lives have been taken with them.

"They may not be the weapons you came with, but hopefully you'll find something that'll suit you," Hook says.

"Keep an eye on him," Pete says to Maddox with a nod toward Hook.

"You're kidding me. I lead you to a treasure trove of weapons, and you think I'm still a threat. Five of you against me. I'd say the odds are in your favor, don't you think?" Hook says.

Pete ignores him and steps toward the daggers and throwing knives, opting for his preferred weapon of choice. Not surprising is Maddox's choice of a gun, while Alyssa selects a deadly-looking sword.

Last is Lily, as she scrutinizes the weapons. Finally, she makes her choice of a sword for herself as well. The blade is not nearly as fine as her original sword encrusted with precious jewels, but I have no doubt that she can inflict an equal amount of damage. She gives me a passing glance, her eyes falling on mine.

"You have to take one," Lily says softly to me, concern crinkling her brow. "You're going to need it."

Scanning the options, I'm at a loss for where to start. I've never been a fighter. Lily knows me well enough to know that the Hippocratic oath runs through my mind as I consider wielding something that could kill a person. I've never killed anything, at least not on purpose. Not by my own doing. Sure, I've lost many patients along the way, but none were because I didn't help, or because I hurt them myself. Her concern is for my life, while mine is that I don't know that I have it in me to take another's.

Lily picks up a small gun, loads it with ammunition, and hands it to me.

"Aim for the knees," she whispers. "You don't have to kill anyone. Just make sure you incapacitate them enough that you have the upper hand. The same goes for the Haploraffen. Look for any exposed gaps in their armor."

Nodding, I grimace, because harming another is no better an option. She places a hand on my cheek. "Don't worry. I've got your back. Pete will be with you, and when you return, I won't let anything happen to you. But keep hold of that just in case you find you need it."

My anxiety slips with her touch and the kindness in her words. I wish I could have a moment with her alone—I miss those.

Pete's voice distracts me. "Just what do you think you're doing?" I turn to see he's got a dagger pointed at Hook.

"Arming myself like the rest of you," Hook says, rolling his eye as he takes in the various weapons.

"Yeah . . . no. I don't think so," Pete says, giving him a slight shove.

"What? Do you expect me to go in there with only my bare fists?" Hook asks.

Maddox is cleaning the ornate gun he's chosen. "He's got a

point, Pete. I, for one, have no intention of saving his hide should we find ourselves in battle."

Pete tosses an annoyed look. "Fine," he says, picking up a small pistol. "I know your weapons of choice tend to be the big, bad, ugly guns that can wipe out dozens of people with one squeeze of the trigger, but I think this is more your style."

Scowling, Hook holds out a hand, waiting for Pete to give him the weapon.

Pete hands the gun to Maddox, who then tucks it into an empty holster at his hip. "I think we'll hold on to this for safe-keeping," Pete says. "You can give him the gun when the time is right."

Scowling, Hook doesn't respond to the slight. "How long do you think it'll take you to get to the lab and get what you need? More than likely the Bloodred Queen is in her throne room. With the Haploraffen guarding her, it's going to take all of us to get close."

Alyssa becomes particularly quiet.

"You okay?" Maddox asks.

"It's not going to work," she says, shaking her head. "Even if we kill the Bloodred Queen and Katt, who's going to rule?"

"King Osbourne," Maddox says. "Once we get rid of them, we'll send a team out to go find the king."

"But we know nothing about where he is. And even if we could find him, Hunter had the key," Alyssa says. "The odds of finding and rescuing him are impossible."

"We have Jack," Pete says quietly.

I nearly choke. "Are you out of your mind? You're talking about Jack, the one who led Hook to the Lost City? The one who betrayed not only the Marauders, but everything you and I built."

Hook stares down at his feet, clearly uncomfortable.

"I know it sounds crazy, but hear me out," Pete says, holding his hands up. "Jack . . . well, he is with us."

Confused looks pass between us.

Maddox clears his throat. "Uh . . . would you care to elaborate?"

Pete pauses. "I made a deal with him."

"You what?"

With gaping mouths, everyone stands speechless, looking at him. As if time has frozen and no one wants to move for fear that what he's said is true.

"The last night in the village, before it was attacked, I struck an agreement with him. He'd use his position as King Osbourne's son to infiltrate Lohr and provide us with what we needed to make our strike," Pete says. "Even though plans changed when Katt took us captive, nothing about that has changed. The deal still remains."

Maddox brings a palm to his face. "How can you guarantee that?"

Pete shakes his head. "He has no other choice."

"No choice?" I ask, the betrayal evident in the tone of my voice. "What could you possibly have to exchange for his allegiance?"

"His life," Pete says. "I made a promise to him back in Everland that the day I got my hands on him he'd wish he was dead. That was a promise I intended to keep.

"He also realized that unless his father came back alive, there would be no one to take the Bloodred Queen's place. It could never be Jack on that throne. Not after everything that's happened," Pete says. "The country will never accept him as their ruling monarch. And as convincing as Katt is, there's no way she'll keep him around. Not when she can rule by herself."

"Not according to Katt," Hook says. "She seems to think that she needs him to rule. Who would take a princess of a broken country as their ruler?"

"For now, that's to our advantage," Pete says. "That means she'll keep him alive—for a while at least. Which is exactly what we need. Jack has to play along with Katt until we can position ourselves to take out both Katt and the Bloodred Queen. He knows it and promised me that if we get his father back, he'll do what he can."

"And you believed all that babble?" Maddox says.

Alyssa shakes her head. "I have to say I agree with Maddox. Jack has never been one to trust. More than likely he's after the crown himself."

"He wants the crown no more than when his father died," Pete says. "If ruling was his motivation, he'd have done it a long time ago."

"I don't know. If it isn't the crown he's after, then what does he gain?" Lily says. "What can we offer him to keep him loyal?"

"His dad," I say.

Everyone looks at me.

"Exactly. What more does he have to lose?" Pete asks. "The Bloodred Queen either thinks or wants him dead. Katt's all about power. She'll never let him rise to the throne unless it benefits her. And he knows if he betrays me, I'll slit him open from navel to neck."

"I sure hope you know what you're doing," Hook says, finally piping up. "Because if he aligns himself with either of those women, I'll kill him myself."

"We'll deal with Jack if and when the time comes," Pete says. "Right now, Doc needs to get to the lab."

"What about the rest of us?" Lily asks.

"Find Gwen," Pete says. "Do whatever you can to thin the number guarding her. When you find her, bring her to our agreed meeting spot above the throne room."

"I'm going to need more than just that toy gun," Hook says, waving a hand toward the pistol in Maddox's belt.

Maddox grabs another gun similar to the other. "If you're a good boy, maybe I'll give you two," he says smugly.

"What about you?" Alyssa asks.

Pete lets out a sigh. "This whole thing started with the virus in Everland. It's going to end with the virus, but this time we're delivering the cure. To everyone!"

· GAIL ·

Slipping the doorknob into its matching groove, I grip and turn the handle. The hinges on the large door whine as we enter the tower.

Once an extravagant tower most likely belonging to some wealthy family, it is a skeleton of what it probably used to look like. Wind howls through the moss-lined windows. Chunks of stone and wood lie in piles throughout the vast foyer. It is evident that no one has occupied this structure in years, and yet I can almost sense the presence of those who once lived here. Although I don't believe much in ghosts, I have an eerie sensation of being watched. Instinct drives me to nock my bow.

Ginger gives me a puzzled look. "No one is here. No one other than the king anyway."

I scan the window carved high into the structure. "Just being cautious," I say.

"You saw that creature. Anyone else who dared to get close to the tower's walls didn't live to tell about it," she says.

"With the Guardian of the Gates destroyed, no one is protecting the tower now," I say.

Ginger considers that, then pulls out her ornate gun. "Fair enough. Let's find the king and get out of here," she says.

We ascend a spiral staircase that climbs several stories up, ending at a wooden door. Ginger lets out a breath and turns the knob.

A break in the clouds casts sunlight into the room from the arrow slits in the walls. The rays fall onto a casket made of thick glass and numerous metal parts. Gears grind, moving pistons on either end of it. Tubes loop around the elaborate box, circulating a golden gas into the coffin. The edges are sealed with a decorative gilded lip.

Resting on a red satin pillow and blanket is a man clothed in chain mail and armor. Flowers, herbs, and berries encircle him. A golden crown constructed to look like briar branches with ruby gems sits on his head of long salt-and-pepper hair. Having been left on his own for years, his beard is wild and unkempt. It's hard to believe that Osbourne is still alive.

Ginger and I step to either side of his coffin.

"Ready?" she says.

Nodding, I watch as Ginger pulls the necklace with the key over her head.

"Want to do the honors?" she asks, handing me the chain. I gratefully take it.

An intricate lock is affixed to the edge of the casket. Made up of loops and swirls, it almost appears to be a replica of a royal crest. I slip the key into the notch. It fits perfectly. Holding my breath, I turn the key.

A loud clang rattles the room. What I thought were decorative accents to the gilded seal click, releasing like intertwined hooks. One by one, the elaborate swirls shift from a horizontal design to a vertical one. When the final ornament unclips, the lid of the coffin rises up on spiraled supports in each of the four corners. An earthy smell tickles my nose as the cover stops a meter above, like that of a canopy bed.

Ginger and I watch the king, his body as still as it was moments ago. Wondering if I've done something wrong, if there is more to reviving the king than simply opening his casket, I look to Ginger.

Worry furrows her brow as she reaches for the king's hand. "King Osbourne, can you hear me? We've come to get you out of here."

When her fingertips touch his skin, the king's eyes fly open and he gasps in a large breath. Both Ginger and I jump, startled.

The pupils of his bright green eyes dilate. He blinks once . . . twice . . . and then turns his stare to me.

"She will destroy the world," he cries in a raspy voice.

· KATT ·

The Bloodred Queen's claws clack across the floor as we make our way to the dungeon. While I had intended to save Jack for last, it was the only way to convince her that the king was indeed alive. Although I hold myself together, I'm giddy to introduce her to my companions from Umberland, one in particular. I check my watch; the Haploraffen guard should have returned the young doctor and Pete to their cells.

"You've found others?" she asks, her words slithering from her lips in a reptilian hiss.

"I've done even better," I say. "I've captured the doctor who made us into this." I hold my scaled hand up, the tips of my claws painted crimson red.

The Bloodred Queen's yellow eyes widen as her slitted irises constrict. "The boy who stole my beauty? The one who's made me into this hideous beast?"

"That's the one," I say sweetly.

"Take me to him," she demands, increasing her pace.

We pass through a series of hallways until finally we reach the door leading to the dungeons below the castle. Four Haploraffen guard the door to the prison. They bow as the Bloodred Queen passes and descends the stairwell. She gasps when we reach the bottom. Sitting on the floor, tinkering with the machinery of an incapacitated Haploraffen, is one of the Lost

Kids. Pickpocket startles when he sees us and bolts to his feet. Before he can get far, the Bloodred Queen knocks him to the ground.

"How did you get out?" I ask, peering at the open doors of the prison cells. "Where are the others?"

"Are you the doctor?" the Bloodred Queen says, gripping the boy by the front of his shirt and lifting him effortlessly into the air.

He shakes his head. "No. I . . . I'm just a . . ." Pickpocket gazes at me with pleading eyes. "I'm a prisoner. I . . ."

"Is this the one?" the Bloodred Queen says, her frightening stare fixed on me.

"No," I say, still startled to see him out of his cell. This wasn't the plan.

The Bloodred Queen throws him against the stone wall with such force, his bones break with an audible snap. Pickpocket slumps to the floor, his lifeless eyes wide.

"You're useless is what you are," she says, sneering down at the boy's body.

My heart skips several beats when her stare falls upon me. She advances on me, each clack of her clawed feet counting down the seconds to my own death. "You promised me the doctor. Where he is?"

Bumping up against the prison bars, I can smell the raw meat of her last meal on her breath. Speechless, I shake my head. "He must be still in the lab. He's under guard to create the antidote for us . . . for you!"

"Stupid girl," the Bloodred Queen spits with a flick of her forked tongue. "If this one has escaped, I can only assume you had other prisoners who have found their way out as well. If you value your frail, insignificant life, you'll find them. You'll bring that doctor to me so I can repay him for what he's done. I'll disfigure him until he's as beastly looking as I am. And if you don't bring him, Princess Katt, you'll take his punishment in his place."

My legs grow weak.

"Yes, Your Majesty," I say with a bow of my head.

The Bloodred Queen turns toward the exit. "You have until dusk."

When she's gone, I'm left alone with the broken Haploraffen and the body of Pickpocket. I kneel next to him, my pulse still racing. I've seen my fair share of death. In fact, I'm guilty of the demise of so many, but to watch it happen at someone else's hands, and so violently, makes the air feel thin around me. The deaths in Everland were so massive and so quick that there was no room to feel anything. My sister and I were quickly swept away and taken to the safe lands of Alnwick. We never saw enough of the destruction to really see the casualties.

Maddox saw a number of deaths by his own hand, but he was a mercy killer. The lives he took were at their request, to end their suffering.

And then there are the victims of my orders. But even those lives weren't taken by me. Those losses were caused by the tim-sah in Umberland, those who succumbed to Doc's antidote, the lizard protein taking over their bodies and turning them into reptiles. They weren't even human anymore. And the Haploraffen were responsible for the deaths in Evergreen.

However, peering down at this dead Lost Kid, I remember there is one who died by my own gun, and he was the youngest of all the deaths I've witnessed. I did what I thought was right at the time, but his dark wide-eyed shock when I shot the young boy still haunts my dreams. Maybe five or six years old. Way too young and too innocent to have died the way he did. He was never my target, but as he stepped in front of Pete, he took the bullet meant for the leader of the Lost Kids. Pete should have died that day.

Tired of the war and the uncertainty of our world, I rise, more determined than ever to take the crown as my own. I'm done with the Bloodred Queen's rule. It's time for a new era.

The four Haploraffen guards stand rigid as I cross the threshold from the prison.

"Retrieve Gwen from the belfry and prepare her for a tribunal. Unless the rebels surrender themselves to me, her next dose will be lethal," I say.

"Yes," the Haploraffen say in unison.

They turn to do my bidding.

"One more thing," I say. "Bring the priest and my future husband, Jack. Tonight will be the start of a new monarchy."

Alarms blare loudly, announcing our prison break. I'm surprised we've managed to be away this long without being discovered. Given detailed directions to the lab by Hook, Pete and I follow the dark pathways within the walls of Lohr Castle, the flame of a torch lighting our way. When we reach the small opening in the wall, Pete peers through the peephole.

"Looks clear," he says. He presses his hands against the door and slides it to the side. On our hands and knees, we crawl into the room, then stand. Pete places his torch in the sconce on the wall.

The stainless-steel fixtures and countertops give the lab a sterile feel. Cabinets filled with vials and equipment rest along the far wall. Two small windows allow in minimal sunlight, its rays landing on carefully placed pots of exotic plants I can't identify. In brilliant colors, blooming with unusual leaves and petals, the collection is extraordinary. Only a skilled apothecarist could possess plants like this. They are not like anything I've ever seen in any science book.

Whoever works here has secrets. Secrets they'd protect.

Suddenly, the hair on my arms stands up, and I have second thoughts about being here. I take a cautious step back. "Pete, I have a really bad feeling," I say.

"You aren't the only one," he says, gripping the hilt of his dagger.

Scanning the room, I notice that the knots on one wood-paneled wall are not wood. Instead they appear to be hollow, each pointing directly at the numerous potted plants throughout the room. Pete steps close to one of the strange plants and reaches to touch the bright orange petals.

"Pete, no!" I shout.

He ducks just in time as a dart shoots from one of the holes and sticks into the opposite wall. "Stay away from the plants," I say, bolting to my feet. "They're rigged."

"Obviously," Pete says, pulling the dart from the wood panel and handing it to me. "Where did that thing come from?"

"Blow dart," I say, inspecting the small projectile.

A door bursts open, and a bearded man holding a double-barreled rifle peers into his scope, his aim pointed right at Pete's head.

"Don't know how you got in here, but get your things and leave," he says.

Holding my hands up, I take a step forward. "Look, we need your help. We—"

"I said we don't want you here," the man hisses.

A thin woman slips out from the next room and sidles up next to the man. With her hands on the man's shoulder, she peers around him. "Hase, they're just kids. Put your weapon away."

"I will do no such thing," he growls. "If you are here on the queen's bidding, you can just escort yourselves back where you came from. We don't have the cure, and we'll let her know when we do."

"We're not with the queen," Pete says.

"Then you're with the one from England," Hase says. "I should've known. Your accents give you away."

"We are from England, but we've come to help create and distribute the cure," I say. "I'm a doctor. I developed an antidote. One that is successful, but it was destroyed when our home was attacked."

Pete passes me a glance, sorrow blooming in his expression. We've had our differences, but one thing we have in common is all the homes we've lost and tried to rebuild. Our home with our family, with the Lost Kids, Umberland, and in Evergreen. At this point, I'm not sure home is a place anymore.

"You're awfully young to be a doctor," Hase says suspiciously.

"Who are you to judge?" Pete says. Gripping his dagger tighter, Pete's frustration is more than clear. Before I let him escalate it further, I step in front of him.

"I was a physician in London before it was destroyed by the Horologia virus. I was able to acquire research and produce a cure. Only, because I was hoping to accelerate the healing process, I created something far worse than Horologia. I was working on a second cure, but Katt, the princess of England, stole the research. Luckily, I could recall most of the data. With that and the poison apple from the Labyrinth, I did create an antidote," I say.

Hase gives the woman next to him a puzzled stare. She shrugs.

"You, a child, created a cure?" Hase says, turning back to me.

"He's telling the truth," Pete says, holding out a hand. Although the intricate designs stain his skin, the scars still remain. "I was infected, too, and now I'm better. He's the real deal."

"Look, I need that apple and the virus if you have it," I say, desperate. "I've been told they're here in the lab. I need to re-create the cure and destroy the virus—for good."

The older couple give each other a knowing glance, but don't answer.

Pete holds out one of his daggers. "You will show Doc where the apple and the virus are. If you don't, I'm going to have more than just words with you."

Hase squints and aims his gun at Pete. "I don't think you're in a position to make demands."

"If this young man can help create the antidote, let's give him a chance," the woman says.

"Maus, I'm not handing the apple or the virus to a couple of teenage kids," Hase says.

"We could take it by force," Pete says, twirling a dagger.

"Not likely," Hase growls, gripping the gun tighter.

"We've been working on this cure for months and have been largely unsuccessful," Maus points out.

Hase wrinkles his brow. Maus places a hand on the barrel of his gun and pushes it down, directing the aim of the weapon to the floor.

"We have nothing to lose," she says.

Reluctantly, he nods. Maus scurries to a cabinet and opens the glass doors. She moves equipment from the bottom shelf and lifts a hatch on the floor of the piece of furniture. Reaching in, she pulls out the ragged research book that once belonged to Gwen's mother and hands it to me. Excitement wells within me.

"See what you can make of this," she says.

I thumb through the pages, grateful to see that the familiar charts, notes, and annotations are just as I remember them. It's no different from the day I first laid eyes on it. Opening the cover, the Professor's name is elegantly inscribed on the first page.

"What can we do to help?" Maus says.

"I could really use that poison apple if you have it," I say.

"Do we have it?" Hase asks, suddenly giddy. He slings the strap of his gun over his neck and waddles over to another set of shelves. Shoving one of the cabinets to the side, Hase reveals a large hole cut into the wall. Pulleys and ropes support a platform large enough to hold one person. The lift looks rickety, but when Hase invites me to climb in, I don't hesitate. At this point, what do I have to lose?

"Take this," Maus says, handing me an oil lantern as she lights the wick.

Pete gives me a wary look before I am lowered down the shaft. The fire within the lantern threatens to extinguish as a breeze sweeps through the chute. Taking in a breath, I fight the choking sensation of confinement. I'm grateful when the lift comes to a stop. I slip from the platform and nervously watch it rise back up the shaft.

Holding the lantern up, I take in the room as firelight flickers off the steel fixtures and lab equipment. Shadows skip along the walls, taunting my vision. A lever to my right protrudes from the wall. Scratched into the wood wall panels are the words *on* and *off.* Hesitantly, I lift the switch, moving it to the *on* position.

The familiar smell of methane fills the room as the click of flint against steel breaks the silence. Panic rises within me, but it is quickly replaced with profound awe. Lanterns strung along the wall light one after the other. Within seconds the room illuminates brightly under the glow of a sophisticated indoor lighting system.

The distinct sound of lit Bunsen burners is washed away as the others join me in the basement. Although biology is my expertise, I've spent hours poring over chemistry, physics, and engineering books. None of what I've read would prepare me for the idea of an automated lantern system like this. Even more curious are the dozens of contraptions, machines, and tools scattered throughout the room. None of them are traditional lab equipment. Instead, they appear to be handmade for specific purposes.

Pete appears equally mystified by the instruments and modern lighting. His awe is captured in his surprised expression and loss for words. His demeanor quickly changes as he scans the room, appearing wary.

"What's the matter?" I ask.

"Just keeping an eye out for any more crazy plants," he grumbles.

"As you should," Maus says as she hurries by us. "One can never be too careful with concentrated sulfuric acid. That dart was meant for the Bloodred Queen's cronies."

"Sulfuric acid?" Pete asks. "What does that do?"

"To you? You'd be dead within minutes," Hase says nonchalantly. "To the Haploraffen? One dose instantly reacts with their metal inner workings and starts a chain reaction of corrosive destruction."

"Serves them right, those Haploraffen," Maus grumbles. "Nasty beasts, I tell you."

"Why haven't you used the darts on Katt or the Bloodred Queen?" Pete asks indignantly.

Hase opens a wooden cabinet and sorts through several beakers filled with a variety of colored chemicals and plants. "Bah! Do we look like killers?" Hase squints at us over his shoulder. "Merciless, maybe, but not murderers."

Pete crosses his arms over his chest, clearly aggravated.

However, I can't say I blame them. So far, I've not been in a situation that required me to kill anyone, but given the opportunity, I'm not sure I could. I'm here on this earth to save lives, not destroy them.

"We have done nothing to anyone who hasn't deserved what they got," Maus says, opening the front hatch of what looks a tin oven up against the far wall. She slips on thick gloves, tightening the straps at both wrists.

"Shush, our company doesn't need to be burdened with our sins," Hase grumbles.

"The apple?" Pete says.

"In a rush, are we?" Maus says.

"That apple is invaluable. It's the only one left of its kind," I insist.

"You don't really believe that, do you?" Hase asks, selecting a beaker with a yellow liquid in it. "Months have gone by since Hook brought the poison apple here. It would have rotted away by now."

Pete snickers. "I don't have the book smarts that you do, but even I know that can't be the one Hook got."

Giving him a quick glare, I turn my attention back to Hase. "If that's not the one from Hook, where did you get it?"

Maus loops her arm into mine and leads me to a steel door. "Silly boy. By extracting the seeds and growing a new tree."

"But it takes years for a tree to bear fruit from seed form," I say, bewildered.

Maus pats my arm. "Not if you're the Bloodred Queen's apothecarists."

Wrapping her wrinkled hand around the handle, she pulls open the door. Inside, similar automated lanterns light up a room, only there is just one thing inside: a tree bearing golden apples not unlike the one Maus holds.

"An underground greenhouse," Pete says. "Brilliant!"

Although much more sophisticated, the technology is like that of our underground garden back in Everland. Cogs and the Tinkers spent weeks building a section of the cave network into our own greenhouse to be able to grow fruits and vegetables.

"But how were you able to grow it so fast?" I ask.

"The same way the Labyrinth was built overnight," Hase says. "With growth enhancer. The same chemical used by the Bloodred Queen's herbalist and groundskeeper."

Pete and I exchange a glance, but say nothing. Maddox's parents were the royal family's herbalist and groundskeeper. That is, until the night the Labyrinth was built. The queen's army was sent for them and they were never seen again.

Maus closes the door to the greenhouse and takes the apple to the oven-like contraption.

"What exactly does that machine do? Is it safe?" I ask, peering over her shoulder.

Hase pats my shoulder. "Are you questioning my wife? I wouldn't do that if I were you, son. She's a spitfire," he says, poking her in the ribs.

She swats at his hand, snatches the beaker from her husband, and shoos him away.

My stomach twists as Hase fills a test tube halfway full of the liquid. He caps it with a stopper. Tubing snakes from the cork and into the metal container. With a flick of a striker, the Bunsen burner beneath the test tube lights with a blue flame.

I know how to concoct the cure; however, I hold the Professor's notes close. Their value is priceless, and once we're done with our mission, I intend to return them to their rightful owner: Gwen Darling, daughter of the woman who ultimately will save the world.

Maus pulls a pocket watch from her apron. From where I

stand, I can almost hear every tick of the second hand. A bell tinkles above a spout on the top of the contraption that spews steam.

"Let's see what we've got here," Maus says.

She opens the door. My breath catches as smoke billows from the oven. Maus waves it away, coughing. "Hase, when are you going to get the exhaust fixed on this infernal machine?" she complains.

Rolling his eyes, Hase grips a lever protruding from the side and pulls it forcefully. The whir of a fan followed by the grinding of metal on metal erupts from the machine.

I'm afraid to look, half expecting the apple to be nothing but ash. As the smoke clears, the apple lies unharmed. I blink in disbelief. Maus pulls out the apple with her gloved hand and places it back into its glass domed case.

"So . . . where's the juice?" I ask.

Maus straightens her wire-rimmed glasses before pulling a beaker from the back of the machine. Inside, an iridescent liquid glimmers in the lamplight.

"That's it?" Pete asks.

"That's it," Maus says.

I step toward her, take the beaker, and place it on the counter. "May I?" I ask, gesturing toward her gloved hands.

She nods.

Gently, I take off each glove, exposing her blistered fingers. Sores ooze with blood and pus, new scabs barely covering open wounds.

"I can help you," I say, noticing the gold tones in her hazel eyes. They are identical to so many other patients who have been on the brink of succumbing to a disease I caused. The mutation of the Horologia virus is evident in her stare. I saved most in the village before the Bloodred Queen's attack on it, but there are still more out there who desperately need my help.

Maus smiles. That instant, she seems years younger, almost childlike with the glint in her eye. She wraps her arms around me, and I think of the hundreds, maybe thousands of patients I held as they hung on to a hope I could not provide them while taking their last breath.

I choke on my next breath, hoping that Maus is not the next victim of this horrific disease. "Let's create that antidote and get you fixed up."

Reaching for the beaker filled with the extract from the apple and the vial, she hands them to me. She says nothing, but the plea in her eyes is more than words can convey.

We need a cure and an end to the tyranny. And we need it now.

· GAIL ·

With his face buried in his hands, King Osbourne shakes his head. It's taken a while to help him through the disorientation. He's insisted that this all must be a bad dream, that all we've told him about the state of the world, or of what we know of it, can't possibly be the truth. As he takes another sip of water from Ginger's canteen, I wonder what it must be like to wake up and have no recollection of the last five years of your life.

"Easy now," Ginger says as the king reaches for another piece of shortbread from her supplies. "It's going to take some time for your body to adjust to food."

He snatches the biscuit and tosses it into his mouth. "You try going five years living off those Zwergs' voodoo, witchcraft, or whatever sorcery this is," he says, tossing a twig with flowers to the floor, appearing irritated. I don't recognize the plant. In fact, none of the blossoms or leaves are remotely close to anything I saw within the Labyrinth. I realize with a start, this is the farthest from home I've ever been.

"Thankfully, that sorcery is what kept you alive," I say, placing a hand on his arm. "Your Majesty, I don't think you can appreciate the suffering the Bloodred Queen has caused until you see it for yourself."

King Osbourne raises a brow. "Is that what they call her now?"

"She's certainly earned the name," Ginger mutters, removing her glove. Her fingers are covered in scabs and blisters. "This is only a fraction of what we've experienced here on the Emerald Isle."

Grateful that I have yet to show symptoms, but not wanting to bring attention to it, I shove my hands beneath my cloak.

"What she's done to England and Gail's people in Germany is unforgivable. We need you back ruling Germany," Ginger says.

"I can't imagine what London must have looked like during the days following the attack. The kids from Everland and Umberland say there's nothing left," I say.

Sorrow graces Ginger's expression as she sits on the edge of the king's coffin. "How many died? Suffered from ailments far worse than this?" she asks, peering at her disfigured hands. "How could anyone do something so cruel? She's hardly a queen of any type."

Remembering my father's last breath, a lump grows in my throat. I'll never see my father again. Or my mother. My friends. Everyone I loved is gone. "She's wicked," I say, choking on my anger.

The king's green eyes moisten as he stares at Ginger's disfigured fingers and my clenched fists. "She more than wicked. She's a witch," he says, his jaw rigid with fury. Fueled with rage, he attempts to climb from the bed, lifting his armor-plated legs with his hands as he swings them over to the side.

"Help me out of this blasted sarcophagus," he grumbles. "I'm far from dead."

Ginger grips him by the arm. "Your Majesty, you're still weak."

The king pulls from her grip and glares at her. "Weak, you say? I was weak when I gave that wretched woman my heart. Withered muscles are nothing compared to selling your soul to the devil."

Exchanging an uncertain glance with me, Ginger says nothing.

"Well, what are you two waiting for?" he asks. "Take me to Lohr."

After years of lying idly, the king struggles to stand. He weighs at least fifty kilograms more than me, but Ginger and I each take an arm and try to help him to his feet. A shadow at the narrow windows draws my attention, but when I turn, there is nothing there. The hair on the back of my neck prickles. I stay alert, expecting something to break the quiet. Other than a distant dripping, the tower remains silent.

"So, any suggestions on how to get back to Lohr?" I ask.

The uncomfortable feeling of hidden eyes upon me returns, but only for a moment. The minimal bit of sunlight is obscured, leaving the three of us in shadows. Glowing red eyes fall upon us like fiery beams. My breath quickens, audible even within the buzz of the machines that slowly fills the air.

Suddenly, an explosion rocks the tower, sending us all toppling to the floor. Wooden beams and slate tiles barrel down on us. When the rocking stops, I struggle to get up, knocking the rubble off me. Ginger hurries to pull King Osbourne back to his feet. Sunlight beams from where the roof once was.

The winged monkeys beat the air, stirring up dust in their wake. Terror fills the king's expression. It's the same look I felt cross my own face yesterday when I first encountered these wretched beasts.

"We've found him," one of hideous creatures says.

The winged monkey perches on the edge of the broken tower wall. The citrine-colored stone set in the middle of its forehead illuminates in a fiery orange glow. It is the only machine with an adornment of any type.

"Take him to Katt," the beast growls. "Leave the others."

Ginger pulls her weapon from its holster and takes aim. "Get behind me!" she yells.

The king falters, falling back onto his coffin. Assured that he's all right, I nock my bow and send arrows toward the intruders. One strikes a machine in the neck, bringing it crashing to the ground. Another arrow misses, but Ginger's blaster leaves a sizable hole in its chest.

"Cover the king," Ginger demands. "Don't let them get near."

With a quick pull of a lever, the barrel of her gun turns, collapsing into itself. When it's no bigger than a handgun, she pulls the trigger. Lightning bursts from the end. As it hits the first machine, the monkey lights up in flames. She aims for another and looks over her shoulder.

"I *said* cover the king," she commands, the militant soldier in her taking charge of the situation.

I climb onto the casket, continuing to send arrows into the growing army. Ginger screams as one of the winged monkeys digs its spiked claws into her shoulders and lifts her into the air. She kicks wildly, aims her gun up, and blows a hole through the entire machine. Both Ginger and the creature drop to the floor, the tower shuddering as they land.

Reaching back to my quiver, I find it empty. The machines hover above the casket. With the steel spikes on my bow, I battle them away as best as I can. But they outnumber me.

King Osbourne shrieks as one of the beasts snatches him. As weak as he is, he hangs like a rag doll in the machine's clutches, hollering in pain.

Several more fly toward us.

"Those two are of no significance to us. We have the king. Return to Lohr," the leader of the army shouts.

Sending gusts of dust and pebbles in a maelstrom within the room, the metal primates turn and fly out the window with King Osbourne in their clutches.

Ginger continues to shoot her weapon, but it's far too late.

Panic grows as I watch the king become nothing but a speck in the sky. The one thing I was tasked to do, to save the king, I've failed at, and now there's no way back home.

My blood turns cold as the deafening silence burns holes into my already broken heart. With all that I've lost, all the hard work it took to find the king, I'm left empty-handed and alone. Well, mostly alone.

Ginger curses vehemently as she holsters her weapon. "Those blasted monkeys!"

"What are we going to do?" I ask.

Yanking an arrow from a broken machine, she grunts. "I'm not worried about us. It's King Osbourne. All these years I've dedicated my life to the day he was to return to his throne, and when that day comes, I lose him in just a few hours."

My chest aches listening to her. While my journey, my call to save the king, has not been anywhere as long as hers, I feel the same sense of disappointment.

"The Bloodred Queen will have the king in her custody soon. What do you think she'll do to him?" I ask.

Collecting the rest of my arrows, Ginger shoves them back into my quiver. "I know exactly what she'll do to him. The same thing she's done to everyone else she deems unworthy. She'll guarantee his death even if she has to do it herself, make no mistake of that."

"We have to help him," I say, rushing to one of the unmoving machines, wondering if we can salvage some part of it to carry at least one of us back to Lohr. Singed wires lie exposed from where Ginger's blaster hit. "How are we going to get back to Lohr?"

Ginger laughs as she trudges over to the glass coffin and steps onto it. "Certainly not with that thing. How did you plan on getting the king back when you decided to rescue him on your own?"

"I didn't really think that part through, but I guess the same way I got here," I say.

Grunting, Ginger places both of her hands on the glass cover and pushes up on it. "You mean that hunk of metal that plunged you into the Manx Sea? You're lucky you even made it here alive in that contraption."

Pressing my lips together, I force myself not to respond. Any retort I come back with will only give her fuel to poke fun at me. While she may be at least ten years older than me, I am not the helpless child she makes me out to be.

"Come help me with this," Ginger says.

"Why?" I say, joining her.

"You don't think the Zwergs would send the king all this way without a way for him to return, do you?" she says.

I climb on the casket and press up on the lid. It takes a few minutes, but eventually the glass cover lifts from the four gold posts.

"Toss it to the ground," Ginger says.

I shove the lid to the ground, cringing as I anticipate the shatter of glass. Instead, it drops to the floor with a loud thud, but remains perfectly intact.

Seeing my expression, Ginger chuckles. "Indestructible coffin. Just because it's glass doesn't mean it can be broken."

She tugs cords from the struts of all four corners until the ropes lie in piles on the floor. As she finishes unwinding the last bit, she directs me to two of the posts at the foot of the coffin that once held up the glass canopy.

"On the count of three, hit those two switches," she says, pointing to small gold levers in the supports. They're so tiny that I missed them as well.

"What are they?" I ask.

"Do you want to get out of here or not? On three. One . . . ," she says, steadying herself on the other side.

I place a hand on both posts, my fingers barely touching the switches. I have no idea what will happen if I hit them too soon, but I don't want to find out.

"Two . . . ," she says, looking over her shoulder.

I swallow, not sure what to expect.

"Three!" she says.

I hit both switches at the same time. A rattle within the metal components of the coffin sends me off balance. The cot in which the king lay lowers until it is level with the ground, encasing us waist high with glass walls. Above us, fabric bursts through the four posts, each quadrant of the gold cloth snapping together as if being held by tiny magnets. Flames billow at the end of each post. Fueled by heat, the fabric rises through the opening in the castle ceiling as it fills like an ordinary balloon . . . and that's when I realize, it is a balloon. An air balloon.

As the fabric lifts into the sky, the coiled ropes pull taut. The glass case rises from the ground. My pulse races as the castle grows distant beneath the transparent floor of our gondola. We lift higher into the sky and I find myself in absolute awe not only of the balloon, but of all the beautiful green landscape that appears below us. Hope wells in my chest as the balloon catches on a brisk wind, sending us east.

"How did you know?" I say, unable to find the words to properly convey my thoughts.

Ginger smiles brightly. "I told you. I came over with the king. When I was sent here, the Zwergs entrusted me with their secrets to secure the king's safety and return. From the coffin, the ship that brought us here, and the Guardian who was designed to protect the king until a designated time."

"All these years, though? With all that's happened under the Bloodred Queen's rule. Why now? Why couldn't he have been rescued before England was destroyed? Before my home was trapped with terrifying walls and then burned to the ground? Why now?" I ask.

The green hue of the Emerald Isle no longer seems to hold the same splendor. In mere moments, its beauty has been reduced to naught as I wonder where my future and the rest of the future lies. With our only hope resting on King Osbourne, who will be the Bloodred Queen's prisoner soon, I ache to know why it's taken so long.

Ginger reaches inside the pocket of her vest and holds her hand out. Lying in her palm is the brass key.

"Because we were waiting for the key," she says.

· KATT ·

I storm from the jail, furious to have found the other cells empty. The Haploraffen guards follow me, equally puzzled by the escape. With all the talk about hidden walkways, I should have known better than to leave so few guards with the Lost Kids. A mistake I don't intend to repeat.

But I still have leverage. I have Gwen and Jack. And as flighty as Jack is with his loyalty, it shouldn't take much to get him to talk.

When I reach the belfry, I halt, stunned at what I find. Appearing to have been ambushed, the Haploraffen guards are slumped on the staircase, riddled with bullets and arrows. The wooden door beyond is ajar. My pulse speeds up as I burst through the doorway.

Gwen lies unconscious in Jack's arms, but that is not what stokes the embers of rage within me. Alyssa, Maddox, Lily, and Hook draw their weapons on me, stepping in front of Jack and Gwen. The fury burns up my legs, body, and neck like deadly vines.

"How did you escape?" I demand. "And where are Pete and Doc?"

Hook grins. "You forget, this castle used to be my playground. I know secrets that even the Bloodred Queen doesn't know about. As for Pete and Doc . . . they're not your worry anymore."

Alyssa takes another step forward, her sword aimed at my throat. "Katt, we're taking over the castle. You will stand down or you will die along with the Bloodred Queen."

"And then what, Alyssa?" I say. "You'll rule?"

They exchange weary glances before their gaze falls back on me.

"Jack is the rightful heir to the throne, for now," Hook says.

Laughing aloud, I shake my head. "You want Jack to rule? How ironic. I was thinking the very same thing, but with me by his side as queen. But what surprises me is how you could trust him at all. After all he's done, all the ways he's betrayed you and everyone else," I say. "He's a traitor . . . not unlike you at this moment."

Hook starts to speak, but Jack cuts his stepbrother off.

"I'm a traitor?" Jack says, stepping from behind Hook with Gwen still in his arms. "You intended to do the same thing. You want me to be king, and you demanded that I marry you. This game is over, Katt. This is no longer about power or who is ruling over who. It isn't going to matter in the end unless we lay down our swords and find a way to save everyone. That's what Doc, Pete, and the rest of them have wanted all along. You and the Bloodred Queen not only have stood in the way, but you single-handedly destroyed thousands of vials containing the antidote."

"I had no idea the antidote was in the village," I say, seething. "Their destruction is not my fault."

"It is your fault, and if you continue on this course, there will be no hope for anyone," Alyssa says. "While Jack hasn't made the best decisions, at least he hasn't abandoned his country just to take over another. You, on the other hand, not only committed treason but also contributed to the destruction of your country. You held one of the highest powers, even higher than me, and instead of stopping the fires that raged through England, you fueled them. You are not fit to rule anyone."

Alyssa's face burns red. She was a strong leader as the Duchess of Alnwick, but never angry. This is an entirely different side to her.

"Enough!" I shout. "Listen up, Jack: The agreement was that you will claim the crown and I'll be your bride. If you break our deal, I will kill your father. And these fools, too."

"You'll *never* be my bride," he says. "You yourself commanded the Haploraffen to bring my father back alive. Now all we have to do is wait. When he shows ups—and trust me, Princess, he will—Osbourne will rule. If not, the crown is mine and mine alone."

"Figures. You've always been about Team Jack," I say indignantly. "You flip sides quicker than a fish out of water, but ultimately, it always comes down to you, what you want, what you think is best at the cost of everyone else. These stories of you playing good guy, bad guy, they only reveal who you really are. A self-serving narcissist."

A laugh billows from Maddox, who has been relatively quiet the entire time. "Says the former princess of England turned White Queen turned to . . . what are you now? The Bloodred Queen's puppet?"

I pull my gaze from him. He doesn't need to know that my final title will be the White Queen, ruler of the world. It was the Bloodred Queen who brought the world to its knees with the virus, not me. And it will be me who the world will look to for a redeemer.

"I've had enough of this," Lily says, moving from her position in the back.

"Guards, detain them," I command. The halo shimmers, casting a gold glow on my face.

Before Lily can reach me, the Haploraffen guards charge the Lost Kids. A short struggle ensues, but they are relieved of their weapons and in the soldiers' custody quick enough. Gwen stirs in the arms of one. Her dose is wearing off. She'll be awake soon.

"Your father is as good as dead," I say, jutting a finger at Jack. "I'll make sure of that."

My fingertips touch the circlet, taking in the vibrations. The quicker the pulses, the closer the Haploraffen are. Turning my gaze to the window, shadows appear in the stone frames. Although darkness skews the details of the machines, their silhouetted wings tuck behind them.

"Perfect timing," I say.

Curses rise from a deep voice. Kommandt and six of its

entourage glide through the window. In the claws of one of the machines is a middle-aged man. They release him a meter above the floor. He grunts as he strikes the ground hard. Although aged, with salt-and-pepper hair and deep smile lines, his resemblance to Jack is uncanny. There is no doubt who this man is.

Jack, as if in a dream state, slips around his Haploraffen guard and over to his father. Panting, the king peers up. His face scrunches before relaxing into wide surprise.

Curious, I allow this to unfold, wondering how this reunion will play out.

"Jack? Is that you?" he says, struggling to stand. Jack helps him to his feet. Osbourne throws his arms around his son and chokes out a sob. Pulling back, Osbourne puts his hands on Jack's shoulders, joy evident in his expression. When his focus falls on the thin crown on Jack's brow, Osbourne beams.

"You're here? So you are now the king? Thank goodness," he says, relieved. "What has become of Katherina?"

Jack frowns. "No, Father. She still rules."

His words are weak, as if uttering his stepmother's title would be offensive in front of the true ruler of Germany.

I don't know what runs through the king's head as he takes in this bit of news, but he seems to age in that moment as the glimmer of hope leaves him. A deep line forms between his eyes while he processes that the woman he once loved, who betrayed him, is still the ruler of Lohr. Of his land. After a thoughtful moment, he holds his son again. "I'm here now, Jack. We will undo all the evil she has brought upon this world. We'll bring peace, and you, my boy, will one day take my place as king."

Jack steps back from his father and peers at each of the Lost Kids before casting his gaze to the floor. "I'm not fit to be a king," he says, his voice cracking. "I've done nothing to make you proud. In fact . . ." He chuckles. "Everything I've done, the people I've hurt along the way, would bring you shame."

Confusion lines Osbourne's expression.

"You are the rightful king," Jack says. "You will find an appropriate successor."

"I don't understand," Osbourne says.

Finally fed up with this display, I shout, "Oh, spare us the tears. Arrest them! I want one guard on each of them this time."

Kommandt glances my way, its steel eyelids blinking as it processes the situation.

"You will do no such thing," Osbourne says, staring down the machine. "I am Osbourne, king of Germany. You will do as *I* say."

"We answer only to one who wears the halo," it says in a mechanical voice, before bowing to me. Two other soldiers join in the gesture of respect. When Kommandt rises, it signals to its guards with a wave of its hand.

"Take your claws off me," Osbourne yelps when one grabs on to him, forcing him across the room toward the door.

"Katt, don't do this!" Jack says. "You yourself said no one would accept a ruler from another country. Once the villagers know that the king lives, they'll fight for him."

Walking coyly up to Jack, I smile and gently place my hand on his cheek. "Not if they realized how he's deceived them. How he abandoned his own people in times of crisis. And not when he abdicates the throne so you can rule," I say. "If he doesn't . . . well, I'm sure we can find a reason that compels him to agree."

"They won't be fooled by your lies. Not for one second," Jack says.

"They will if his son convinces them," I say. "If Prince Jack divulges that the king of Germany ran away when the Bloodred Queen demanded the crown, they'll be struck with disbelief—but only momentarily, when they realize they are not alone. That in the king's son a new world order will rise, but one of healing, peace, and prosperity."

"Even if they believe that story, they'll still never accept you. You've been at the Bloodred Queen's beck and call. And surely news of Evergreen has traveled by now," Jack says. "If they don't know what you've done to Evergreen, it won't be long before they do."

Poised, I jut out a bottom lip. "But I was only doing what I was told," I say in a singsong voice. I press a hand to my chest, blinking as if in disbelief. "The Bloodred Queen made me do it."

"They'll never buy it," Jack insists.

"And that's why wedding bells will toll this evening, my handsome prince. Just as we planned." I laugh. "They will have no choice but to fall in love with me. And neither do you."

"You're wrong. They've seen this game played out before with the Bloodred Queen. They won't be fooled again," Hook says.

"You better pray they do," I say. "Otherwise, you'll all end up dead."

With a wave of my hand, I shout my next orders. "Take them away."

Kommandt nods, and the soldiers drag the prisoners away in a song of protest.

"There is one other matter to deal with," Kommandt says with a bow.

"What is it?" I ask.

"In recovering the king, we encountered two other individuals attempting to protect him," Kommandt says. "We left them behind once we acquired Osbourne, assuming them to no longer be a threat. However, it appears they are on their way to Lohr."

I tap my bottom lip in thought. "There's also the issue of Pete and the missing doctor. They can't have gone too far."

"What are your orders?" Kommandt asks.

"Find them. When you do, bring all the prisoners to the courtyard for execution. As for Osbourne, let the queen know he's in custody, awaiting her orders. Tell her I look forward to seeing her at the executions."

"What about the others headed this way?" Kommandt asks.

"Make certain the rebels never make it to Lohr," I say. "And just to be sure, send out the queen's Henchmen."

· GAIL ·

Flames and smoke billow from the hills to the west, obscuring the mountains beyond.

We travel in silence as the beauty of the Emerald Isle renders me speechless. This high up I bid farewell to the green rolling fields. Plots sectioned off with stone walls give the landscape the appearance of a quilt pieced together with squares. Speckled throughout are remnants of old Emerald Isle castles, rising like ghosts from a forgotten story of the past. We drift over the extravagant structures, their roofs long consumed by nature and her destructive ways as she reclaims what was once hers. I squint, imagining lords and ladies entangled in dance, twirling across the old ballroom floors.

If they only knew what the future held for their kin and the homes that once sheltered them from the storms.

Hours pass by as we drift over villages with stone huts. Some occupied, others not. Grave markers, tombs, and Celtic crosses outnumber the people we see. The scent of fire and burnt grass permeates the air as we drift over Ginger's home. We are high enough from Wicklow that I wouldn't be able to see signs of life even if the aftermath of the metal monkey battle didn't dominate the landscape. I let out a breath, feeling sorrow for the Wickloreons. My last view of their village is not unlike the last moments of my own home.

Ginger does not look back. Instead, she keeps her focus fixed to the east, but the stray tear does not go unnoticed. How she consistently keeps a brave face astonishes me.

My stomach turns as the destruction fades into the horizon. How much more devastation will this world see at the hands of the German queen? Disease, bombs from airships, a deadly labyrinth, fire-breathing mechanical primates. There is so much death branded by her hand that I'm certain the earth will forever be stained by the blood of the innocent.

Floating over the eastern coast of the Emerald Isle, I bid it a bitter farewell. As beautiful as the country is, I'm disheartened by damage caused by outsiders. By the Bloodred Queen.

A choppy blue sea passes beneath, until we reach England's borders. I brace myself. After hearing the stories from the people of both Umberland and Everland, I'm certain the destruction in England is no less horrifying than the Emerald Isle's or the Labyrinth's.

I'm wrong.

The blackened landscape of what once was London is a stain on a grassy patched landscape much like the Emerald Isle. This is the all too familiar mark of the Bloodred Queen.

A burnt field sits behind the castle. Piles of wood, metal, and other parts scatter the landscape. It is a landmine of destroyed zeppelins, evidence of the queen's assault. All the iconic London structures I learned about through stories told by my parents stand charred and broken along the skyline. Big Ben, Westminster Abbey, the Tower of London, and Westminster Bridge. They are almost unrecognizable. While the loss of my home along with the attack on the Wickloreon village was deplorable, this . . . this is like that but on a much larger scale.

This is ground zero. Where the genocide began a year and a half ago. I cannot imagine how the people of Everland suffered, nor will I bring myself to try. The only sound is the hiss of the torches keeping the balloon afloat, but even in the quiet I can almost hear the ghosts of those who lived here crying out.

Rage consumes me as I understand just how much we all have lost.

"I will avenge you," I whisper into the wind. "You will rest in peace or I will join you in your sorrow in death trying."

Despite the deadness of winter, the countryside of Germany is a welcome sight, but only temporarily. The scarred remains of the Labyrinth and the charred tree in the center are a reminder of the sheltered life I lived within its borders. As the balloon flies over the destruction, even Ginger appears heartbroken at the sight.

"So, this is where he was all these years?" she asks.

She speaks of her father, but I don't know how to respond. I'm not entirely sure if the grave below was once his home. All I know of her father was that Jack was given the key by him during his battle within the Labyrinth. Beyond that, he was just a stranger.

"I hope he went quickly," she says, leaning on the glass gondola, seeming lost in the vast rubble.

I feel for her. The ache of my own father's death weighs

heavily on me. As hard as it was to witness his last breath, at least it was quick. Ginger will never know how her father died or if he suffered. We continue in silence, honoring all those who died mercilessly within the walls of the maze.

Lost in the image of the destruction below, we don't see the attack until a bolt of fire whizzes by. A half dozen of the machine monkeys descend upon us. Ginger and I both snatch up our weapons and return fire, but it is too late. Fiery cannonballs soar toward us, nearly setting the silk fabric ablaze. The gondola shakes, threatening to toss us both over the side. Steadying myself, I try to ready my weapon, but the balloon suddenly loses altitude. The windowed view of our quick decent is nauseating. While Ginger may claim the glass container is indestructible, I doubt even this box could withstand a fall from this high without shattering.

Ginger tosses her gun back into its holster. "There's too many of them. Get ready to crash," she shouts.

"Get ready to crash? Just how do you expect me to prepare myself for that? Close my eyes and wish for a soft landing?" I yell back, slipping my bow over my head.

Ignoring my sarcasm, Ginger attempts to keep the fabric inflated by switching the levers on the post to increase the flames, but it is futile. The glass gondola hurdles toward the earth at an alarming rate. Scanning below for a landing place, I find nothing but dense forest, although much of it charred. My heart races, knowing that landing in the trees is going to be a bumpy ride, and more than likely will tip the gondola, making our prospects for survival bleak.

A burst of blue appears through the blackened, bare trees. Hope eases my panic ever so slightly as the body of water draws closer. While landing in the river is still not my first choice, it certainly is better than being smashed onto the forest floor.

"We're going to jump," I tell Ginger as she struggles to keep the pilot lit. "Can you aim the balloon over there, just beyond the tree line?"

Briefly taking her attention off the billowing fabric above us, relief dances in her expression. "Thank goodness you can swim, kid," she says, alluding to my arrival on the Emerald Isle. That day seems like years away.

It takes a few minutes before the gondola passes over the shoreline. Ginger and I steady ourselves, waiting for the water to draw close, but not far enough from shore that the swim will be impossible. When we are only a few meters above the water, Ginger and I throw ourselves over the side of the basket and into the icy water.

My lungs seize as the chill steals my breath. Battling the current, I'm eager for air. When I break through the surface, I gasp, willing my frozen lungs to expand. It takes several attempts before I'm able to breathe normally. If I never crash-land in cold water again, it'll be too soon.

"Ginger!" I yell, searching for her, but she's nowhere to be found.

Water foams around me in white peaks as the rapids carry me down the river. My bow and quiver threaten to drift away, but I cinch them tighter. As a wave crests, taking my body with it, I see Ginger off in the distance struggling to get to shore. With every bit of strength left within me, I battle the current, swimming in the direction of Ginger. About fifty meters away, the earth meets the torrential water. Ginger gets her legs beneath her and she crawls to shore. I manage to follow.

Lying on the soft dirt, our breaths come quick and shallow. My muscles are fatigued and I have no desire to move anytime soon. I roll over onto my back, trying to regain both strength and breath, but time is not a luxury we have. When I open my eyes, the machines are flying above us. I nearly choke when a fiery ball heads in our direction.

"Run!" I shout.

Ginger and I leap to our feet and dash into the forest as cannonballs whiz by us, striking the earth in a blaze of fire. We follow the forest line along the river, hoping to lose our attackers. The trees and dry brush burst into a wall of flames, chasing us as the draft from the beating wings of the creatures fuel the blaze forward. Heat blooms on my backside, letting me know that slowing down would be disastrous.

"Head that way," Ginger shouts. "Back to the river."

Struggling down a sloped embankment, I nearly lose my balance. When I glance over my shoulder, the inferno is only a few meters away.

"In the water, under there," she says, pointing to overgrown foliage near the river's edge.

We stumble into the water, dropping to the rocky floor. The wall of fire roars behind us.

"Get down! Don't come up until I say," Ginger says.

Hardly able to catch my breath, I nod and submerge myself into the frigid water. Although the water is less than a meter and a half high, I still feel as if I'll drown. The current wraps around my body, like hands threatening to drag me into its path. I shiver as the glow of fire erupts overhead, a blanket of it consuming the precious air above the water's surface. I know we've been under less than a minute, but it feels like it's been much longer.

I struggle to hold my breath, eager for the gold-and-orange glow to dissipate. When it does, I don't wait for Ginger. Ready to take in a breath, I break the surface, but as I do Ginger pulls me deeper into the smoldering brush. She wraps a hand across my mouth as I let out a loud gasp.

"Shut up!" she hisses.

I fight the panic building within me, reminding myself to breathe through my nose. While it might not be the gulp of air I need, it'll have to suffice.

The painted early evening sky is speckled with the machines. Their wings beat in sync as they retreat to where they've come from. Toward Lohr Castle.

Ginger lets me go as I pant, grateful for air.

"Looks like that's the direction we're headed in," I say.

"It appears so," Ginger says, stumbling from the river's edge. She pulls her weapon from its holster and turns the barrel toward the ground. River water pours from the gun. "So much for modern weaponry. It can do just about anything, but get it wet and it's useless."

She pulls a pin from her hair and uses it like a tool, unscrewing the outer shell of the weapon. Removing the cover, she unveils several hidden compartments. She reaches inside and holds up a dozen short poles.

"We're going to defend ourselves with those? I think I'll take my chances with soggy arrows," I say, pouring water out of my quiver.

Ginger frowns. With a flick of a wrist, a sharp blade explodes from the shaft. She tosses it to the ground and, one by one, she does the same with the others.

When she drops the last one to the ground, she gestures. "Pick one," she says.

Lying at my feet are a spear, a pair of maces, a variety of axes, a sword, and several other bladelike weapons.

"I'll stick with the bow," I say. "I've never used any of those."

"Suit yourself." Ginger opts for the two short-handled maces. The heads of each are equipped with jagged teeth. "You ready?" she asks.

Nodding, I let her lead the way into the forest. Thankfully, this section has not been destroyed by the fall of the Labyrinth. The lush trees provide excellent cover if the Lohr's army returns.

The last of the fading sunlight peeks through the bare branches. Lost in my thoughts and the gurgle of the nearby river, I tune out the evening songs of the forest animals. On any other given day, I'd find solace in the melody, but today, there is very little to find comfort in. We have no idea what awaits us in Lohr. While we can hope that there are allies along the way, there is no guarantee they will join us in rescuing King Osbourne and overthrowing the Bloodred Queen. And even on the slight chance they do join us, the castle will undoubtedly be guarded. Coupled with the fear that she has already murdered the king and we're too late, nothing quells the anxiety brewing in the core of my belly.

Ginger, on the other hand, appears quite content. As if the growls and caws of the forest's inhabitants are common wildlife. But I suppose for her, they are familiar, at least to some extent. While she may have lived the last five years on the Emerald Isle, most of her life has been spent here in Germany.

A rumble beneath my feet disrupts my musings. Ginger reaches for a tree branch to catch her balance. I'm unable to hold my footing and tumble to the ground.

Flocks of birds lift into the air from the treetops, their wings dusting us with a gust of leaves and other debris. We are plunged into an unnerving quiet. Not even the wind leaves a whisper as it brushes against my cheek.

A rusty screech of metal grinding against metal rings out through the dense forest as whatever is causing the commotion rumbles our way.

"Get up!" Ginger shouts, pulling me to my feet.

We sprint through the trees, dodging in between them.

"What is that?" I ask, breathing heavy and looking over my shoulder as the whine of rusty metal draws close.

Panting, Ginger leaps over a log. "That is one of the king's most deadly weapons. It was meant to protect the castle from invaders. I've only seen it in action once, and trust me, you do not want to be on the other end of that thing's fury."

"But what is it?" I ask again.

Ginger doesn't need to answer. I am bowled over as a steel spear pierces through the forest floor next to me. The barbed shaft trembles, standing half a meter above the moss-covered ground. A second spike shoots from the earth, almost impaling my leg. Another nicks my right thigh, tearing through the leather pants just below my hip.

Howling, I roll over, but then another spear bursts into the dirt. Rushing to my hands and knees, I attempt to crawl away when three more spikes land in the ground in front of me.

"Get out of there!" Ginger yells.

Panic-stricken, I jump to my feet right before an enormous explosion erupts behind me. Trees soar over my head like rockets, their roots waving in the burst of hurricane-like wind. Clumps of clay, dirt, and shrubbery shower down on me, obscuring my vision. The ground trembles again. Turning away from the commotion, I dash to my left but am blocked by another blast that throws dirt high into the air.

A low growl shakes the ground beneath me once more. As steam hisses from the newly formed hole in the earth, a creature rises until its head is just above the lip of the cavern. Blue sparks flash in its hollow eyes.

Although it's certainly a machine, the figure before me also appears human in form.

Ginger grips my elbow. "Meet Timothy, the former royal

woodsman for the king. Now let's get out of here before he decides to chop off our heads."

I glance over my shoulder as we run. He leans his head back and howls. With screams so piercing, both Ginger and I are brought to our knees. I writhe in pain on the cold, damp ground, my palms pressed against my ears.

Again, the earth shakes, as the steel woodsman jumps from the pit and onto the ground. Standing two meters tall, he roars. Through jagged metal teeth, rays erupt from the machine, like lightning from a raging electrical storm. Each blinding beam chars the vegetation and sears limbs from trees. What is left of the foliage floats to the ground in nothing more than a blanket of ash.

The forest grows still once again as the woodsman's eyes spin like that of a telescope, focusing in on his prey . . . *me*.

I scramble to my feet as the contraption shrieks, wielding a sharp ax. Dirt flies in the air as I dodge the blade. With his weapon stuck halfway in the ground, I take the opportunity to wield my bow and send arrows into the chest of his armor. The diamond tips pierce the thick metal with ease. The shafts of a half dozen arrows protrude from the woodman's shell, but the damage doesn't slow him down. When the ax is freed from the earth, the woodsman returns his attention to me. Clearly, I won't be able to stop the machine on my own, and Ginger has disappeared. With the odds against me, I decide to rest my fate on the only thing I can do . . . keep running.

I take off. But metallic footfalls shatter the forest floor, sending wet earth exploding in every direction. The woodsman's blade just misses me with every swing.

"Ginger!" I scream, unable to hear myself above the tempest surrounding me.

A piercing screech, even louder than before, tears through the trees. I whirl around, expecting to find the machine close behind me. Instead, several dozens of meters away, Ginger sits on a tree limb, fairly obscured among the leaves. Having surprised the woodsman, she grips the one mace still left in her hand. The other is embedded in one of the woodsman's eyes.

Jagged shards are all that is left of the lens. Circular metal rings hang from the few brackets that remain. Ginger hurries off the limb and starts to climb back down. Before she makes it even halfway, the machine slams into the tree. The trunk splinters. Ginger grips a branch, terror filling her expression as the treetop lists to the side before crashing to the earth. Ginger's flailing body hits the ground hard.

"No!" I scream, running to her. She doesn't respond to my touch. Blood gushes from a deep cut just above her brow.

The woodsman screams again, hovering over us. In his remaining eye, blue electricity sizzles angrily, building in intensity with each passing moment. Despite the heat emanating from the machine, my skin crawls with an icy chill. I slip my hands under Ginger's armpits and try to pull her.

"Ginger, wake up! You have to wake up," I say, panic trembling in my voice.

She doesn't respond. The creature growls as I struggle to tug

Ginger to safety. With a gasp, I watch the machine shift to the side and hit a lever on his ax. I can't breathe, can't take my eyes off the weapon as the blade swings wildly around the shaft. The woodsman raises the rotating blade and sends it hurtling toward us. I throw myself on top of Ginger and use my momentum to roll her out of the way. The ax drives into the soft earth where Ginger's body was, centimeters away from my face.

Snatching up the ax, the woodsman lifts the weapon once more.

"Ginger, wake up!" I shout, shaking her.

The machine barrels toward us. With no other choice but to fight, I take aim and prepare for battle. With each arrow I shoot, the diamond tips puncture the metal, but again only slow the woodsman down minimally.

His only functioning eye sizzles with blue light.

"Not with the barbecuing again," I say, rounding the machine, eager to get him away from Ginger's still body.

As if on cue, electricity blazes again from his lens. I tumble to the left, out of the fiery path, as the spark scorches the earth where I stood.

"Come on. Cut me a break," I say, holding the grip of my bow tightly.

Behind the woodsman, Ginger, seeming somewhat dazed, struggles to her feet. She retrieves her weapons and calls out to the machine.

"Timothy, she's awfully small to be considered a challenging target, don't you think?" Ginger says.

The woodsman peers over his shoulder and scrunches up his face, rage etched in his expression with each shift of the metallic plates that make up his face.

"Remember me? I know it's been a while. You were my favorite of the king's woodsmen. Always kind and giving. I know what they've done to you is horrible, but I'm sure somewhere in that hunk of metal you possess some semblance of a heart. Let us be on our way," she says. With an ax in each hand, she twirls them, circling the machine.

The woodsman pauses for a moment, his single lens fixed on Ginger.

"Aw, you do remember me, don't you?" Ginger asks. "Of course you do. How could you forget all those times I stole your ax as a kid? You'd pretend to be mad, but I knew you never really were. Can I tell you a secret? I did it on purpose just to watch you attempt to make that silly, angry face. You never pulled it off well."

Peering at his ax, the tin man seems to contemplate her words.

I'm confused by the one-sided conversation, but I don't ask questions. Those will come later. Instead, I also circle the woodsman, prepared to fight.

"Come on, Timothy, we don't have to fight. I know you're in there," Ginger says.

The machine gazes at Ginger for a moment, then raises his ax and violently swings it Ginger's way. She dodges its sharp blade. His actions are quick, but Ginger is quicker.

When the creature whirls, his face is met with the blunt end of Ginger's mace. She spins and smacks the jagged end against the woodsman's leg, leaving a sizable dent. Ginger leaps in the air, hopping over the woodsman's weapon as it comes slicing toward her.

I keep my aim fixed, waiting for the first opportunity to shoot. With another swing of the mace, this time using the sharp teeth, she slices through the leg of the machine. Wires dangle and spark from the breached metal parts.

"Please stop, Timothy! It doesn't have to be like this," she says, hurt evident in her tone. She swings her mace, leaving slashes along the machine. The damage is severe, but still the woodsman battles as if uninjured. All I can think to do is to continue to inflict harm to the exposed parts. I send several arrows flying, each one striking the metal components fueling the machine. While the arrows make movement cumbersome, the tin man fights on.

Ginger strikes the woodsman across the head, momentum turning his body in my direction. It takes a second for me to nock my bow and send an arrow to his chest. The diamond tip buries itself into a gash left over from one of Ginger's hits.

He screeches as steam and smoke billow from his torso. Finally, he lets out a sorrowful groan before falling quiet.

I release a breath I didn't know I was holding. Ginger turns her green gaze my way as she returns both of the short-handled maces to their holsters on her back. She wipes the sweat from her forehead with her shirtsleeve, brushing away her auburn disheveled hair. Clearing away the dust and wrinkles from her vest and pants, she takes in a sigh.

"Godspeed, Timothy. Maybe you'll finally be at rest," she says, placing a hand on the tin man's face.

"Timothy?" I finally ask.

"Yes," she says, helping me gather my arrows. "That thing you see there used to be a real living man. One of the king's closest soldiers. The king loved him like a brother. Timothy was hard not to love. He was caring, humble, generous. There wasn't a soul in all of Lohr who didn't take a liking to him. No one except the Bloodred Queen.

"Timothy supposedly died young from a heart condition, but most of us believed his demise was the queen's doing. King Osbourne was distraught with grief. Willing to do anything to bring his friend back, he sent the body to the metalworkers along with his personal physician to see if they could revive him with a machine heart. Instead they created this thing. When the king realized that the person who once was Timothy was long gone and all that remained was his shell, he armored the creature and made him part of the Henchmen."

Ginger hands me my arrows and trudges ahead.

"The Henchmen?" I ask.

"Yes. The elite of the king's army," Ginger says.

My nerves spark again at the idea that there are other creatures, or men, out there as fierce as this one. "Just how many Henchmen are there?" I ask, scanning the treetops.

"There are only three Henchmen. Two now that the woodsman has been incapacitated," she says. "But if the woodsman found us, the other two are not far behind, and that's not even the worst part," she says.

"How can things get much worse?" I ask.

"If she's dispatched the Henchmen, the Bloodred Queen knows we're here," she says.

· □□□ ·

apping the last vial, I let out a breath. It's been several hours, but with the massive selection of ingredients and supplies Maus and Hase have accumulated, along with the help of Pete, we've created several batches of the antidote. Now all that's left is to get it to those who need it.

"How do you think Pickpocket is doing with that Haploraffen?" I ask.

Pete shakes his head. "I don't know, but I don't trust those wretched things. We shouldn't have left him alone."

I nod, an odd feeling brewing in my gut. Rubbing my hand across my forehead, I weigh our predicament, wondering if we should meet Hook and the rest as planned, or search for Pickpocket. "Someone needs to check on Pickpocket and it should probably be me," I say wearily. "I'll be no use when you infiltrate the queen's throne room anyway. And the sooner I get the Haploraffen armed with the antidote, the better. You go meet up with Hook."

Maus laughs. "That's your plan? Somehow convince those winged beasts to willfully join your agenda and release the cure around the world? We're doomed," she says, throwing up her hands and turning. She grabs a scoop from a bucket of herbs on the bottom shelf of a wooden cabinet. "If any of you need me,

I'll be out digging my own grave. Good thing the snow hasn't settled in."

"Pickpocket is reengineering one of the Haploraffen now," I argue. "He just needs time."

"Time?" Maus asks. "You think time is what will gain the Haploraffen's allegiance to you? If it were as simple as tinkering with their mechanics, don't you think someone would've already ended the Bloodred Queen's reign? Nice fantasy, boys, but it'll never happen."

"But . . . ," Pete starts to protest.

Maus sighs. "The Haploraffen only answer to the one who wears the golden halo. Without it, you'll never get anywhere with them. No amount of tinkering will change that. And suppose you do gain control of the Haploraffen Halo; they are always loyal to the Bloodred Queen first."

"So, we kill the queen, take the halo, and rescue Gwen. Sounds simple enough," Pete says.

Maus shakes her head. "And how do you plan to do that? The Bloodred Queen is all exoskeletal armor and strength. Her scales are nearly impenetrable."

"We're aware of that," Pete retorts. "But have no doubt, that ruthless woman is going down, even if I have to melt the darn plates off her body one by one," Pete says.

Hase taps his chin. "It's not a bad idea."

The old man shuffles to another cabinet and turns the dial of a lockbox. When it clicks open, in it is a glass container that looks to be coated with something on the inside. Wax, maybe? He carefully removes it and offers it to me.

"What's this?" I ask, preparing to take the cap off to get a whiff.

"No! I wouldn't do that if I were you," he says. "That's hydrofluoric acid."

My stomach feels sick at the error I almost made.

"What does it do?" Pete asks.

Maus hands me a rucksack and fills it with old rags. "Put it in here to keep it safe. Until you need it," she says.

Cautiously, I place the container into the bag and zip it up. "Aside from burning flesh on contact, inhaling it is poisonous and will kill you within days."

"Sounds awful, but just the thing we need," Pete says. "Once we're rid of the Bloodred Queen, it's only Katt we need to take care of. She might have the Haploraffen Halo, but not for long."

Maus laughs. "This almost sounds like an impossible task, boys. If you're caught . . ." He makes a slicing motion across his neck.

"We should probably stick together, then. Both Pickpocket and getting that acid to the Bloodred Queen are priorities. We'll join the others later," Pete says, worry evident in his tone. "Maus, is there any other way to get these vials distributed, if the Haploraffen don't work out? Like, what about more of the Marauders' airships?" Pete asks. He knows as much as I do that at the speed and distance they're capable of traveling, it's a viable option.

"Pfft! Those hunks of junk have been gone for a long time. The Bloodred Queen's entire armada left and never returned. They were sent to bring down London and return once German rule was established," Hase guffaws. "Seems the zeppelins went down with London."

Pete rolls his eyes. "She sent her entire fleet? Amateur move."

I'm sure he finds some satisfaction knowing that he and the Lost Kids are responsible for the airships' destruction, but I'm irritated. Zeppelins would be helpful right about now. "What other choices do we have?" I snap.

My question is met with silence and sullen expressions.

"I'm afraid there's no other way, Doc," Maus says, frowning. "When the Bloodred Queen learned of the destruction of her zeppelin fleet, she decided that if she wanted things done right, she'd do it herself. Instead of using an army of men, she had the Haploraffen created to be controlled by her using the halo. Armed with the latest technology, they have one job: to do everything she bids. Often, that means patrolling countries that are dependent on her promise for a cure. Other times, it means the destruction of those who defy her. Sadly, she might very well have the deadliest military in the world, and until you gain control of them, you'll never get the antidote out."

"I may not be able to hold up my end of the bargain with Hook," Pete says to me, balling his fists. "What I wouldn't give to spill her blood."

He's as desperate as I am to weaken the Bloodred Queen's stronghold. It amazes me how alike we think, but how vastly different we are. The Bloodred Queen's rule must end. He seeks her blood, while I seek to take away her power. I fight with medicine and the need to restore life to health. He fights with blades.

I loved his sister, Gabrielle, so much it nearly killed me that I couldn't save her. He loved her so much that, given the chance, I'm sure he'd have killed me because I didn't save her—if he didn't need me so much.

Pete has been so many things to me. My patient, my friend, my enemy, my leader, my closest companion. Had Gabrielle not died, he'd have become my brother. Although Gabrielle's life was stolen from both of ours, of all the things Pete is to me, whether he accepts it or not, he's family.

"The Haploraffen are our priority," I say. "We need that crown."

"And for that, you'll have to take it off Katt's head yourself," Hase says, nudging me in the ribs with his elbow. "Grab yourself a scooper. Looks like we'll be joining Maus. The dirt is as hard as stone, and I'm only digging my grave. You're on your own to make your bed before you meet your maker."

"What about Hook?" I ask, ignoring Hase. "Maybe he can manipulate his position as the queen's son to get close to the crown?"

Pete grimaces. I know the thought of him working with Hook any more eats at him. The hero and villain of Everland working together is absurd. But at this point, that's where we are at in this. Our options are running thin. And we've already involved him . . . at least at the end of Lily's and Alyssa's swords and Maddox's gun.

"What? We just tell Hook that he needs to get that crown because whoever wears it controls the deadliest army in the world? Seriously, Doc, you may be smart, but that's the dumbest thing you've ever said," Pete says.

"You're practically doing the same thing with Jack," I point out. "In fact, maybe this deal you've made with him should include retrieving that crown."

"The deal I made with him was to play along with Katt. Make her believe he's on her side until we're ready to strike. That's it," Pete says. "I don't trust him with that crown either."

"But you'll let him rule Germany?" I ask.

"Not alone," Pete says. "Of anyone, the German people would accept him as ruler long before they'd accept anyone else. Under our supervision, he could run the country until we find the king ourselves. But neither Hook nor Jack will be in charge of the Haploraffen Halo."

"At this point, what choice do we have? We've already brought them into our fold," I say. "They may be the only way we get close enough to it."

"Hook's insane as it is. Despite all she's done, she's still his mother. His own flesh and blood. Who in their right mind would kill their own mother?" Pete says, kicking a cabinet.

Maus gapes at his burst of anger.

Sighing, I afford him a moment, knowing that lately his whole life has been taking care of one child after another who have lost their mothers and fathers, including him. The thought of purposely killing one's own parents—it's incomprehensible to him. And that is his weakness.

I hesitate, knowing my next words won't be taken well. "I trust him," I say.

Pete raises a brow. "Trust him? How can you trust a guy like that?"

"He's got nothing to gain by keeping the Bloodred Queen alive and everything to lose if he does. Think about it," I say, pacing the room. "What other options does he, or we for that matter, have? We've seen the evil the Bloodred Queen has caused. Of anyone else, he's suffered the most by her hand. Who gouges out their own child's eye?"

Maus and Hase watch the discussion as if it were a fascinating game of cricket, not saying a word.

"And then what? We include him in not only killing his mother, but what lies behind the power of the crown. How do you think that's going to go?" Pete says. "He'll just do the same thing his mother did."

"Do you have another suggestion?" I ask.

Pete bites his lip thoughtfully before he pulls his daggers from their sheaths and twirls them. "Sounds like Hook and I are taking down a queen and retrieving the Haploraffen Halo," he says.

"Deal, but I'm going with you," I say. Turning to Maus and Hase, I gesture to the toolbox filled with the antidote. "Can you keep these safe until we return?"

Maus smiles a wide grin and pats me on the cheek. "Of course, my boy. In the years we've been confined to this lab, we've had many hidden secrets. What's one more? Especially one that will save the world. Good luck to you both!"

As we depart, I take a passing glance over my shoulder, hoping that whatever happens this night, Maus and Hase survive it.

· GAIL ·

Ginger is deadly silent, having not said a word in over an hour. She forges through the overgrown foliage. The unknown of what awaits us gnaws at my gut like a parasite. I want to ask questions, but it's clear that Ginger is not in the mood for discussion.

Our encounter with the tin soldier has left her rattled, and her anxiety is contagious. She has been steadfast, courageous in the face of adversity. Now fissures mark her steel countenance. I have no idea who the other two Henchmen are, but if they're anything like the tin soldier, we may not make it to Lohr Castle alive.

We've traveled over an hour with no hint of civilization in sight. Other than the song of birds and the occasional squirrel, the forest has been relatively still. The back of my neck prickles when the birds abruptly become quiet. Ginger halts and peers up into the trees. She reaches behind her and pulls out a mace.

An ominous growl behind me draws my attention. Quickly, I aim toward the sound rumbling from the thicket. A second snarl comes from the brush to my left. Within moments unseen beasts surround us.

"Ginger?" I say, hoping she has something encouraging to say.

"Shh!" she hisses, her eyes darting.

Dry leaves crunches nearby. Ginger pushes me behind her, shoving me into the dense shrubs as she faces the creature heading our way. She grips the handles of both maces, ready to defend us.

A large man emerges from the bushes. His thick dirty-blond hair hangs in waves past his shoulders. A scruffy beard and mustache frame his dangerous smile. A deer-hide hunting vest barely covers his muscular build.

Ginger stands a little taller. "Leon," she says, frowning.

"Ginger," he says, shaking his head. "Why am I not surprised? You've always been trouble. Looks like nothing has changed."

"What are you doing here?" Ginger asks, twirling her maces with ease.

Leon pulls two butterfly swords from their sheaths. "Funny. I was just about to ask you the same."

Gripping my bow tight, I keep my arrow fixed on Leon.

"Let us pass," Ginger says, moving to go around him.

Chuckling, Leon sidesteps, appearing to look for the first opportunity to strike. "Now, you know I can't do that. Letting outsiders into the Lohr's territory? That would be against the rules."

"I'm not an outsider," Ginger says. "Lohr is my home."

"Lohr *was* your home," Leon says. "But you disappeared. Most of us thought the Bloodred Queen disposed of you when she murdered the king. Seems we were wrong."

"Seem so," Ginger concurs.

"It's a shame that you're the one I must kill today. Especially in light of our history with each other," Leon says, drawing closer to Ginger. She responds by taking equal steps back.

Growls continue to surround us, but neither Ginger nor Leon appears concerned.

"Where have you been hiding out all these years?" Leon asks. "Spain? France? It's incredibly difficult to court my future bride when she disappears without a trace."

His nonchalant tone slips as anger seeps through his words.

"That's funny, I don't recall ever accepting your offer for courtship," she says. "In fact, if memory serves me right, I clearly told you that I'd *never* be your wife. Eighteen was much too young to be a bride, much less the bride of a man who betrayed his king."

The corner of Leon's mouth turns up just before he attacks her with his swords, his movements swift. She wards him off with each blow, knocking away his advances with her weapons. Standing back, I take in a slow, steady breath, keeping my aim on the struggle and waiting for a clear shot. Ginger swipes at Leon with her mace, but misses.

"I wouldn't call it a betrayal," he says. "More like a promotion. A man can only ward off predators from the castle for so long without losing himself to the wild. Without questioning his purpose. There's no honor in battling beasts. No courage in scaring off the occasional wild boar or bear. Under the Bloodred Queen's rule, I'm an executioner. I might not be king of the castle, but I'm certainly the king of the forest. And you, my lady, are in my territory." His words grunt out as the two parry with each other in some beautifully terrifying battle dance.

Cautiously, I step through the brush, but when a branch breaks beneath my boot, Leon turns his attention to me. Before

I can react, one of his swords flies and shears off one of my braids. The blade splits the wood in the trunk behind me as my braided lock falls to the ground.

"This is not your battle," Leon says. "But don't worry, I'll get to you."

Ginger swipes at him, landing a blow to his thigh and pulling his attention from me. He howls in response and lunges for her.

Blocking his move, she spits out, "I am not a child anymore, Leon. You don't frighten me."

Suddenly, Leon sucks in his bottom lip and whistles loudly. Three wolves emerge from the surrounding brush, each baring sharp canine teeth.

"I'll make you a deal," Leon says as they continue to battle. "I was sent here on the Bloodred Queen's orders to kill you and your little friend. However, I'll spare your life under the condition that you cooperate with me. Come back to Lohr alive as my bride or die as my enemy."

Ginger swings her mace, aiming for Leon's head, and misses. "Never," she says, her teeth clenched tight.

"What a waste. Your father would be ashamed of you," Leon says as he swings his butterfly sword.

Ginger easily dodges it. "My father would only be ashamed of me if I let the sun set on your beating heart."

Shaking his head, he takes several steps back, out of Ginger's reach. With a quick turn, he waves a hand over his shoulder. "*Töte sie.*"

Ginger throws the short-handled mace, landing its sharp

teeth in the thick neck of one wolf before the kill command is completely out of Leon's mouth. A second wolf pounces, pinning her to the ground. Drooling, the animal snaps. I lift my bow, but I am knocked to the ground as well. My weapon slips, landing a meter from me.

The wolf circles back on me, snarling. I flip to my hands and knees and scurry to my weapon. Before I reach it, the wolf sinks its teeth into the heel of my boot and shakes its head violently. I try to pull myself loose, but the canine's jaws are locked tightly. I make a second attempt to grab my weapon, but it's still too far away.

With the heel of my other boot, I give the wolf a swift kick in the face. It yelps, releasing my boot from its hold. I have mere seconds to snatch an arrow from my quiver. When I whirl back toward the wolf, I don't have time to aim. Shoving the arrow at the rabid beast, I hit the animal directly in the eye. Blood splatters my face, and I cough. The beast howls and retreats, pawing at the arrow. Finally, it turns and runs into the forest.

Rising to my feet, I search for Ginger. She's pulling her mace from the third wolf's body when she is jerked to her feet and thrown to the ground. This time Leon pins her beneath his massive knees, both hands gripped tightly around Ginger's throat. She kicks and wriggles, but he's at least seven stones heavier than she is. Hitting him with her fists proves futile. Her green eyes bulge as she gasps for air.

Snatching up my bow, I line up my shot. While I'd like to see him suffer, he isn't worth wasting one more breath on. When the base of his skull is within my aim, I release the arrow.

It flies straight and true, piercing the base of his skull. His blond locks bloom with a crimson hue as his body wavers and topples to the side. Gasping, Ginger writhes beneath Leon's corpse, eagerly taking in air. I rush over to her and struggle to pull Leon off her entirely.

Propped on her elbows, she takes several breaths. "Nice shot, kid."

I help her to her feet. "I'm assuming he's one of the Henchmen?"

Ginger nods, standing and picking up her mace.

"Two down, one to go. It should be fairly easy from here on out, right?" I ask, slinging my bow over my shoulder.

"Those two were pussycats compared to the last Henchman," she says.

Throwing my bow over my head, I roll my eyes. "Why do you keep saying that? Can't we have one adversary that isn't impossible? I just want to get to the castle, save the king—again—and go home." I pause. "Although I'm not all that sure where home is anymore."

Ginger pats me on the back. "The only way home is to follow your heart."

"What does even that mean?" I ask, exasperated.

"You'll figure it out when the time is right," she says, smiling.

Turning, she trudges forward into the brush.

I throw my hands up in frustration and follow.

· KATT ·

My lips shimmer with a pale pink lipstick within the mirror. Loose tendrils frame my face. With my long dark hair cascading down my back and the Haploraffen Halo on my head, I'm as pretty as any queen should be. As any bride should be.

I rise from the vanity chair, taking in my formfitting bodice adorned with pleated, stained leather along the boning, bits of delicate chains, and polished gears. Ivory taffeta and lace billow from my skirt and bustle in elegant layers. Polished silver chains wrap around my waist and cascade over the fluffy fabric, serving as a train. If only my mother, my father . . . even my sister could see me, the youngest of the royals from England dressed as a bride and future queen of Germany. Somehow, I imagined my wedding day to be remarkably different. Considering all that has happened over the last year and a half, there's no room to want for more.

Keep your eyes on the goal, Katt. The crown.

Behind me stand my two handmaidens. With iron muzzles screwed into the joints of their jaws, they blink, speaking with only their eyes and hand motions. One kneels in front of me with a pair of lace-up, brocaded boots. I carefully slip my feet into them. She ties my shoes, but startles when the chamber doors spring open. Kommandt steps inside.

"The prisoners are ready," it says.

"Has your army found the other two?" I ask.

Kommandt shakes its head.

"Keep looking," I say sternly. "They must be found."

"They are searching for them now," he says. "Neither they nor the apothecarists appear to be in the lab."

I tap my claws on the vanity. "And what about the Bloodred Queen?"

"She is being updated as we speak," he says.

Standing, I walk from the room to the balcony, passing the fluttering curtains. As the moon rises over the town of Lohr, torchlight flickers to life throughout the village. The whir of machinery provides an ambient melody as they gather the villagers for an announcement. Their defeated expressions are a stain left by the Bloodred Queen's rule. A stain I intend to wipe clean. I can almost imagine their confused but joyous expressions when they realize they've been called to a wedding, an execution, and a coronation. Yes, their world is going to be a much different one under my rule.

"Does the Bloodred Queen expect anything?" I ask.

"Only what you've asked us to reveal: King Osbourne's execution," it says.

"Perfect," I say. Her death will be just one more reason the German people will accept me as King Jack's bride and their queen.

Turning on the heels of my buckled bridal boots, I peer at my reflection. My complexion has taken a green tone to it. "Find

Doc and have him brought to me immediately. Hunt him down. He can't have gone far. Tonight he lives and the others will die."

"As you wish," Kommandt says, turning toward the entrance to my room.

I straighten the halo trimmed with tulle and antique white roses. "One last thing."

It pauses at the doorway, waiting for my response.

"Toll the bells. It's time for a wedding."

· GAIL ·

It's been several hours since our encounter with Leon, and other than the harmony the forest life brings, it is silent. While Ginger forges through the forest, I'm a prisoner to my thoughts.

I've never murdered anyone before. Sure, I've killed animals for food, but only what was necessary to feed the villagers back at home. Even Timothy was mostly made of metal, and I'm not all that sure there was anything human left of him. But Leon was flesh and bone. While I know that I had no choice—he would've strangled Ginger if I hadn't—I still feel the weight of taking another person's life.

"Who was Leon?" I ask, finally unable to resolve his death.

"He wasn't a good man, but he also wasn't always that bad," Ginger says. "My pa told him if he could catch me to put a ring on my finger he could have me. Fortunately, I was fast, and Pa taught me to fight as good as any of the Zwergs. Several of his proposals ended up with an open wound and his tail tucked between his legs."

"Doesn't it bother you?" I ask.

Ginger stops and turns back to me. "Bother me?"

"Yeah, the fact we've just taken his life," I say.

"First off, *we* didn't kill him. *You* did. And thankfully so, because if you hadn't, that would be my dead body lying out there for rats to devour. I don't know about you, but being a feast for rodents and bugs was not on my agenda today," she says.

"Second, of course it bothers me. Who wants to end the life of another, whether good or bad? Even those beastly tin monkeys don't deserve to die," she says.

Timothy's death weighs heavier on me.

"But what choice do we have? We either surrender to the fact that each battle is our last or fight and be haunted with the lives we've taken," she says.

Not feeling at all better, I frown.

"So, yes, I feel bad. Taking someone's life is never an easy burden to carry. But you also *saved* a life. Two, in fact."

"Two?" I ask.

"If you hadn't done anything, if you let your conscience dictate that his life should've been spared, I would be dead, but you would be next," she says. "He was ordered to get rid of us, not just me."

She's right, but I think his death will always burden me. He is the only human I have murdered. Recently, I've seen my fair share of lives being taken, but their blood has never been shed by my own hands. Not until now.

She can tell by my silence that I'm not convinced. "Look, we live in a time in which only those who fight survive. Certainly you've seen this yourself over the last few years?" Ginger says.

Nodding, I think of how my world became exponentially more dangerous the day the Labyrinth walls burned to the ground. No longer were we fighting bears and wolves. Machines and hybrid beasts became our new worry, and they were deadlier when not confined by the maze. And now it's those who are flesh and bone, like Leon, that I have to fear. Is there no stop to what will become an enemy?

"But is killing others the only option?" I ask.

"Isn't that what has been done to your family? To your village?" she asks.

I swallow hard, trying not to think of the day I found my village in ruins, with no survivors.

"This war wasn't started by people like you or me. It was started by someone who had absolutely no regard for the lives of others. Not for King Osbourne, not for the people of England, not for your village or mine on the Emerald Isle. How many more lives must be taken before we stand up to the evil in this world? At what point do we cross the line of respecting humanity, no matter how awful it is, and finally stop the death that it brings?" Ginger says.

I glance at her out of the corner of my eye, unsure how to respond. How to put into words how I feel seeing this side of the battle. She's right. Evil should never win, but I still can't resolve in myself that murdering them is the only way.

Something behind her catches my eye. The brief glint of moonlight flashes off a blade.

I'm not sure if it's the expression in my face, the reflection in my eyes, or just sheer instinct, but Ginger reacts. Pushing me out of the way, she spins and drops to her knees, pulling both maces out in one movement. Stumbling back, I feel the whoosh of the blade as it barely misses me. Ginger swings her weapons, but the silent figure leaps, her blades flying beneath his feet.

"I was wondering when you'd make an appearance, Crowe," Ginger grunts out, dodging the sharp scythe.

"And here I am," Crowe says, his words muffled. Sickles, pruning shears, and a pointed trowel hang from his belt.

My feet are frozen in place as I take in the person . . . or is it a creature? Although it has the form of a human, it is far more frightening than any person I've ever met. Mesh bandages appear grafted on to Crowe's face and exposed arms, giving him the impression of having burlap skin. Aviator goggles obscure his eyes. A thick cord is stitched through his lips, sealing his mouth shut. This creature is clothed in ripped and dirty rags. If his appearance isn't horrifying enough, the scythe in his hands is stained with old blood.

Ginger throws herself to the ground and rolls as the creature swings his scythe again, just centimeters from her flattened body. The momentum throws Crowe off balance, giving Ginger time to get to her feet. They barrage each other with swift swipes of their weapons, each managing with extraordinary agility.

"Nice lip enhancement," Ginger says, her mace colliding with the sharp blade.

Crowe growls, swinging violently at Ginger. She grunts with every strike of the weapons.

"Who would've thought it'd be the Bloodred Queen that would find a way to keep your lying mouth shut," she says.

Launching at her, Crowe swipes his blade at her wildly. Ginger manages to fight him off, but in doing so backs herself up against a tree. With a swift shift of his scythe, he knocks her weapons from her hands. I almost see the corners of Crowe's lips turn up into a threaded smile as he raises his blade. The metal shimmers in the moonlight.

Hearing Ginger's quick breaths, I ready my bow. My hands shake, and I can't keep my target within view of the tip of my arrow. Taking a breath, I steady myself and align the creature in my view. Before I have time to release the arrow, Crowe brings his sharp blade down toward Ginger's head.

She ducks, and the scythe sticks into the thick trunk of the tree. Crowe tugs his weapon free with ease. It gives Ginger enough time to plan her escape. She dives for one of her maces. Snatching its handle, she rolls, anticipating Crowe's next maneuver. His weapon plunges into the soft dirt seconds after she moves. Too quickly, he pulls the blade free and aims for her again as she grabs her second mace.

Ginger hollers as the sharp edge rips through her shoulder, pinning her to the ground. Blood fills the gash in her flesh and spills down her arm. "Kill him!" she screams, barely holding his looming attacks back.

My arrow flies, but my hand trembles so much that it misses and buries itself into a nearby tree. I aim again, but when Crowe's eyes turn to me, I know I may only get one more chance. With Ginger wriggling beneath him, he swipes at her again, this time grazing her face. Her weapons drop to either side of her as she reaches for the gash across her cheek. Taking a final blow, he embeds the tip of the blade into Ginger's right forearm. She howls in pain.

Crowe stands and leaps toward me. Again, I send another arrow his way, but my weapon is swiped from my hands and I am knocked to the forest floor. I gasp, sucking in air as the wind is knocked out of me. Crowe sits on my chest, pinning my arms with his knees. He reaches for the sickle clipped to his belt.

"No one tries to kill Crowe and lives," he snarls, his sewn lips barely moving.

As the sharp point descends toward me, I squeeze my eyes shut, waiting for my last heartbeat. Instead, his scream rings through the forest, like the cry of a banshee. His body jerks when his own weapon pierces his back and comes out of his chest. When his body slumps to the side, Ginger stands behind him, holding his scythe tightly gripped in her hands. She leans the weapon against her shoulder.

"Not anymore," she says.

· ☐☐☐ ·

Following Hook's instructions, we make our way toward the hideaway near the throne room. Haploraffen guard the maze of hallways, clearly on a mission. With the sound of the alarms earlier, I'm almost certain they are hunting for Pete and me and possibly the others. Lily and her safety sits at the forefront of my mind, but I force myself to stay focused. While everything within me yearns to protect her, she's strong enough to hold her own. Glancing at Pete, I see a multitude of expressions knotted across his face. I can only imagine it has something to do with Gwen.

Slipping through the corridors, we find ourselves hiding in darkened corners and behind open doors. Pete and I watch two Haploraffen hurry by before we find our way to the door of the prison cells.

Expecting a fight, my breath catches to find the prison door unguarded and wide open. Alarm bursts in Pete's eyes as well as we race down the stairwell. The air of death hits me before my eyes fall on the broken body of Pickpocket.

"No! Pickpocket, wake up!" Pete cries, collapsing at Pickpocket's side. "Doc! Fix him!"

The pallor in Pickpocket's face and lips speaks volumes. He's been dead long enough that there is no bringing him back, but a sense of urgency drives me to my knees. Examining his body, there is no rise or fall of his chest. I try to breathe for him, but I know it is futile. His head lies at on odd angle, confirming a snapped neck.

I sit back on my heels, unable to catch my breath as another of our friends lies lifeless.

"Doc! Help him!" Pete begs.

"He's gone," I say, my voice frail. Sorrow threatens to derail me. An injury like this would've been violent enough that he would've died instantly. I'm grateful he didn't suffer.

Pete buries his face in his hands and sobs, his quiet voice whispering through the prison cells. With all those he's lost, I wonder how much more he can take. I've lost so many as well, but each death seems to steal a piece of him.

Getting to my feet, I say, "Come on. We're getting out of here."

"We can't leave him here," Pete replies, anger coloring his words.

"Pete, we can't take him." I say the words softly, unsure if Pete will lose it more or realize I'm right.

He hangs his head, rubbing the back of his neck. When he looks up at me, he nods. He closes Pickpocket's eyes. "You were the best. You'll be missed, mate," he says in a strangled voice.

"Good-bye, Pickpocket," I add. Then I hold out my hand, and Pete reluctantly takes it. I yank him to his feet, and we race back up the stairs. When we reach the landing, we are greeted by a large portrait of the Bloodred Queen hanging on the opposite wall. She appears young in this picture, her skin without a single flaw. Her eyes are familiar, the same shape and hue as Hook's.

Sliding the portrait to the side reveals an opening into the passage Hook said would be there. We descend several floors before finally reaching a wooden door at the bottom of the stairwell. Pete cautiously opens the door.

Other than a crudely made rocking chair constructed of rusty pieces of armor, the room is empty. A set of soldered-off lances are mounted onto two old breastplates that function as both a seat and chair back. Beneath it, four greaves provide the legs to the chair. Otherwise the room is completely empty.

"They should be here by now, shouldn't they?" I ask.

"We agreed to reconvene at dusk, even if they couldn't find Gwen," Pete says. His voice cracks, and I understand how hard this must be for him. "The longer they stay out, the higher the risk they'll be caught."

"You don't think . . . ?" I can't finish my sentence. After seeing the condition Pickpocket was left in, I can't begin to think of Lily being out there without me. The only peace I have right now is knowing she's with Alyssa, Maddox, and, if he stays true to his word, Hook.

"Unless they show up in the next few minutes, I think it's safe to assume we're on our own," Pete says, his voice wavering.

Leaning my head to the left, my neck cracks. As the stress of our situation continues to mount, the muscles in my body ball up. I just want this day to end with Lily safe in my arms and the rest of the world at peace. Right now, that vision seems impossible to attain.

Something catches Pete's eye on the wall opposite the makeshift chair. Dark fabric hangs over a small section of the stone. When Pete pulls it back, a narrow slit in the rock gives us a view of the room beyond.

From our vantage point, we are overlooking the royal throne room. Sitting in a wrought iron throne and facing a mirror is a monstrosity far worse than any nightmare. With scaly green skin and golden reptilian eyes, the Bloodred Queen smiles serenely, running a brush through her long dark hair. I swallow hard. What I'm looking at is my fault. I am the cause of her malformations. She might be the enemy, but my broken antidote has made her what she is today. Accident or not, I've failed my oath as a physician and it's something that will haunt me for the rest of my life.

From inside the chambers, two Haploraffen approach the queen.

"The prisoners are ready," one of them says.

The Bloodred Queen whirls her chair around. "It's about time. How many are there?"

"As of right now, six in total," the Haploraffen says. "We are still on the hunt for two more."

Pete gives me a worried glance. "Sounds like she's found the others," he whispers.

Counting off on my fingers, I try to figure out who the last captive is. "Gwen, Alyssa, Lily, Maddox, and Hook. That's only five. Who's the last one?"

"Jack?" Pete suggests.

"I suppose it's possible," I say. "If either Katt or the Bloodred Queen have found out you two have a pact, Katt could've changed her mind on his usefulness."

"Where are they?" the Bloodred Queen says.

"Katt has prepared them for a public execution. She requests your company to decide the individual fates of each," the lead Haploraffen says.

The Bloodred Queen stands. "*She* requests *my* company? That twit needs a lesson on who is in charge here. Take me to the prisoners."

Bowing as the queen climbs down the stairs, the Haploraffen rises. "They await your decision in the courtyard."

"Any traitor to the crown must die," the Bloodred Queen says, exiting the room with the guards following behind.

Pete releases the fabric back into place and plops onto the rickety chair. "This is not looking good. How are we supposed to take out both Katt and the Bloodred Queen by ourselves?"

Lost for words, I say nothing. My priorities are muddled in my head. Lily is a prisoner, and my heart begs to rescue her and the others. However, with a public execution in order, there's no way to get to them without being noticed. They'll be heavily guarded. And we still need to kill the queen and figure out how to distribute the antidote. Helpless, I look at Pete.

He seems to be pondering the same thing. "Maybe we can recruit some of the villagers to help us free them."

"We'll never find enough people in time. And even then, we're risking their lives for everyone else's," I say.

Appearing defeated, Pete drops his face into his hands. "There's got to be a way."

And then I realize there is. I take a moment to myself, feeling the air expand my lungs, because uttering the next words may take my breath away.

"There is a way," I say quietly.

Pete stares at me, anticipating my explanation.

"You need to kill Katt and get the Haploraffen Halo," I tell him.

He runs a hand through his hair, trying to make sense of my suggestion. "You heard Hook. They listen to her but are first and foremost loyal to the Bloodred Queen. While she's alive, we have no chance. And if Hook is really taken captive, then we can't count on him to do her in."

I pause, preparing myself for the protest that is about to come from Pete, before saying, "I'm going to kill the queen."

Pete stares at me as if I've lost my marbles.

"Doc, I know we've had our differences, but you don't need to be a martyr," he says. He drops his gaze to his hands and shakes his head. "I know I've been awful to you and have treated you like pond scum, but that doesn't mean I don't care for you. In fact, I appreciate you more than you know. You're like a brother to me. You and I go back further than anyone else here."

His words are bittersweet. They are the affirmations I've waited a year and a half to hear, but they sting as they take hold of my thoughts.

"I can't lose you, too," he says with tears in his eyes. "You're my best friend."

Sucking in my bottom lip, I struggle to find words, and all I can manage is a smile. Pete returns the gesture, rises, and pats me on the back.

"We kill the queen together, or we don't go at all," he says.

"No. You need to get our friends out of here," I say. I hold the rucksack with the hydrofluoric acid. "This is dangerous stuff. It needs to be handled carefully by someone who's experienced. When this bottle is opened, anyone nearby who touches or inhales it will be poisoned and eventually die."

"You're not sacrificing yourself," Pete says.

"I'm not intending to," I say, frustrated. "But with only two of us left, one needs to kill the Bloodred Queen and the other needs to get that crown from Katt."

He is silent.

"Go, Pete," I plead. "Get the crown. Save Lily and Gwen and the others."

Again, tears brim in his eyes. He pulls me into a bear hug and releases me. "See you in the courtyard," he says, his voice cracking.

Turning, he exits the room and doesn't look back.

· GAIL ·

Dusk has finally settled, leaving all of Lohr in the darkness of nightfall. A stormy and starless sky offers no light, leaving torches to illuminate the castle. Haploraffen sit atop the walls like gargoyles watching over the entrance. Others shout at the local people. Like cattle to the slaughter, they stumble along, hurrying to keep pace with the queen's mechanical soldiers.

After an hour of walking, Ginger has left me within the tree line of the forest. While I'm not afraid of the dark, I have the sensation of bugs crawling all over me. It's just my imagination, but the noises, the shadows . . . they are unsettling.

Bells toll, demanding the presence of all those who hear its ring. A mother shushes her crying infant, worry evident in her tired eyes. Children cast their gazes to the ground, frightened to peer at the terrifying soldiers.

A young girl assists a woman as she limps down the footbridge toward the castle courtyard. When the lady falls onto the stone path, the crowd comes to a halt. The girl kneels by the woman, attempting to bring her to her feet.

"Get up," the mechanical soldier growls, lifting a spiked claw.

Wielding my bow, I nock an arrow and step from the tree line. When the soldier's head is within my aim, I ready myself to release the arrow. Letting out a breath, I pull back the bowstring and remind myself that the soldier is just a machine. You can't kill something that's made up of wheels and gears.

"What are you doing? You're going to get us killed," Ginger hisses as she grips my elbow and pulls me back into the tree line.

"I'm not about to stand by and watch them brutalize the people of Lohr," I say.

Two other villagers rush to the woman's side and help her to her feet.

"While I admire your bravado, if you go all heroine on me, those soldiers are likely to take you prisoner. Then I'll have to rescue the king *and* your impulsive behind," Ginger says sternly. "Now put that thing away."

She hands me a hooded cloak. "Cover yourself with this."

"Where did you get these?" I ask as I slip the dusty fabric over my shoulders.

"Doesn't matter," Ginger says, slipping into her own cloak. Something's not right. Her words are clipped, and she refuses to meet my eye.

"You stole them, didn't you?" I ask.

Ginger tugs her cloak around her. "Listen, kid, we don't have time nor do you have any grounds to discuss morality. We've both taken a life or two in the past few days. Stealing a few wraps is hardly our worst crime."

Her words cut, but she's right. What are a few missing coats in the grand scheme of what we're doing? I clasp the cloak tight to my chest and follow Ginger as she pulls the hood of hers over her head and weaves into the crowd.

The young villagers are thin, with sallow, sunken cheeks. None are much older than Ginger. All bones and dirty rags for clothes, they appear to have given up what little hope they must have once had. We mingle with the people as soldiers line the entrance to the castle.

"What's going on?" Ginger asks a toothpick-thin boy.

He shakes his head. "Don't know. Mostly the queen just ignores us. This is new."

"Shut up! Both of you!" a soldier says, giving the boy a shove. He stumbles, nearly running into the girl in front of him.

We follow the crowd into a large square filled with torches. When every villager is within the courtyard, the guard slams the metal doors shut, barricading us inside the large area. A large wooden platform stands in the center. A half dozen stakes rise from the stage. Gwen, seeming confused and disoriented, tugs at her shackles. To the left, Alyssa stands expressionless, resolute in her fate. Maddox and Lily are also bound, along with Hook.

With so many from my village here, I wonder how many others have survived. A hint of hope rises as I wonder if my mother made it out, but it's quickly replaced with a hollow in my gut. Something deep within me knows she didn't make it out of the fiery inferno. If she had, she'd probably be standing with the rest of the prisoners. I swallow the lump in my throat.

It's the man on the middle platform who makes the crowd gasp, sending contemptuous shouts to the machined soldiers that guard him. Seeming frail and bewildered himself is King

Osbourne, shackled, but not to a stake like the others. Instead, the winged creatures surround him.

Standing at the castle doors is a beast more hideous than any I've seen either in the Labyrinth, on Emerald Isle, or on our journey back to Lohr. Her eyes glow gold in the torchlight. The green hue of her scaly skin gives her a sickly appearance. Dressed in a scarlet gown, the Bloodred Queen watches the activities, surrounded by her mechanical soldiers.

Tinder and wood are piled high beneath their platforms. Haploraffen stand shoulder to shoulder, encircling the shackled prisoners. Within the soldiers' barricade, a half dozen of the winged machines hold torches, ready to set the platforms ablaze.

"The king lives!" many in the crowd shout, their voices conflicted with both hope and worry.

"He's alive."

Some cautiously kneel, knowing that a gesture of respect is due, but their expressions show fear as their stares fixate on the guards. Panic floods me, seeing him a prisoner of a kingdom he once ruled. Believed dead and now alive and mercilessly shackled in front of his people. If he's killed for real this time, then all is truly lost.

"Come on," Ginger says, leading me through the crowd. "Stay quiet."

The shriek of the bells finally ends, but its ominous ring still echoes in my ears. Hundreds gather in the small arena, leaving very little room to move.

Osbourne tries to console the crowd. They holler his name,

reaching their hands toward him, but the brutality of the queen's soldiers is no match for the weak and hungry members of the community.

"Shh! Please do as they say," Osbourne says.

"Silence them!" the Bloodred Queen shouts.

Pain etches Osbourne's face as the soldiers bare their sharp claws and force the rioters back. Fights break out, and several villagers charge the platform to reach Osbourne, but the unarmed villagers stand no chance against the Bloodred Queen's army. Many lie bludgeoned on the dirt, unresponsive.

As the violence escalates, shouts thunder through the crowd and fists rise in the air. In unison they scream, "Long live King Osbourne!"

Osbourne tries to subdue the people, but the rise of fury drowns out his pleas.

"This is not good," Ginger says, taking in the disorderly crowd.

"The alternative is no better," I say. "Either they fight or continue to be ruled by the Bloodred Queen."

Their chants grow louder in unison. "Long live the king!"

"Silence!" the Bloodred Queen shouts again.

A girl, not much older than I am, saunters onto the upper balcony dressed in layers of ivory lace and taffeta. A gold circlet rests on her forehead with yards of tulle and ribbon flowing behind. She holds out a gloved hand. Jack takes it and leads her to the railing of the balcony. As he scans the crowd, a look of fury crosses his face—like nothing I've ever seen before. It seems like he's struggling to get himself under control. Finally his features slide into place, and the only sign of anger is in the set of his jaw.

A hush rumbles through the arena, and even the wind seems to go still.

"Jack," the Bloodred Queen hisses. "You ought to be standing with your brother."

"Not today, Your Majesty," the girl says sweetly.

Jack ignores them both, keeping his eyes on the crowd.

"People of Lohr," she says. "I am Katt, princess of England. Jack and I come before you with troubling news. Osbourne White, your king, has betrayed you all."

The crowd's shouts dissolve into confusion. Even I wonder if I've heard right. Standing before them are King Osbourne and his son: one bound as a prisoner, the other wearing the royal crown. It doesn't make any sense. Jack drops his gaze, seeming unwilling to refute or confirm her claim.

"For five years you were led to believe he was dead, his body entombed within the royal crypt. But those were cowardly lies. Lies that even we in England believed," Katt says.

"Instead, under the tyranny of the Bloodred Queen, he ran, his cowardly tail tucked behind him. That man turned his back on you, citizens of Lohr. Abandonment hidden in the face of fear. Desertion of his very people, and—his only son. It is only right that he abdicates the throne and pays for his crime."

"Why isn't Jack stopping this?" I ask, my heart crashing against my ribs.

Ginger shakes her head. "I don't know, but this isn't the Jack I remember from several years ago. He'd never turn on his father."

"That's not true!" Hook shouts. "You were there when he was declared dead. He didn't abandon you, me, or these people. The Bloodred Queen poisoned him. Tell them the truth! These people deserve to know what happened to their king."

Katt's brows rise. "Poisoned? Then how do you explain his reappearance?" She waves a dismissive hand. "Perhaps he's immortal? No, maybe he's a saint or, better yet, an angel."

"He's the devil!" the Bloodred Queen hisses. "And so is that boy you stand next to. Jack is a traitor to the crown and all those he's vowed his loyalty to. I don't know what your intentions are with him, but I promise you, you will be his next victim."

Anguish grows on Jack's expression. He glances at his father and back at Katt.

"Son, don't listen to her!" Osbourne shouts. "You are not what she says. You're a good boy with a heart of gold. You've always been driven by your empathetic spirit. You're kind, sometimes to a fault, but you've never been a traitor."

Jack grips the edge of the balcony, seeming to struggle with his thoughts.

Osbourne continues. "And I would never leave you. Not of my own volition. I love you, Jack. More than anything in the world. You are my greatest success in all I've done in my time as king and as a human being."

Shaking his head, Jack's cheeks flush.

"Son, I don't know what that girl has told you, but none of this true," Osbourne pleads.

Jack's next move startles me.

Slamming his hand on the railing of the parapet, he growls. "Five years, Father! You've been gone five years and look what has happened. The Bloodred Queen has nearly brought the world to its knees. Millions have died at her hands and you weren't here." His voice cracks. "You weren't here. Not for them." He waves a hand over the crowd. "And not for me."

Osbourne's face pales as he shakes his head. "You know I would've been here if I could. I'd never abandon you or my kingdom. Nothing for anything in the world."

Jack takes in a visible breath before he stands tall. "For the crimes you've committed against the country, I relieve you of your power over Germany and take it as my own."

Cries erupt from the crowd of villagers as they surge toward the machine-powered line of defense.

"How dare you!" the Bloodred Queen shouts. "I am the queen. Seize them!"

Her words are lost in the commotion. Between the protests from both the villagers and the prisoners, and the guards' shouts to stand down, I can no longer hear anything she says.

The guards warn the villagers to keep their silence, but their anguish cannot be quieted. Reverberating through the open space, the clang of iron manacles rings through the air.

"Your life shall be spared, but you will live in exile," Jack says.

Katt sidles up next to Jack. "The others who stand before

you are prisoners of Lohr, charged with crimes against both England and Germany. For the destruction they directly or indirectly contributed to my country, they are hereby sentenced to death by fire," she says.

"What?" Jack says, turning her way. "That was not the agreement."

Katt grins and whispers something into his ear. Jack's face pales as his gaze falls on the Everland kids.

"Son, I demand you let these people go," Osbourne shouts in an authoritative voice. "You may have issue with me and the queen, but these prisoners and the villagers have done nothing. Set them free immediately!"

"You know nothing of them or your son!" Katt says. "Gwen and the rest of the Lost Kids left him for dead in Everland. Hook tried to kill him with a poison apple, the same one you ingested. The dissension between Jack and the prisoners still stands."

"Jack, my boy, this is not the right thing to do," Osbourne pleads.

Jack's eyes glitter in the torchlight, wet with unshed tears. "Father, it is the only thing I can do to save the world," he says, the hurt in his voice more than obvious. "I'm so sorry."

He straightens his coat. "For crimes against the crown, I sentence you to be stripped of your title and exiled from Germany, never to return."

· KATT ·

*P*atience, I remind myself. *Smile.* Bat my eyelashes and jut out my pouty lip. Be the sweet, kind princess that they desire. Make them believe that he's in control. That he's in charge. He's the one who is sentencing their beloved king to exile. Like a black widow, lure them into a well-spun web. Spin my snare of illusions so grand they can hardly see the truth so close to their own faces. Entice. Tempt.

Dismay bubbles through the crowd. Haploraffen soldiers continue to subdue those who revolt, leaving dozens wounded.

The Bloodred Queen watches in disbelief, but her commands cannot rise above the discourse.

"Enough!" Jack shouts, but his voice is lost in the commotion. He turns to me, disgust etched into the curves of his face. He points to the halo on my head. "Katt, this has to stop! The Lost Kids were never a part of our agreement. I've done exactly what you've asked. How much more cruelty do you intend to impart on them? None of them deserves this. Not my father, not the Lost Kids, and certainly not the people of Lohr."

I smile as sweetly as I can. "You've just sentenced the highest ruling person to exile. I guess that makes you king now. Quelling the chaos is your responsibility, isn't it?"

Pressing his lips together, he reaches for my halo crown, but I command the monkeys to restrain him.

"What do you have to gain from any of this?" he says, struggling against their grip.

I lean close. "We've been over this, Jack. No one likes the Bloodred Queen. She's as good as dead. When she's distracted enough by all that's going on, I'll have the Haploraffen stand down and let the villagers take care of her. Then there's your dear old daddy, who obviously is the rightful ruler. We can't have him standing in my way. The Lost Kids are just a nuisance, and if they don't die now, they'll always be biting at my heels. Is your father's life not worth it?"

I brush his cheek with my hand. "And then there's you. Take a look at what you've caused. You've given the people their king back and ripped him out of their hands just as quickly. They'll never respect you, not really. But if you take on a bride—and not just any bride but the only surviving princess from the country where this whole war started—they'll see our homelands as unified. As a means to end what the Bloodred Queen began. Trust me, I'll be the best queen they've ever encountered. Soon their loyalty will lie with me. Eventually, the world will see me as the bringer of peace, and world power will be mine."

More screams draw Jack's attention.

"Those soldiers are going to kill someone," he growls. "Stop them!"

With a wave of my hand, a Haploraffen guard drags in a young man dressed in clerical robes. His eyes are wide with fright, but it only fuels my cause.

"If you want this all to stop, claim the crown. Announce

yourself as king and marry me right here in front of all of them," I say. "That was our deal. Now carry it out or everyone dies."

It takes several seconds before the rage drains from his expression and defeat takes its place. Without another word to me, he returns his attention to the soldiers and citizens. Again, he attempts to calm the crowd, but to no avail.

"People of Lohr, hear me out," he shouts.

Alyssa stares up at me, her fury visible even in the dim light. She frowns but says nothing. She doesn't have to. Memories of my old childhood friend flood my thoughts. Both our families of royal blood. My mother the Queen of England, her mother a princess and younger sister. Long gone are the summer days of hide-and-seek in the hallways of Buckingham Palace. Of tea parties in the royal garden. Of pretend play, imagining being the Queen of England herself, decreeing Mondays to be the weekly plum tart day. Giggling at jelly-stained lips to mimic my mother's perfectly painted face.

I'm not sure if the shine in Alyssa's eyes is a reflection of the tears in my own or just the lighting, but her gaze remains fixed on me. Unblinking.

While she may not rule over Lohr, or even Germany, she will rule one day. It's in her blood. It's in her soul to care for people. She may not govern a country, province, or even a city, but she will be a leader again. Alyssa would never allow for a one-world government and therefore will always be the enemy.

It's either her or me.

Surprised at the realization, I struggle for the breath caught in my chest.

My crown hums, casting a gold glow in my vision. The Haploraffen shovel one last mound of hay beneath the wooden platforms, nearly done with the preparations for the prisoners' execution. Soldiers collect the burning torches. The wails of the community grow, begging Jack to show mercy. For me to stop this atrocity, but their pleas are left unheard.

Jack's breath comes shallow and quick as he struggles in the grip of the Haploraffen soldier. Watching the Haploraffen battle the villagers, his voice breaks. "Please, Katt, I'll do anything, but you have to stop this."

He's soft. He cares for these people, for his father—too much. There'll never be room for both of us on the throne. Where he is filled with mercy and compassion, he lacks authority and an iron fist. They'll never respect him. He might not recognize it, but I do. While the idea of a united king and queen is the happy conclusion of every fable, this is no fairy tale.

The Bloodred Queen attempts to bring control, but the chaos is far louder than her orders. I almost feel sorry for the crowd. It'll be hard for them to see their beloved king die not once but twice, and this time so cruelly.

At the end of this night, I shall be queen.

Jack watches helplessly as the Haploraffen continue to show force against the villagers' protests. Metal against flesh, they stand no chance.

Jack scowls at me, his fury skewering me. I tilt my head and smile, a silent nudge to comply. The Haploraffen behind him dig their claws into his back. He wriggles in the soldiers' grip. "You should be the one bound to those stakes," he growls.

"I wouldn't be so bold if I were you," I say. "Threats won't win favor for you or your father."

"Oh, trust me, Katt, your day is coming," Jack says harshly.

"You think so?" I ask.

"You've gone too far," Jack says through clenched teeth. "If you kill those people down there, you'll never earn their respect."

"We'll see about that," I say. "Are you ready to say your vows?"

"I'll never marry you," Jack says.

"I can still kill your father, Jack," I reply.

"You're as much of a witch as the Bloodred Queen," he spits at me.

I laugh loudly. "We should do something about her as well, shouldn't we?"

Turning to Kommandt, I make my next command. "Order the Bloodred Queen's guards to take up their posts around the prisoners. No one is to rescue them."

Kommandt scowls. "That will leave the Bloodred Queen vulnerable," it says.

"Yes, and unless you hear otherwise, that is what you're commanded to do," I say.

"Down there, no one could hear anything," Jack says.

"Precisely," I say.

The leader of the Haploraffen turns to one of its soldiers.

Returning my gaze to the Bloodred Queen, I watch as the soldiers leave her to join those protecting the prisoners, leaving her defenseless in the open.

· GAIL ·

Machine-driven guards and people battle all around us. Ginger and I dodge the onslaught of metal against flesh. The villagers use anything they can get their hands on as weapons. I hardly catch a glimpse of Katt and Jack up on the balcony, surrounded by the Haploraffen. At the front of the castle, the Bloodred Queen is wide-eyed and alone. Even if I could wield my weapon without drawing attention, I don't know that I'd have an open shot to take out Katt . . . or Jack, for that matter. At this point I don't know whose side he's on.

An explosion from the balcony startles me and everyone else around me. Smoke billows from the cannons of a Haploraffen guard that stands near Katt.

"Lohr, your anger is justified," Katt shouts. "Your fury is justified. As the princess of England, I feel your frustration. Like your land, the Bloodred Queen has destroyed my country, my home. Because of her deeds, my sister, the Queen of England, is dead. She is the reason I suffer," Katt says, holding up a scaly hand. "She's the reason you suffer. I've come to Lohr seeking both shelter and the cure, the very cure that many of you need."

A hush grows over the crowd as their eyes fall on the queen.

"You will pay harshly for your crimes," the Bloodred Queen hisses.

Ginger shuffles next to me. Reaching inside her dark cloak,

she draws her weapon. It's then I see movement just over her shoulder. About fifty meters away, Doc struggles to pull a gun from his waist.

"Ginger," I say softly, pointing to the lone boy standing away from the crowd behind her. "I know him. He's from my village."

"Looks like we're more than an army of two," she says, watching him draw closer to the Bloodred Queen. "Or maybe not. Head over and help the poor guy before he shoots himself in the foot."

"Where are you going?" I ask.

"Katt's in control right now and I'm going to end that. Do what you can to get close the Bloodred Queen. When the opportunity strikes, you both shoot at her until she goes down. When the shooting starts, it's going to get confusing quick."

I nod. "Good luck," I say.

"You too. We're going to all need it," Ginger says.

Slowly making my way toward Doc, I keep my eyes fixed on Katt and Jack. She's obviously been shouting back at the Bloodred Queen, and her words spur the crowd to turn their anger toward the queen. They are hesitant, though, their concern for the gravity of King Osbourne's situation is priority.

"Doc," I whisper when I'm close enough.

He startles, but relief washes over his expression. "Gail, how did you get here?"

"Long story," I say. "One that will have to wait until we kill the Bloodred Queen."

"She can't be killed. Not with weapons," Doc says. "Her scales are like armor."

Defeat sinks my heart. "Well, what do you suggest, then?" I ask.

Katt's voice rings out over the courtyard, so sweet that it's almost sickening. "It is clear that your adoration for Osbourne is significant. You remind me of my own people back before the Bloodred Queen called my home her own. Back before it was Everland."

"Come with me," Doc says, leading me by the elbow to a clearing in the crowd. He tucks his gun under his arm, reaches for his rucksack, and opens it. Carefully, he pulls out a dark container. "This liquid will dissolve her scales, making her as vulnerable as you or me. We just need to figure out how to do that, but we can't touch it or breathe it in."

"Well, certainly not with that thing," I say, taking away his gun. "Seriously, stay away from weapons. They're bad for your health."

"Prince Jack has asked me for my hand in marriage," Katt is saying, her rant continuing.

Astonishment rumbles through the throng of people, and I glance around at what's happening.

Katt's expression of compassion is so fake, I'm not sure how everyone else doesn't see through it.

"Now that I've seen your suffering under the Bloodred Queen's rule, I know that I can help bring an end to it," Katt says. "I've accepted his offer under two conditions. The first is that one life be spared. Osbourne White deserves to live. The king may have let you and the world down, but his crimes do not deserve a death sentence. He shall be spared, as his son decreed."

Osbourne shakes his head in disgust and Katt takes a dramatic pause.

I return my attention to Doc, knowing we need to do something while Katt's still listening to herself talk. "I have an idea." Reaching inside my pack, I pull out the gas mask I used back on the Emerald Isle, along with several arrows, ready to dip them into the liquid. "Give me the acid."

Doc is hesitant. "This is too dangerous to leave in your care."

"Do you have a better idea? How are you with a bow and arrows?" I ask, offering him the fistful of arrows.

He shakes his head. "I've never used one."

"Then I guess this one is on me," I say.

Reluctantly, he hands me the container. "It burns on contact. The vapors alone will harm you."

"I got it," I say. I point to the crowd of people, many of whom lie wounded on the dirt. "Now, good doctor, I think your people need you."

Doc smiles. "Good luck."

I yank the mask over my head as he hurries to the closest victim and begins attending to her wounds.

"My second request was for the death of the one who first started this war," I catch Katt saying.

I slip behind a pillar, drop to a squat, and open the vial, dipping the tips of three arrows into the liquid. When I'm done, I recap it and gently place it back into my rucksack to be sure it doesn't break. Picking up the first arrow, I move into position and take aim.

Again, doubt riddles me. Killing another person is beyond what my father ever taught or wanted for me. I'm a hunter, not a murderer. But he's not here to give me advice. I know if he were, he'd tell me to follow my gut—my heart. He'd remind me this one life has stolen millions of others and, indirectly, stole his, too.

Pulling the bowstring back, I lift my aim to the center of the Bloodred Queen's heart.

"The death of the Bloodred Queen," Katt shouts.

I couldn't agree more.

"This one's for you, Pa," I say, letting my arrow fly.

· DOC ·

Screams erupt throughout the courtyard as Gail's arrow pierces the Bloodred Queen's heart. Although her scales are thick, the tips penetrate far enough that the damage is done. The queen howls as she is struck again in her gut and thigh. It doesn't take long for the acid to do considerable damage. Her scales sizzle as the acid burns through them. Coughing, she falls to the ground.

The physician within urges me to end her suffering, but I recall the torment of so many by her own hands. I look away, trying to focus on the young girl with lacerations who lies in front of me. However, the Bloodred Queen's agonizing screams won't let me let it go. It's a slow and painful way to die. I search for my gun and realize that Gail has it.

Shouts explode from the parapet, drawing my attention. The crowd gasps as Pete bursts from inside the castle and lunges for Katt. A struggle ensues and the villagers take this cue to launch an assault on the Haploraffen guarding Osbourne.

I curse and search frantically for Gail in the crowd. When I spot her, I see she's swapped her bow for my gun, a weapon I know she's not familiar with. Her hand unsteady, she takes aim at Katt. Gail's voice is far louder and defiant than the throng of villagers.

"Long live King Osbourne!"

· KATT ·

Daggers tightly gripped in his hands, Pete crashes through the castle doors and into me, knocking me against the railing. The Haploraffen Halo tumbles off my head, clattering to the ground. Pete throws his arm around my neck, putting me in a headlock.

"Pete, you don't want to do this," I wheeze out.

Driven by anger, betrayal, and maybe even rage, he whirls me away from the onlooking crowd and holds his dagger to my side.

"Katt, I've been waiting three months to do this," he says, seething.

Before I can move or protest, he plunges his dagger into my side. Pain floods me, pulsing through every nerve in my body. "That's for Pickpocket," he grunts. Then he twists the hilt hard, sending a new rush of agony over me. "And Bella," he adds.

I try to gasp, but Pete's still cutting off my air. Instead, I flounder as a bright burst of pain explodes in me and then intensifies. My vision blurs, and I'm sure I'm about to pass out.

The sound of a gunshot cracks, diminishing the fog in my head and air gushes into my lungs. I'm not sure where the shot came from or who was the intended target. Pete shoves me away from him, pulling out his dagger as I fall, and I crumple to the floor, my muscles failing me. While agony still throbs from my knife wound, I don't think I've been struck by the bullet.

The crown sits nearby, and I reach for it, grunting through another bolt of agony, but he snatches it before I can. When I scramble to get it back, the pain is too much. Examining my knife wound, I gasp at the amount of blood pouring from it. I try to stanch it with the skirt of my dress, but as the white fabric grows red and my heartbeat echoes too loud in my head, I know I'm in trouble.

Turning my gaze up, I find Pete standing against the railing. Wide-eyed. Jack holds him, his face pale with worry.

"Pete?" he asks.

Pete drops his gaze to his chest and pulls the lapels of his hunter-green coat back. A scarlet stain blossoms in the shoulder of his beige shirt. When he lifts his chin, he crumples to the ground, his daggers skidding across the stone floor.

Jack cradles him in his lap. "Pete, hang on. You're going to be okay."

His green eyes stare at me as he gasps for breath.

"Well played, Lost Boy," I say, my words merely a whisper.

· ☐☐☐ ·

My gut twists as Pete collapses. Leaving my current patient behind, I race into the castle, up the staircase, and out onto the balcony. It feels as if it takes forever before I'm finally there.

"Doc, you've got to fix him," Jack says, nearly sobbing as he grips Pete tight to his chest.

"No! Pete!" The grieving voice rises from the throng of people. Gwen's choking sobs bellow throughout the arena. She struggles with her shackles. A cloaked figure darts from the crowd, past the motionless Haploraffen, and up the platforms. When her hood slips, a young woman snatches the keys from one of the guards. Oddly enough, he doesn't protest. With the Haploraffen Halo lying next to me, the soldiers wait for their next command.

From the corner of my vision, sudden movement draws my attention. Katt—on her feet again. How the former princess of England still lives defies my understanding. Judging by the amount of blood staining her gown, she doesn't have much longer.

I dodge Katt's sharp claws as she brings them toward me. One nicks my face, sending needles of pain through my cheek. I drive a heel into her gut, causing her to double over and slam against the wall, but it stalls her for only a second. Alternating hands, she swipes at me, her long fingernails like blades eager to spill my blood. With each swing, I back up, avoiding her advances. She surprises me when she knocks my feet out from under me with a kick. I fall hard and, despite the pain rocketing throughout my bones and flesh, I attempt to get back up.

I'm not quick enough.

Katt leaps, snatching up the crown from the ground and returning it to her head. She shouts in pain again, probably at the sudden movements, but she manages to knock me back down, pinning me with her muscular legs. Panic sets in as I struggle, the weight of her so heavy it's as if she's made of stone.

The pupils in Katt's gold eyes are nothing but slits. "Just where do you think you're going?" she asks. "You'll never win. This crown was meant to be mine."

She raises one clawed hand. "Good-bye, Doc."

She howls as Jack kicks her off me with the heel of his boot while still clutching Pete to him.

The next few seconds feel as if they are minutes. I reach for Pete's dagger and aim for Katt's chest. My hand shakes as the Hippocratic oath rings loud in my mind. *Do no harm,* I tell myself. Squeezing the hilt, I do the most merciful thing I could for the tortured soul she's become.

A rose-shaped stain of blood appears on her chest where the blade has struck. She slumps over, motionless. The gold circlet sits crookedly on her head. I slip it off and shove the crown in my rucksack, determined not to let anyone see it. Not until the right time. This is the only promise for human survival.

Jack sits speechless, refusing to let Pete go.

Gwen bursts through the door, eyes swollen and tears pouring down her face. She throws herself over Pete's body.

"Pete, stay with me. You'll be okay," she says through hiccuping cries.

Jack finally releases him as Pete reaches for her face, his breaths so shallow, so gurgling, that I'm surprised he is still conscious. "Don't cry, Lost Girl," he says.

"Don't you dare die, Pete," Gwen sobs. "I will never forgive you if you leave me, too."

"Help me get him inside, now!" I say.

Gwen and I lift the leader of the Lost Boys to his feet. Jack stands, watching his fallen leader in disbelief.

"Jack? You know what you need to do?" I ask.

He nods. "Take care of him," he says, before turning back to the parapet to address the crowd.

· GAIL ·

Down in the crowd, no one moves. Nobody speaks. I drop Doc's gun as panicked guilt hits me. Time slows and we all hold our breath, unsure where the next one will bring us. We can't look away from what's happening on the parapet. Gwen's sobs are a melancholy song in the thick air of death, betrayal, and uncertainty. She struggles to help get Pete to his feet. My heart breaks to see the bold and fearless girl I know she is succumb to grief.

When I take in the scene, I feel as if I'm in a dream. A horrifying nightmare in which the bloodbath of the last year and a half has ended bittersweet. While so many have lost their lives to war, to disease, to tyranny, we still have hope in the beating heart of the man who once kept our country—and to some degree our world—together. But somehow, there is no optimism in this scene. It still feels like we're drowning.

"Release the king!" Jack shouts.

Ginger, having battled her way through dozens of immobile Haploraffen, finally reaches the king. Taking the keys from an incapacitated soldier, she sets Osbourne free.

As Ginger unlocks Hook's shackles next, he pushes her out of the way, grabbing a knife from the sheath on her hip.

Looking beyond the dazed and confused villagers, something darts quickly between them. A snake striking its prey.

Instinct courses through me as I pull out an arrow and nock it, trying to find the queen among the crowd. After all the arrows I put in her, I thought she was incapacitated.

"If I go down, you go down, son," the Bloodred Queen says, popping up in front of Hook, her fangs oozing with a black liquid. I swing my bow, trying to line her up without hitting anyone else. But in one swift movement, she drives her knifelike claws into his gut just as he plunges Ginger's blade into her eye. The Bloodred Queen screams.

"You'd kill your own mother?" she shrieks, surprise twisting her grotesque features.

"Love is blind," Hook manages to utter through clenched teeth. The seconds drag before both collapse to the wooden platform floor, unmoving.

A hush blankets the crowd, and time seems to stand still.

The wicked queen is dead—and her only son lies lifeless next to her.

· GAIL ·

A crisp wind kisses my cheeks and ruffles my hair. With each step of my silver boots, the song of the dry leaves announces the onset of autumn. As I stroll along the cobbled stone of Lohr's magnificent rose garden, I'm reminded of the battle that changed all our lives just one year ago. With King Osbourne's return to his rightful place on the throne, some semblance of order has returned to not only Lohr but much of the world.

Having missed breakfast, I know Jack would be at only one place on this day.

Upon hearing my footsteps, he rises from the brilliant blue bed of cornflowers. The simple headstone within it bears no comparison to the sacrifice he made. Hanz Otto Oswald Kretschmer's spirit blooms within the garden, as if he's never left.

"You all right?" I ask, placing a hand on Jack's shoulder.

Jack turns to me, and the sorrow in his expression is evident. He nods. "Oddly enough, I miss him despite all he's done."

"You can't blame him for the things he did," I say.

"I don't. My father loved us both equally. But when my father was gone, all either of us had was his mother. And while she was no parent to me, she was exceptionally cruel to him." Jack shakes his head. "Who does that to their own blood-born child?"

I have no words of wisdom to offer him. Both my parents adored me and made a point daily to let me know that fact. And yet neither lives.

How the innocent die and the wicked live is beyond any belief or folktale my parents passed down to me. Why Jack would lose his mother to childbirth or I would end up parentless is beyond explanation. Why either of our parents died while the Bloodred Queen lived . . . I guess that is a question we'll both deliberate on forever.

Lily smiles adoringly at Doc while they stroll through the garden. The Haploraffen Halo shines brilliantly on Doc's brow. The Haploraffen remain under his control, acting as delivery machines to ensure the cure reaches the countries that need it most. Both Lily and Doc chose to reside in Lohr: Lily to protect King Osbourne and Doc to cure the world. Having an innovative lab and the help of Maus and Hase, Doc continues to create and distribute medication to the nations still recovering. He was able to destroy the Horologia virus using the same hydrofluoric acid that dismantled the scales on the Bloodred Queen.

Although Alyssa and Maddox have returned to Umberland, restoring their home has been slow. After the few months it took Pete to recover from his wounds, both he and Gwen followed and have been loyally by their sides through the rebuilding process. As for me and Pete . . . while he was quick to forgive me for shooting him during the battle, it has taken a lot longer for me to forgive myself. I'm a hunter by instinct, but the shedding of another's blood has left a black stain on my heart.

Ginger was appointed general to the king's army, tasked to locate and destroy the rest of the beasts released from the Labyrinth when the walls burned down.

Most important, peace has returned worldwide.

The devastation of the Horologia virus and its aftermath was far worse than we had anticipated. Millions died before the cure could reach them. Thankfully, survivors across the world have banded together in universal support. King Osbourne continues to be the driving force in returning our world to what it once was. Or perhaps something better. Although not officially the world leader, many still look to him with reverence. As the leader paving the way in world restoration, in most of the countries infrastructure, medicine, and government have been rebuilt.

Bells ring throughout Lohr, beckoning all who can hear their chime to converge in the arena where the Bloodred Queen fell. This time not to witness the end of her tyranny, but to commemorate a new beginning for our world. To rejoice in the rebuilding of this place we call home.

ACKNOWLEDGMENTS

With *Ozland* completing the Everland series, I can't begin to express my gratitude for the amazing people who have supported me on this journey. It's been an incredible time of growth, change, and wonder for me.

My three sons continue to be my biggest cheering squad and motivation. To Gavin, Keaton, and Riley, being your mom is the best gift I could have, and you are my greatest achievements. You'll always have a home in my heart.

Mom and Dad, you have been the sunshine amidst the tornadoes I've encountered in recent years. Thank you for getting me through my darkest days.

Jones, thank you for helping me heal my wounded heart. When the forest grew dark, you were the road that led me to light. I love you. Erik and Alyssa, I kind of love you both, too.

Harriet, I miss you. I wish you were here.

To my awesome BBB's critique group, Jennifer Fosberry, Erika Gardner, Amy Moellering, Cameron Sullivan, Georgia Choate, and Jerie Jacobs. Without the ongoing support of my Bacon Babes, I would've lost my mind, my heart, and the courage to soldier on.

To Department 384, while we called Disneyland our home away from home, it was you that made it magical. I miss you all.

To Ed Westmoreland and the staff at Eddie Papa's, can you believe it? You've seen me through numerous sliders, glasses of wine, and three books. Thanks for being my home office.

The cogs in the big publishing machine are magical. That's the only explanation I can come up with for how seamlessly the series began and ended.

To my incredible agent, Thao Le, thank you for being the Glinda in my life. You've believed in me even when I doubted myself. You'll never know how much I appreciate you. Also, much love to Sandra Dijkstra and agency members Andrea Cavallaro and Jennifer Kim for being on team Everland!

Jody Corbett, my incredible editor at Scholastic, I don't know where to begin. You've been more than someone who added the missing comma or corrected my grammar. You've challenged me to dig deeper, ask questions, and discover the story I didn't even know was there. You're not only my second pair of eyes; you've become a dear friend. Thank you for always, always being my consistent ray of hope when my own personal storms blotted out the sunshine.

To my Scholastic marketing and publicity team, Rachel Feld and Brooke Shearouse, thank you for getting the word out about the series. Without you, I'd have a lot of pretty books, but no one to share them with.

Christopher Stengel, my unbelievably talented designer and art director extraordinaire, I might be biased, but I've never seen a series with such beautiful cover art. I cannot convey how fortunate I am to have had your talents.

And of course, many thanks to those at Scholastic that continue to provide ongoing support, including David Levithan, Tracy van Straaten, Lizette Serrano, and everyone else behind the scenes. Also, I must send love out to Lori Benton, John Pels, and Paul Gagne, who handle all things audio books.

To the other residents of Scholastic-land, you seriously deserve a standing ovation. I applaud you for all of your hard work in making the Everland series happen. Thank you to the sales team, including Elizabeth Whiting, Alexis Lunsford, Annette Hughes, Chris Satterlund, Betsy Politi, Jackie Ruben, Jody Stigliano, Meaghan Hilton, Sue Flynn, Nikki Mutch, Charlie Young, and Roz Hilden.

Special thanks to the original storytellers: J. M. Barrie, Lewis Carroll, and L. Frank Baum. Because of your imaginations and the fantastical worlds you created, you made my childhood richer. I hope the Everland series makes you proud.

Finally, to the readers who had the courage, the heart, and the mind to lose themselves in my wild, fun world—thank you. Life is full of surprises. I've certainly discovered that over the making of this series. Never ever give up on your dreams, fervently follow your heart, and be stubbornly courageous. Whether we have crossed paths or not, I believe in you.

ABOUT THE AUTHOR

Wendy Spinale is a former character actor for the Disneyland theme park (so she is very familiar with the world of make-believe). She is the author of *Everland* and its follow-up, *Umberland*, as well as *Lost Boy*, a prequel novella to *Everland*.

Wendy lives with her family in the San Francisco Bay Area.